COWBOYS CAN'T KISS

Copyright @2025

Cowboys Can't Kiss by R.M Neill

All rights reserved. May not be reproduced in any form, stored in any retrieval system, or transmitted in any form by any means —electronic, mechanical, photocopy, recording, or otherwise —without prior written permission of the publisher. For permission requests contact:

www.rmneillauthor.com

This is a work of fiction. Names, characters, places, and incidents either are the products of the author's imagination or are used fictitiously. Any resemblance to actual person, living or dead, businesses, companies, events or locales is entirely coincidental.

AI was not used to create the cover art or any part of the story within. This story was created entirely by the author and their sometimes too vivid imagination.

Cover by: Jillian Liota, Blue Moon Creative Studio

Edited by: Jenn Reads Books

This one is for you, dear reader.
Thank you for being here.

Contents

One
Riley

"No, you can't fuck on horseback."

Internally rolling my eyes, I stare at the man across from me.

"Have you ever been on a horse?"

"No, but how hard can it be?"

Pinching the bridge of my nose, I count to five before replying.

"It's actually quite hard. Not to mention I'm sure the horse wouldn't approve of being used as a...sex surface. That's rude and I won't help plan it even if I found a horse who would stand still and let it happen."

The man frowns and points a single thick finger at me.

"You said you'd help me plan a romantic date for my girlfriend. I'm paying money for this and I want to fuck on a horse."

Seriously? This guy probably thinks buying his girlfriend a new vacuum is romantic, too.

"You're paying for my advice and my assistance. I assure you, no woman will want to expose her private parts while on a horse and risk getting horsehair rammed up her insides. Let's not even touch on the fact you keep referring to it as fucking. That's not romantic, Anthony."

His brows furrow, and if I were a cartoonist, I'd draw little plumes of smoke coming out of his ears as he processes my words.

"Horses lose hair?"

"A shitload of hair. It can be itchy."

He scratches at his crotch and I think that's successfully moved us from the topic of sex on a horse.

"Maybe I should think of something else. What do you think, Riley?"

"Well, you said she likes aquariums. Is this just a romantic date or a proposal? What's your end goal?"

He smirks. A look he likely thinks is sexy, but it's... yeah, eww. That's not a good look.

"Sex, Riley. It's always the end goal. Is there anything else?"

Anthony folds his hands over the crisp blue pin-striped *Tommy Hilfiger* button-down that clings to his torso like a second skin and smiles. It's one of those secret smiles. One that's reserved for inside jokes with his buddies.

I don't know what it is about this guy, but my cringe meter is on overload, and I want to extend my sympathy to his girlfriend.

"I think you've misunderstood what it is I do. Romance isn't about sex. It's creating a bond. Connecting with someone special and building a relationship. Incredible memories you both cherish forever."

He nods along like he understands. Fifty bucks says he doesn't.

"Yeah, that doesn't sound like me."

You don't say.

"Just help me plan an exotic place for sex. Oh! Think we could reserve the aquarium and we could bang in that dark room with the jellyfish?"

That's it.

Pushing my chair back, I stand and force a smile.

"I'll refund you. We aren't a good fit. That's not what I do."

He huffs and stands as well, his lips curled in a sneer.

"I knew you were too uptight. Romance is dead, Riley. I'm not sure why I even thought this was a good idea."

"Then you don't need my help to get laid, Anthony. Have a good day and good luck."

Of course, he leaves and gives me the middle finger because he's classy like that. Just as classy as wanting to fuck on the back of a horse. Immediately, I open our contract and pull up his email to refund the consult fee he paid. He was definitely not a fit for me.

Honestly, I thought it would be easier planning romantic moments for people than dating them. But all it serves lately is to remind me how lonely I am. Maybe I should have stuck with the escort service. At least I had company. Mostly fake company, but still. A guy can dream that one of his clients would give him a *Pretty Woman* moment and whisk him off to a life of romance with a handsome, less famous version of Richard Gere.

At least my next client is a couple who asked me to plan their wedding reception. They're already in love and just want a magical romance filled day.

And I will deliver. Romance is what I live for. Just not for myself.

Right after, I call my Aunt Agnes.

She picks up on the second ring.

"Is this my favourite nephew?"

Snorting, I shake my head even though she can't see me.

"It's your only nephew."

"Still my favourite."

"I'm just checking in. Have you taken your meds?"

Aunt Agnes is terrified that she'll forget her pills one day and die in the bathroom naked. Her words, not mine. Now I call her every day at lunchtime to remind her of her meds. Which is good for us both, really. She reminds me life is for living and not always about work. I ignore the reminder most of the time because I'm stubborn like that.

"I did! I'm having grilled cheese for lunch and my pills went down first. Are you eating lunch today?"

Checking the clock, I'm surprised the morning has passed.

"You know what? I think I will. I'll go to the little bistro around the corner. They have an amazing goat cheese and beet salad."

She makes a gagging noise and I laugh.

"You need to eat meat, Riley. Not salads all the time."

"I like salads. And I eat plenty of meat. Don't worry about me."

Besides, the bistro is the one place in this town where I can avoid cowboy hats and belt buckles and men spitting their chewing tobacco in cups. If it wasn't for Aunt Agnes, I'd never have moved back here.

Cowboys are not my favourite. Not since Chase.

Oh, they're delicious to look at. A hundred percent. But you'll never be first place in a cowboy's life. Even one who's not a pathological liar. It was a hard lesson to learn, but one I remember well.

"At least take a break from work and get out. Will I see you tomorrow?"

My cheeks stretch with a smile. "I wouldn't miss it."

"Go eat your lunch then, Rye. I love you."

"I love you too, Auntie. We'll talk tomorrow."

Now that I'm thinking of that salad, I grab my phone and keys and slip out of my office. The bistro is a block away and sits on the corner of a busy downtown street. It caters to the business crowd, especially for lunches, and closes late afternoon. The best part about it is it's almost always filled with people in dress clothes. Bankers, lawyers, receptionists, and anyone else working in the downtown core.

It's all business-y businesses. Professionals with suits, ties, and pressed shirts with polished shoes. There's no business to draw the cowboys here, not even a farm supply store. It's firmly out of cowboy territory. A definite plus for me.

The aroma of roasted garlic greets me as I open the door and the chatter of customers fills the air. It's a busy afternoon and with all the tables full, it looks like I'll have to take my food to go and skip the glass of wine I hoped for.

"Hi, Riley. Nice to see you again. Your usual?"

Smiling at Hannah, I nod. "Although it seems like you're full. I'll take it to go, please, and instead of wine, I'll have a peach iced tea."

As she punches in my order, she nods. "It's ridiculously busy today. I'm sorry, there are no free tables." She hands me the payment terminal and I tap my card.

"If a table empties before my order is ready, I'll nab it."

Stepping off to the side so she can keep up with her customers, I scan the small bistro and watch for anyone nearing the end of their meal. I have a few prospects, but worst case, if no table opens, I can also eat in the park today. It's been ages since I've had a picnic lunch.

"Here you go, Riley. Don't be a stranger."

Turning, I find Hannah holding a bag with my order.

"I wouldn't dream of it. I'll call ahead next time."

Aunt Agnes was right. I need to get out more and lunch in the park sounds fabulous. Romantic, even if I don't have someone to share it with. Self-love is still romantic, and I'll die on that hill if I'm ever challenged about my relationship status. Loving yourself is just as important as loving another person.

The small park downtown is deserted and I settle at the lone picnic table there.

As often happens when I allow myself to stop and think, the familiar heartache rears up when I wonder about what could have been. How life might be different if I hadn't let my guard down. Maybe I'd have the white picket fence and 2.5 kids. Instead, I hide a shattered heart and refuse to entertain those dreams again.

Fucking cowboys.

"No, Riley. Don't go down that road. He was a bastard to his core. You can do better than him," I mumble as I unpack my lunch.

"Sounds like someone made a mistake."

A deep voice sounds from... the ground? Easing off the picnic table, I peer over a small plot of flowers to find a pair of feet with dress shoes poking out. The branches of the willow tree hide the body the feet belong to.

"Um, I'm sorry. I thought I was alone."

"So did I. Don't be sorry. Want to talk about it? I'm a good listener."

My lips twitch in a small smile. I feel like I'm one of Lucy's patients in a Peanuts cartoon without spending the nickel.

"Why are you on the ground?"

The man laughs softly, and it's a gorgeous laugh. Deep, even though it's not a full laugh. It's... inviting.

"Like you, I also had a bastard in my life. Today was a hard day."

"Oh. I'm so sorry."

That laugh comes again, but it's tinged with sadness. Unsure if I want to eat or talk to this stranger who has my interest piqued, I open my salad and poke at it. Maybe he has a broken heart that just won't mend too?

"It's okay." His deep voice now carries a smile and my lips tilt in response. "I'm just stretching here and enjoying the quiet. Then a gorgeous man came and sat next to me."

Holy wow. That's rather forward. I don't even know what to say. Which is dumb. I should know how to respond to someone flirting with me. I was an escort, for Pete's sake; I can flirt with the best of them. Not to mention I've been a wedding and romance planner for several years. But I shove salad in my mouth to delay saying anything.

"I'm sorry if that made you uncomfortable. You seemed down, and I wanted you to know that whoever did you wrong made a mistake."

My hand trembles as I raise another forkful to my mouth. "You don't even know me." The salad I usually love falls on dead taste buds. This stranger on the ground has me unsettled, and I don't know why.

"Would you like me to?"

"To what?"

"Would you like me to know you?"

Do I? What if I like him? It's easier to stay in touch with my romantic side by selling it to others. Living through someone else's dream. He could be another liar. Or he could be a friend. I don't have many of those here.

Perhaps....

"What if I say yes?"

There's a long pause and I lift my butt from the bench to see his feet wiggling back and forth. I don't know why, but that makes me grin like a fool.

"I might be happy to hear a yes."

"What if I say I like this mystery and I'm not ready to see who you are?"

There's another long pause and his feet stop wiggling. My alarm sounds from my phone and I curse under my breath. Where did the last forty-five minutes go? I have a client in fifteen minutes.

"Um, I'm sorry, but I have to go. I have a client coming and..." God, this is so stupid. Do I really want to get to know this guy I just met who is lying on the ground in a park without a care in the world? Should I try to forget the shit in my past and move on? Surely I can be brave again, right? Besides, it's hard for my inner romantic to ignore the romance of meeting a stranger blind.

"Would you meet me here again tomorrow?" the stranger asks. His voice carries a hope that sings to my romantic heart. It's crazy. But maybe it's a sign. Maybe I should finally listen.

"Yes, I would."

A whoosh of air sounds from beneath the tree. "Okay. It's a date. Enjoy the rest of the day and I hope you ate your salad. The bistro has good food."

With a goofy grin on my face, I pack up my garbage.

"I ate enough, thank you. I'll see you tomorrow. Same time."

As I rush out of the park, unsure of what just happened, he calls out, "I'll be here!"

"So you're going to meet some rando in the park? This isn't a joke?"

Laughing, I rest my feet on the coffee table and put my best friend, Gabe, on speaker.

"No joke. My aunt keeps telling me to get back out there and not to live for work and all that stuff. I should listen. He's taken enough of my life away."

Gabe growls over the phone, and I miss his protectiveness. For a best friend, he can't be beat.

"Every time I hear his name, I wish I could punch the fuck out of him."

"He's not worth the effort, Gabe." Sighing, I let my head fall back on the couch. "Is it too much for me to hope this stranger might be my Prince Charming? Can't someone make an honest effort to romance the romance guy?"

"You need hope, Rye. It's what makes you, you. There's not a single person I know who deserves a happy ending more than you. If you don't show up tomorrow, you'll never know."

Gabe is right. I know this. If I wasn't such a sucker for fairy tales and romance, I'd run far away. My heart is still so bruised I've kept it in bubble wrap and never, ever thought about giving it to someone else.

Maybe it's finally time.

"Okay. I'm doing it. I'll fill you in."

"You'd better. I live through you. I have ten more years of fourteen-hour days and zero time for relationships. Until then, I need your stories."

Laughing out loud, I shake my head. Gabe works far too much, but he's the best lawyer in the city. He knows he can't dedicate the attention needed to form a lasting relationship right now, which makes me sad because he'd make an amazing partner for the one who catches his eye.

"As long as I amuse you, Gabe."

He stifles a yawn and papers shuffle in the background.

"Listen, doll, I need to finish this paperwork before I call it a night. I loved talking to you tonight, and I miss you."

"I miss you too. I'll let you know how it goes."

After we say our goodbyes, I pour a glass of wine and flip through channels for a little longer before heading to bed with the sound of a deep laugh and a smooth voice to lull me to sleep.

Two
Jackson

Leaning on my pool stick, my gaze scans the bar. It's filled with old-looking rich guys. Not just a few, but dozens of them. Which is not the type of fun I'm looking for.

To be fair, my fun isn't a roll-in-the-sack with a stranger, anyway. I prefer to know someone before we get naked together.

"What's with all the old men in here with sticks up their asses?" Hunter laughs as he follows my gaze.

"I know. I'm not looking for a sugar daddy."

A man walks by with a full three-piece suit and pauses at our pool table.

"Are you real cowboys?" he asks, and I have to hide my smile. The awe in his voice is the same as any buckle bunny, and while I'm sure he's a fabulous guy, he's not my type.

My type left me hanging at the park three days ago. So much for finding a connection in alternate places.

Tipping my hat, I grin. "Yes, sir. Just here unwinding after a rodeo."

"Heavens! A rodeo!" The man's cheeks flush red and he can't seem to decide where to look. Which is kind of adorable.

"Yep. As real as the horses we rode in on." Hunter grabs his belt, drawing attention to his championship belt buckle. It's been a long time since he was at the top of the standings with his former team-roping partner, Alec. But a buckle earned is still reason to brag, no matter how long ago it was.

The suited man's eyes light up. "Would you care to join me for a drink?" he asks Hunter directly, but motions to me. "Both of you are welcome."

"That's mighty kind of you, sir, but I think we'll finish our pool game. Thank you for the offer."

The man nods and glances behind him where several other gentlemen wearing suits sit at a table. The group watches our new friend like they sent their best Romeo over to pick up the cowboys.

"If you change your mind, please join us."

"We'll keep that in mind."

After the man leaves, Hunter leans close and whispers. "Shit. What is that about? Think he's just wanting a walk on the wild side? Who wears a suit to a bar?"

With a laugh, I line up to take my shot and resume our pool game. "I don't know, but that's strange. He's into you, though. That buckle still works for you."

My combo shot sinks a ball and Hunter huffs. "Lucky shot. And I don't need a belt buckle to get laid."

"I never said you did."

Another ball goes in, and I grin at Hunter.

"Lucky in pool, but not in love, Jack?"

"That's a low burn, friend."

Hunter shrugs and I miss my next shot.

"Truth isn't it? Didn't that guy stand you up this week?"

Hunter lines up his shot and sinks a ball as I grab my beer.

"Yeah. But really, is it a ghosted date when he doesn't even know who I am? I only half expected him to be back."

That's a lie. I hoped like fucking hell he'd be back. As soon as he sat at the picnic table mumbling to himself, I was intrigued. With his light brown hair, cute-as-a-button nose, and those lips! The most kissable lips I've ever seen. The man still carried himself with a confidence I appreciated, even if he seemed a little down.

Hunter scoffs as he takes a shot and sinks another ball. He shoots a finger gun my way and I roll my eyes.

"I call extreme bullshit. You moped about him not being there for the next three days. You're such a bleeding heart, man."

His next shot misses and a flash of disappointment crosses his face as he curses.

"I didn't mope." Lining up my cue, I take the shot, sinking a ball and moving around the table. "I lamented the loss of a cute man who doesn't even know what I look like. I can search for him, but how would he find me?"

"It's easier to not look for relationships. I don't know how many times I keep telling you a cum and go is better. Especially when you travel so much for rodeo."

"Strong relationships can last through that, Hunter."

My last ball sinks and Hunter scowls. He hates it when he loses.

"Eight ball, off your green stripe and side pocket."

Just as I'm making my shot, Hunter whistles and says, "Hot damn. Now that's an ass."

His distraction doesn't work and my shot goes in as planned. Hunter doesn't even notice. He's staring at the man who just entered the bar. Wearing a very well-fitted pair of dress pants and a button-up, he's also very overdressed for a honky-tonk place like this.

"Maybe he's with the group of old rich dudes."

After ordering at the bar, he turns around and leans his elbows against it as he surveys the room.

"Holy shit," I breathe. Hunter raises an eyebrow.

"You okay there? He's hot, but you look like you might throw up."

That cute little nose and lips. It's my guy. Park guy who didn't show up for our date. He still grabs my attention more than anyone I've ever met. A slender hand runs through his short hair as his gaze lands on me and Hunter before skipping past us.

"It's *the* guy. That's the guy from the fucking park, Hunter."

"No shit?" Hunter rakes his gaze over the man again, and I fight the urge to shove him and shout, *'mine!'* "Good taste, Jack. What are you going to do?"

"I...I don't know. What should I do?"

Hunter snorts and takes a swallow of beer. "You're asking me? I don't even like to know their names, buddy. You're the tender heart of the bunch."

My hands are so sweaty I need to wipe them on my pants.

"Okay. I'm going to introduce myself."

Hunter smacks my back with a little too much force. "If you need a wingman, give me the signal."

Without another word, he picks up his beer and joins the group of older dudes who invited us over. Knowing Hunter, he's just looking for free beer and a chance to talk about how great a cowboy he once was. Well, still is. He's my partner, after all.

"Okay, Jackson. Manifest what you want," I mutter as I weave through the crowd towards the gorgeous man. "Manifest."

He's still waiting at the bar when I arrive and my tongue sticks to the roof of my mouth. What if I screw this up? He might not like what I say. Of course, I need to actually say something first. Where the hell did my manifesting go?

He turns from the bar, drink in hand, and almost spills it on me.

"Sorry, excuse me."

Oh my god, how cute is he close up!?

Like an idiot, I don't move. I don't even speak. What the hell is wrong with me?

Tipping my hat, I squeak, "Have an enjoyable evening." But he's already out of hearing range. Seriously? An enjoyable evening? What the actual fuck was that?

The man disappears across the bar, joining a small group of people, and a hand clamps down on my shoulder with a laugh.

"That was more painful than watching you break a barrier early for a no score in a big money event."

Groaning, I shake off Hunter's hand.

"Don't remind me of how awful I am with this stuff. I couldn't even say hello. No, I had to sound like Batman's butler. Have an enjoyable evening," I mimic with a terrible British accent. Hunter chuckles as he steers me out of the bar.

"You can't be smooth at everything, Jacky. But I found the solution for you." He passes me a business card and I raise an eyebrow.

"Wild Romance?" Flipping it over, my eyes scan the words and I turn to Hunter. "You think I need a romance coach?"

"No. Well, not really. I mean, you always get flustered when you want to talk to a guy. I think you're plenty romantic already." He stops walking and lays a hand on my arm. "Which makes me want to gag for the record. But I was chatting with the dudes in suits, and it turns out they were here tonight because this Wild Romance guy helped the man propose. It's a bachelor party, Jack." Hunter throws his head back and laughs. "I wish I was making this shit up."

"Why are you laughing at a bachelor party?"

"Because the man swears this guy on the card made it possible." Hunter taps the card in my hand. "He talked about going for what you want and some shit like that." He starts walking again and I follow him down the sidewalk towards his truck. "Jackson, the man is probably sixty-five and marrying a thirty-year-old bombshell. He says the sex is amazing." He looks over at me and holds up a hand. "I nipped that conversation in the bud. No way do I want to hear about an old dude banging. Like, high five brother, but keep it to yourself."

Reading the back of the card, Hunter's rambles fade away as I wonder if he's right. Maybe I could make an appointment and learn how to be more... well, anything better than sounding like a stiff butler. Still doesn't help me find the guy from the park, though.

Perhaps a few meetings with this guy will prepare me for when I meet him again. Assuming he ever returns to the park.

"...So what do you think?"

"What? Sorry, I wasn't listening."

Hunter sighs as we get into his truck.

"I said I'd like to leave for the next rodeo Thursday instead of Friday. We can stay at the place with a hotel and the boarding facility nearby. Then the horses can have a break and we can sleep in actual beds. You in?"

"Absolutely. I prefer beds whenever we can." Hunter puts the truck in gear and we pass under the streetlights as we head out of downtown and farther away from the beautiful man in the bar.

Flipping the business card over, I read it again.

Wild Romance

Specializing in planning romantic events.

Make the ordinary feel extraordinary.

Riley Benton—owner/operator

Fuck it.

I've got nothing to lose.

Riley's contact info is there, so I email requesting a consult and pay the fee when the window pops up.

"So, we're winning money next weekend, I hope? It's a big one."

Hunter nods, smile gone and full game face in place.

"Yep. You're breaking records this year, Jackson. I can feel it."

And that's why Hunter is my best friend and my hazer. A steer wrestler needs a partner with confidence in their abilities. Hunter cheerleads me like nobody else. He may tease me about my romantic tendencies, but he's got my back in the ring.

"Here's to our best season, Hunter."

He pulls into my driveway and drops me off as close to the house as possible.

"Change your outdoor light, Jackson. It's been out for weeks."

"I know. I'll get to it. See you in the morning." Before I close the door, I hold up the business card. "Thanks for this, Hunter. If it works out, you're my best man."

He rolls his eyes, just as I expected. But I know he's rooting for me. He'd be there.

"Get out of here with that nonsense."

After he waits with his lights shining on my door so I can see, he pulls away after I've entered my house safely.

After hanging my hat on its peg and leaving my boots on the mat, I absently walk through my home until I reach the bedroom. Tossing the business card on my dresser, I change into a pair of lounge pants and crawl under the covers. Too much time passes as I lie awake thinking about the beautiful man tonight who I couldn't even speak to properly.

My yoga teacher talks about manifesting a lot. It always helps to put my mind in the right place before rodeos.

Maybe if I try harder and use this Wild Romance guy, I can make it work. I could find the cute park guy again.

Although, I should manifest a good sleep first.

Three
Riley

"Oh, Riley, what a beautiful idea!"

My client wipes a tear from her eye and her fiancée raises a hand to her cheek, wiping more tears.

"When you mentioned you had a butterfly tattoo, I did some research. Your wedding timing is perfect to release monarchs after the ceremony. I can order as many as you wish." I pass another piece of paper to the couple. "If you'd like, we could print cards like this for the guests. It could state your purpose for the butterflies and invite them to be a part of the wish. Or you could keep it private for the two of you."

Melody smiles at Jana. "What do you think, babe? Send our love out on the wings of butterflies or too cheesy?"

Jana kisses the back of Melody's hand, and I swoon. Butterflies for the win. The way these two are looking at each other right now makes my insides liquify. It's beautiful.

"I think it's wonderful, Mel." Jana reaches over to squeeze my hand. "This is perfect, Riley."

There's nothing I love more than planning romantic moments or dates, or like this, a meaningful gesture to take place at their wedding. Is it extra or over the top? Sure, a little. But that's what they hired me for. To coordinate a romantic wedding. What's more romantic than sending butterflies out into the world to spread your love on their wings?

"I'll get you to sign the contract if you want the butterflies, and I'll order them right away. We can work out the information card over email."

"That's perfect." Melody beams as she stands. "We're off to have our dresses fitted again." She pats her stomach. "Jana's cooking might mean I need to let it out."

Jana again kisses the back of Melody's hand. "You're perfect. Stop that. A few extra pounds doesn't change who you are. I love *you*, not the size you wear, Mel."

"Oh my goodness, you two!" I fan my hand near my face. "Get out of my office before you make me cry. You're too sweet."

The two women leave smiling, and I get to work on their contract changes to add the butterfly purchase. After making a note to order the monarchs once I receive the updated contract, I turn to my emails and open the request for a romance consultation.

Jackson Sutherland is a forty-year-old cowboy looking for help to improve his dating game. Says he's always tongue-tied around men and wants help so he can ask them on dates without looking like a goober.

Alone in my office, I bark a laugh. *Goober*. That's funny. I continue reading his consult request, which is an automated form for them to fill out to give me insight into their experiences and specific requests.

Damn.

Jackson sounds perfect as he is, except for the cowboy part. He prefers intimate dates over large group gatherings, doesn't like to drink much, and volunteers at the senior home in the winter. He recently ended a business partnership, and one day hopes to start another, but his partner left a sour taste in his mouth. Jackson also loves dogs, but never had one because of his schedule and someday wants to date an animal lover. He also likes to unwind with yoga and considers himself a homebody.

I'd ask him out based on this questionnaire, but... cowboy. Which is a shame. Using their belt buckles and form-fitting *Wranglers* to get people in the sack, they're all the same. Sure, Jackson might be different, but I'm doubtful.

He sounds great on paper, but I know how it turns out.

After checking my schedule, I email him back with an appointment and a request to respond to confirm his date and time. Almost immediately, my email pings with his reply.

'I'll be there! Thank you so much for your help. I admit I was skeptical doing this, but I've heard good things about you. I'm really excited!'

Jackson's reply makes me smile. I don't respond. Instead, I mark his suggested appointment as confirmed and my thoughts shift back to the man from the park. Work got hectic, and I missed our sort of date last week.

Today I'm making one more attempt to lunch in the park and hope I didn't miss out on a connection. Which is absurd. I don't even know what he looks like, but I liked... him? The idea of him? Something about the mystery man just called to me, and I want to know more.

Checking the clock, I smile as I call Aunt Agnes.

She answers on the second ring.

"Hello, Riley. Are you still working?"

"Hi, Auntie. For a few more minutes, then I'm going back to the park. I'm hoping my mystery man is there. If not, I'll give up."

"Good for you, dear. I think you should keep going even if he isn't there. The fresh air does a body good. Don't give up on love, though."

Aunt Agnes is more of a romantic than me. She was the one who planted a love of romance in my heart. Reading me fairy tales at bedtime will always be one of my fondest childhood memories with her.

"I wouldn't call this love. We haven't even met. Did you take your pills?"

I don't need Aunt Agnes giving me a talk on love right now. She'll get to that at our next *Scrabble* game, I'm certain.

"I did. And I'm having lunch right now. *SpaghettiOs*."

My nose wrinkles automatically.

"Auntie, why do you eat that stuff? I'm bringing you some better meals when I come for Scrabble."

She huffs, annoyed with me dissing her beloved canned noodles.

"I don't want your fancy salads, city boy."

Laughing out loud, I shake my head. "I know. I'll find you something you like."

"Good luck at the park today. Remember, not all men are like that asshole, Chase."

My head knows that, but my heart is an entirely different organ to convince.

"I know. I love you and we'll talk soon."

After locking my office, I slip outside into the warm late spring sun and head towards Avocadabra, my favourite bistro. I called ahead to order this time. Hopefully, I'll have more time to linger in the park and run into my mystery man.

Upon entering the bistro, it's more quiet than usual and the white bag at the counter with my name on it sits waiting.

"Hi, Riley. Perfect timing. I just finished your order. It's a beautiful day for lunch outside. I think our usual patrons feel the same, since it's rather quiet."

"I can't blame them. The sun on my face without the chill in the air makes me so happy. There's just something about it, you know? I should have lunch outside more often."

"As long as you still join us from time to time, I'd support that."

Hannah smiles and passes me the bag as I drop some loose change into the collection jar for the local animal shelter on the counter.

"I'll always be back, Hannah. If not for food, I'd return to see you and your friendly face."

Her cheeks pink as she waves me off and I head to the park with a tight ball in my stomach. What do I say to him if he's there? Technically, I stood him up last week and I'm not like that.

When I enter the park and approach the picnic table, my heart almost stops when I notice the pair of dress shoes poking from behind the flower beds. Sitting on the bench, I turn towards the... feet, since the rest of him remains hidden.

"I'm sorry I wasn't here the next day like I promised. I got held up at work and then I needed to take my aunt to an appointment and...I tried to come back, but you weren't here."

Oh, god. What if this isn't the same guy?

"I'm happy to hear that." My shoulders relax with his voice. Same guy. I'd recognize that voice anywhere. Smooth and deep.

"I mean...not happy you couldn't come, but happy it wasn't me." He huffs. "No, that's not what I mean, either." There's a pause, and I think he might be giving himself a pep talk. There's a lot of mumbling I can't make out, but I swear I heard the phrase, *you can do this.* "I waited for three days." He clears his throat. "I would've waited longer, but I think people were uncomfortable with a man lying in the grass every day. You're here now, though. That's what matters."

Oof. Direct hit to my romantic heart. He waited for three days, then came back again on the random day I tried to find him? I'm not one to believe in signs, but there must be some kind of hocus pocus at work.

"Um...this is going to sound silly, but...I brought lunch. For both of us. Would you like to join me?"

My hands fidget with the handles on the bag. The longer his silence stretches, the longer I wonder if I went too far, and I just made a fool out of myself.

"Do you think it's crazy to meet a stranger for lunch in the park?"

His voice is still steady, but I'm positive there's a waver of hope there. Maybe he feels the same as I do.

"Well, if we have lunch, we're no longer strangers, right?"

His low chuckle brings a smile to my face, and the feet disappear as he stands. Okay, this is happening. When he finally steps out from the shadows of the tree and turns towards me, I pray the gasp in my head wasn't out loud because glory to the beings of creation, this man is gorgeous.

A white dress shirt with his sleeves rolled up shows off *very* muscled arms. His shirt tucks into a pair of black dress pants.

Simple, yet stylish, and his black shoes are still shiny like they were on that first day.

He's dreamy. My teenage heart shoots sparkles, knowing I just met a man to use that word for. His warm gaze wraps around me like a hug from an old friend. As he steps closer, his Adam's apple bobs, and he clutches his suit jacket against his body.

"You're the prettiest thing in this park. I'm really happy you came back."

His eyes widen and he clutches his suit coat closer.

Yeah, okay, that's...wow. My skin feels hot and I dip my head. Lord, I think I'm blushing. I don't blush with compliments. What the fuck is wrong with me?

"Thank you." Clearing my throat, I blurt, "Do you like hummus?"

A bright smile graces his face and he's so handsome I can't help staring at him. There's a slight flash when he turns his head, and I bite my lip when I notice the small diamond earring. It's like the angels cracked open my brain and found all my favourite things and smashed them into this man.

"I love it." The man's voice snaps me back to the present. "Preferably the red pepper hummus from Avocadabra."

"No way! That's my favourite place and exactly what I brought."

We grin at each other like two kids who just discovered they have the same birthday, and I remove the takeout containers from the bag.

"I'm Riley, by the way." I extend my hand to him, and when his calloused palm slides into mine, electricity races down my spine.

"Jack," he rasps, and it takes a moment for him to let go of my hand.

"Um, I...there's water? I didn't know what you'd like."

Jack settles at the table across from me and reaches for the water I offer him.

"Hummus is made from chickpeas. I've always found that interesting," Jack offers, and I can't help but laugh at his choice of conversation topic.

"Food interests you?"

"Well, I like to eat it, so...yeah." He clears his throat and taps a finger against his water bottle. "Did you know baby carrots aren't really baby? They're just big carrots ground down into little ones."

The hummus platter came with vegetables. Baby carrots included. Picking one up, I hold it out to him with a grin. "So this carrot was once an adult and then made to be a baby again?"

"Yeah. And they use carrots that are shaped weird. Like, they don't make it to the grocery store as is. I guess it's a makeover for a carrot."

He's too precious.

Dipping a carrot in the hummus, I crunch it as he scoops a generous amount of hummus up with his baby carrot and pops it into his mouth.

I'm hoping for more random food facts, but he's stopped talking.

"Um...can I ask what made you lie on the ground instead of taking a seat here that day we met?"

Jack pauses his chewing and bites at his lip.

"It was a stressful day. I just wanted to...I don't know, hide from the world for a bit."

He rips apart a piece of pita and dunks it in the hummus. "Did you know pita is one of the oldest breads? It's traced back almost 4000 years ago to the Middle East."

Why do I find his nervous food facts so damn cute?

"I didn't know that. It's one of my favourites. I love eating pitas."

Jack smiles and eats as his knee bounces so much, the entire picnic table wiggles.

"Do you like fairy tales, Jack?"

Jack pauses, chewing slowly, and nods. After swallowing, he chews his lip before answering.

"I don't know if it's considered a fairy tale, but I really like *Lady and the Tramp.*"

His gaze meets mine and I see it. The naked truth of his admission is something he doesn't share with many people, but he did with me. Someone he just met. It might be a movie fact, but to him, it's a big deal.

"I like that one, too."

I smile his way, and he sucks in a breath.

"Maybe one day we could—"

A booming voice jars us from the conversation. "Jack! Where are you? We have to go!"

"Shit." Jack stands and almost knocks lunch off the table in his haste. "Riley, I'm sorry. I have to go. Can we..." He looks over his shoulder towards the man who called for him. "I'll be here again next Wednesday. Maybe we could do this again?"

Walking backwards away from me, he waits for my response and what else can I say but yes?

"I'll be here!"

He gives me a thumbs-up and waves before turning and jogging away.

I stare after him, unsure of what just happened and who Jack really is.

Picking up a baby carrot, I inspect it closer.

"I didn't know these came from imperfect bigger carrots."

Maybe next week I can learn about Jack and not random facts about food.

Four
Jackson

"That steer looks fast, Jackson."

Before Hunter positions his horse in his chute, he nods at me. "Take it quick before he gets away."

"Yep. That's the plan."

I know how to wrestle a steer, but Hunter likes to say things out loud. It's just the way he gets in the zone. But he has a knack for reading steers, unlike anyone else I know. I may do the physical part with the animal, but he's part of the reason I do it so well.

Both of us are in position in the chutes on either side of the steer. Hunter is on the right and I'm on the left. The official signals they're ready, and with a final deep breath, envisioning the time on the scoreboard, I nod to the judge at the steer chute. "Yep!"

Hunter was right and the steer bolts out of his chute like he's on fire. But Hunter and his horse run the steer straight and I'm alongside it in a blink of an eye. I don't hesitate. In one fluid move, I'm off my horse and half on top of the steer. My right arm hooks up and under his right horn, and I grip the other horn with my left hand. My feet plant into the soil and using my body weight, I twist the steer. The animal flips to its side on the ground, all four feet leaving the soil.

The crowd goes wild and my heart races as I wait for my official time.

It was a solid run, and the steer trots away while I whoop and search for Hunter. He's pumping his fist and pointing at the scoreboard.

3.4 seconds.

That's a personal best for me and the fastest time all weekend.

Trotting across the ring to Hunter and my horse, I swing back into the saddle.

"I knew this would be an epic rodeo for us. Keep that up and we're winning the season without breaking a sweat."

I beam at Hunter as the crowd still cheers and shouts my name.

"Fuck, I love this sport!" I shout and tip my head back, howling at the sky.

Hunter laughs as I tip my hat to the crowd and exit the back of the ring. To run a fast time is a great feeling. To run an epic time that nobody will touch has me walking on air. There are still several riders left tonight, and I don't want to assume I've won the event, though. It only takes someone else's best effort to knock me out of top place.

"No one is beating you tonight, Jack. You can breathe."

Hunter chuckles next to me and his horse whinnies like she agrees with him.

"You know I don't like making assumptions."

The next two wrestlers miss their steer, and it's no score for both. My heart kicks up a notch and I smooth a hand down my horse, Lady's, neck. The next man is successful, but far too slow.

I can barely watch the last wrestler. He's away clean. The steer is on the ground with all four feet pointing up. Hunter and I wait and watch the scoreboard.

3.6 seconds. We won!

Hunter whoops and slaps me on the back. "That's what I'm talking about! Meet me at the truck after your victory lap."

I wait at the chute on top of Lady until they announce the second and third-place finishers. When my name is called as tonight's champion for steer wrestling, I ride Lady once around the ring, waving my hat to the crowd.

When I leave the ring, a voice calls my name and I urge Lady to a stop.

"Jackson! Hold up!"

A man wearing a jacket from the rodeo sponsor jogs up to me. He reaches me, and offers me a hand to shake.

"Thanks for waiting. I'm Neill from Neill and Dunn, the main sponsors of the rodeo circuit this year."

Smiling, I dismount Lady and take his offered hand in a firm shake.

"Nice to meet you, Neill. Thanks for supporting the events. I love rodeo and you make it happen."

"Well, I love rodeo too, but I was never good at it. The next best thing is rubbing shoulders with cowboys like yourself." He hands me an envelope. "This is an invitation to the awards banquet after the Kissing Ridge Rodeo. It's new this year and we're inviting all the top performers. My partner wants to meet everyone and their other half."

Neill is a kind man. People share nothing but good words about Neill and Dunn, and their sponsorship of events comes from a genuine love of rodeo. A formal banquet is new, though, and I'm excited it's in my hometown. "Thank you so much, Neill. Can I come alone? This cowboy is whole as is."

I gesture down my body with a laugh. Neill pats my arm with a chuckle.

"Oh, of course! No pressure. Dunn just likes to talk to spouses who never get the attention like the cowboys do. You don't need a date or anything."

"Thank you so much for the invite, Neill. I'll do my best to be there."

"Of course. I'll let you take care of your horse. Enjoy the rest of the evening." He turns to walk away but stops. "And congrats again on the win tonight."

"Thank you!"

Leading Lady out back to where Hunter has his truck and horse trailer, I stuff the invite into my pocket.

Hunter's horse is already tied and munching her dinner. He steps over and helps me unsaddle Lady. "How do you feel about joining the guys at the bar later tonight? Celebrate your big win?"

"You're part of the win too, you know. Just because I do the wrestling part doesn't mean you're not important."

Hunter pauses and his gaze meets mine quickly before he mutters a gruff, "Thanks." He doesn't like being acknowledged for anything good, but he lets me get away with it. It took us years of friendship and practice to gain that privilege, though.

"Yeah, I suppose I could go out for a bit. Not too late, though."

Hunter snort-laughs. "I know, gramps. I'll get you home at a decent time."

Shooting the middle finger at him, I continue brushing out Lady as she enjoys her evening snack. As much as Hunter and the others tease me, they also respect my desire to not stay out all night. Or drink too much. It's never been my scene. When I first met our group of friends, I was hesitant to share my homebody tendencies. But our distinct personalities complement each other, and I'm never made to feel uncomfortable about not following the party crowd. Instead, I'm like the cool dad you can call when you need a sober ride home.

After we trailer our horses, Hunter drives us to the facility where we can house them in a comfortable barn stall for the night. We could drive the five hours straight home, but when we have this available, we both like to take it and get a decent sleep in the nearby hotel before the drive back.

After checking into our shared hotel room with two queen beds, we take turns cleaning up. Hunter plays a country music playlist and sings off-key in the shower while I reward myself with a bag of potato chips.

I wish it was hummus though.

And I wish I was still with Riley. It's only been three days since we first formally met. I felt like I might throw up when he offered me his hand and a beautiful smile. Thankfully, I didn't and stuck to quoting weird food facts instead. Which was only slightly less awkward.

I was running through my brain about how to ask him for his number—and sound mostly normal doing it—when Cameron, my now ex-business partner, bellowed for me and knocked my train of thought into the next station. I didn't get a number, but at least I can meet him again on Wednesday.

"What's got you grinning like that? A bag of chips can't be that good."

Hunter exits the bathroom with a billow of steam. He takes the longest and hottest showers of anyone I've ever met. But at least he stopped singing.

"Remember the guy from the park? The one at the bar who I couldn't even squeak a hello to? He showed up this week."

Hunter pauses toweling his hair and raises an eyebrow. "And?"

"He brought lunch for both of us and hoped I'd still be there." A breathy sigh slips out and Hunter snorts.

"Good god, Jackson. You don't even know his name and you have hearts in your eyes."

"I got his name!" Folding up the chip bag, I toss it on the coffee table while Hunter gets dressed. Sometimes I don't know how much to share with Hunter. He's my best friend, but he's such a cynic when we talk about relationships or love.

"And are you going to share it?"

Hunter pulls a clean T-shirt on and turns back to me.

"I don't know if I should. You're already teasing me, and I haven't even told you what happened."

Hunter stares me down, and I wait him out. Do I want to gush to someone about Riley? Fuck yes, I do. But not if they don't share my excitement. I love Hunter. He's my rodeo partner and closest friend. If I'm going to share with him, I need him in my corner.

Hunter sighs and sits on the edge of his bed. He chews his lips before finally speaking.

"Look, I know I tease you a lot, and most people think I'm an asshole. But...and if you repeat any of this to anyone, I will never forgive you," He mumbles under his breath before meeting my gaze. "Someday I'd like to have a partner who gives good hugs. Not just quick ones, either. A hug where it feels like they're the glue to hold you together and you never want to let go. One day I'd like that."

He dips his head my way. A signal it's all he wants to share right now, but it's a big one.

"Are you sure there's nothing you want to talk about? That's...a big reveal."

Hunter shakes his head. "No. Now spill it. Tell me about this dude who has you sighing like that."

So I do. Hunter listens and smiles when I talk too fast, and he laughs when I tell him about my blurted food facts.

"And you're just going to meet him in the park again? What if he doesn't show?"

"Well, I guess if he doesn't, that's the end of the story."

"You give up too easily, Jacky. If he doesn't show, then you hunt him down. You already know several things about him. Don't give up if he lights a fire in you." Hunter shoves his wallet and phone in his jeans pocket. "If you want something, chase it. It's that simple."

"Is it though? He might genuinely not like me. I can't force him to."

Joining Hunter at the door, I pat myself down to make sure I have what I need, and we exit our room.

"No, you don't force him to. But if you keep showing up and wowing him, he'll give in eventually."

"Be careful, Hunter. That sounds almost like romancing someone. You don't want to ruin your image." I elbow him as we exit onto the street to walk the few blocks to the bar.

"Don't forget you room with me. Sleep with one eye open if you rat me out, Jackson."

"I'd never do that!"

Hunter side eyes me as we walk together. "I know," he whispers, and I let it drop. One day, he'll share more with me. Until then, he's still the best hazer a steer wrestler could ask for.

And he always has my back.

"Jackson! Jacky, Jackmeister." A giggle bubbles out of Jamieson as he sways into me.

"For a bull rider, you're a lightweight with the liquor. Shouldn't you be better at this?"

Jamieson grins at me and pokes my chest.

"Shouldn't you be home and in bed, gramps? I'm no light wand."

"Weight. Lightweight, J."

His blurry eyes refocus on me. "That's what I said."

It's not, but never argue with a drunk unless you're prepared to go the distance and right now, I'm not. I'm tired and the bar scene got old fast tonight.

The boys bought me several drinks that I ended up giving away. Jamieson was also celebrating winning his event tonight, but unlike me, he celebrates hard.

"Where's Griff? You two should head back to the hotel. It sucks driving with a hangover headache. Even when you're the passenger."

Jamieson has a moment of clarity and nods. "You speak the truth, gramps. Imma find Griff."

He wobbles off and I shake my head with a grin. The guy rides bulls like he was born for it. He gets thrown around like a rag doll, sometimes has nasty spills and he bounces back like he's rubber man. But give the big guy a few beers and he's sloppy kissing strangers and falling asleep while standing.

Tough as nails, but zero alcohol tolerance.

"Do you want to head out of here?" Hunter appears and drains his beer next to me.

Exhaustion set in an hour ago, and I nod.

"Yeah. But you can stay if you'd like."

It's then we see Jamieson swaying in some kind of dance with several others, Griff hovering nearby, as they sing something that resembles a sea shanty. Hunter shakes his head.

"Nope. Time to go."

Once out in the evening air, we walk in silence until he points to a hot dog cart vendor.

"Want one? I've fucking famished."

"No thanks. But go ahead. I don't know how you can eat that stuff."

Hunter orders a hot dog as long as his arm and smothers it with every condiment the cart guy offers. My stomach turns looking at it.

"You don't know what you're missing," he mumbles around a mouthful.

"Indigestion. That's what I'm missing and I'm okay with it."

Instead of walking, we step to the side so Hunter can eat the monstrosity without spilling it all over himself. When he's finished, he wipes his hands with the napkin, grimaces, and orders a ginger ale from the vendor.

"That was not my smartest decision." Hunter sips on the ginger ale and I stifle a laugh.

"I'll agree with that."

Five
Riley

"He told you food facts? And you're still interested? How good-looking is this guy, Riley?"

"Listen, it's useful trivia. And he's got Greek-god-level looks. I bet his abs are as chiselled as his cheekbones."

My best friend laughs over the phone.

"So he's hot and nerdy? God, could you imagine him at one of my stuffy law dinners?"

Gabe laughs, and I'd normally join him, but I don't like laughing at Jack. He seemed genuinely nervous and was super sweet. Maybe he had an awful experience with love and that's why he seems so awkward. He certainly has good enough looks to snag anyone he wants.

"Well, maybe I'll ask him out if he doesn't ask first. He's not nerdy. He's just...I don't know. He's kind of charming just the way he is." I'm not lying. He is. I know it's my job to organize romantic events and coach people when they ask for help with romance, but sometimes it's better to keep people in their natural state. Let them lean into that awkward part and embrace it.

Jack definitely charmed me with his carrot facts and his... realness. Maybe I set the bar too low, but it was refreshing. I'm used to men assuming things about me based on my looks and profession. So this was a pleasant change. While he called me pretty, he was sincere, and it didn't give me ick vibes.

Gabe clears his throat, and I sit up, instantly on guard as the tone of our conversation changes. Even over the phone, the shift in his energy is like we're sitting in the same room.

"Riley...this isn't just a personal call. I need to discuss Chase's case."

My blood pressure spikes just at the sound of his name.

"What is it?" I snap out, irritated that Chase's name had to come up while I was daydreaming about Jack.

"His lawyers want to call you to the stand."

"No. Absolutely not. I told you I'm not helping him."

Gabe's heavy breath passes through the phone, and my free hand curls into a fist.

"Riley, I can't stop it. If they subpoena you, then you have to show up."

"What the fuck do they think I can do to help his lying ass? Nothing, Gabe!"

"Actually, there *is* something."

Gabe's voice softens, and I flop back on the sofa with a sigh.

"Gabe, just tell me."

"I know you hate him, but he's being accused of a serious crime. He could go to jail for something he didn't do, Riley. You're better than that."

"And how can I help him with that? Why should I?"

The longer the pause in Gabe's answer, the more my head pounds. Chase is a headache that never ends.

"He was on a date with you the night his wife said he hit her. She logged proof at the hospital for an assault. She didn't press charges then, but she is now. Unless he can prove without question that it wasn't him, it's another charge against him. I don't think I need to tell you, Riley, how serious this one could be for him. Impersonating someone to defraud others is one thing, but domestic assault is a whole other matter."

Running a hand down my face, I drop my head back to stare at the ceiling. Chase Kenney, will you ever leave my life for good? I owe him nothing. He lied about his identity. Cheated on his wife. Made me fall in love with him, and he was nothing but a con artist. A man in the closet living a secret life that I fell for.

Hard.

If it wasn't for Gabe asking a few unsuspecting questions when Chase fucked up, it may have ended differently. Chase wasn't a big, important oil baron. He was just a cowboy who liked to spend money faster than he earned it.

I blame my soft heart for falling for him. It certainly didn't hurt that he had a silver tongue and a face that belonged on a magazine cover, but he wove a story of loss and family drama that I could relate to. Chase knew every button to push for me and I lapped it all up. I ignored every single red flag because he made me feel like I was a king.

When Chase's elaborate façade crashed down, my hope for my own happily ever after burned along with it. Trust was obliterated. My heart that once gave so freely was an empty sack, drained and so scarred I wonder if it will ever beat for someone again.

As much as I dislike the man for making me his target and not seeming to care about any of the collateral damage he caused, Gabe is right. I wouldn't forgive myself if he went to prison for something he didn't do.

"Fine. Just try to make it fast. I'm right into the wedding planning season. I'll be swamped."

"You made the right choice, Rye."

"Yeah, well, he's still a cowboy who needs to be castrated with the next round of calves. I feel like he's a mistake that will never go away."

"He might not, Rye. It's okay to admit you loved him, you know. Yes, he wasn't who he said he was, but you didn't know. It'll get better."

"Yeah, I know...I just...I thought he was my prince, and he broke my fucking heart, Gabe. Smashed it into a million pieces and I felt like such an idiot." My laptop screen saver kicks in and it's a photo of me with Aunt Agnes. The one good thing about this mess with Chase is I quit my escort job and moved back home. Not that I hated being an escort, I loved it. But it's how I met Chase.

I needed the distance from the profession. The constant reminder that he ruined something I loved was too much to handle. Being closer to my aunt is a wonderful bonus. I've missed her. One silver lining in the whole shit show.

And it kick-started me to set up the wedding planning and romance business I'd always had on the back burner. It turned out to be the best thing I'd ever done. I won't go as far as thanking Chase for it, though. I'm just looking at the positive spin of it all. If I don't, I'll only spiral in a loop of self-pity and I'm done going there.

"Well, I think if this vegetable-loving mystery man makes you want to get back to dating, then this is a good thing."

"Speaking of, it's time for me to get to the park."

"I won't keep you then. Good luck!"

Gabe doesn't even say goodbye. He just ends the call and I shake my head.

Stepping into the office bathroom, I adjust my shirt and apply fresh deodorant. I tousle my hair and aim for the trendy, fresh-out-of-bed look. Before stepping out, I rinse with mouthwash.

"Good grief. I'm nervous." Laughing softly, I stare at my reflection. I used to date strangers for a living. Most of them I even had sex with. I was never nervous because there was nothing to be nervous about then. It was a job.

But this is different. He's interested in me and not because he saw my face on a website with hourly rates. He wants me, and I'm meeting him on my time. On my lunch break! It's been a long time since I've felt this excited about a date. If you could call it a date. Jack may have spoken to me from behind the flowers initially, but he wasn't hiding. He's just shy.

A far cry from some of my former clients who had *very* specific requests.

Noting the time, I speed walk down to the park with my lunch bag. The picnic table is empty and no feet poke out from the flower bed.

Okay, no big deal. We missed each other before. Maybe something came up. Last time that happened, we were able to meet up again. If he doesn't show, I'll keep coming back until we connect again.

No big deal.

Except it is.

Because I got my hopes up to see Jack today and he didn't show. The disappointment sits like lead on my shoulders, and I'm not in the mood to psychoanalyze myself about what that means.

With my lunch bag hanging at my side, I finally head back to the office when I can't wait a minute longer for him to show or I'll be late for my next client.

Once back in my office, the disappointment clings to me like pet hair on your favourite pants. It's impossible for me to shake it and I hate that.

And my client is late.

My earlier hopeful mood has vanished, and I want to scream. It isn't like me to mope and have so much...whatever this feeling is.

I'm just about to send off an email to my late client advising that the consult fee is non-refundable when there's a knock at the door and it swings open.

"I'm so, so sorry I'm late. I was helping a friend load cattle and —"

He stands in the doorway, lips parted as he stares. Jack swallows hard and removes his cowboy hat. His mouth moves silently and his free hand waves. It's a little wave, almost like a kid, and at any other time, I'd find it oddly cute and affectionate.

But it's Jack, aka Jackson, and he's not a businessman like I thought.

He's a cowboy... and my late client.

"*You're* Jackson?"

Jackson's brow furrows as he nods. "My friends sometimes call me Jack. I use both. Jackson is on my birth certificate, though. My mom liked it. But yeah, I'm Jackson."

He closes my office door and Jackson's fingers worry at the edge of his cowboy hat.

"Can I still have the appointment?"

Fuck, I don't know. Should he? Why does my mystery guy have to be another damn cowboy?

"Why were you wearing a suit when we met?" I bark. Perhaps too sharply, but I was already into the thought of this guy being something good and he's lied. I suppose that one's on me for assuming.

"Um, I had a meeting with a lawyer those days. Several of them, actually. That's over now."

A lawyer. Great. Another cowboy in trouble. I'm not sure if this day can get any worse.

"You haven't answered my question," Jackson whispers.

My gaze snaps to his, and those eyes, the ones so tender and kind that drew me in, pin me in place waiting for an answer. God dammit, why does he still have to be handsome?

Clearing my throat, I stand to introduce myself.

"Jackson, I apologize for being less than professional." I offer a hand to him, and the moment he accepts my hand in his, my entire body notices the rough callouses on his palm across my smooth one and the way his fingers squeeze mine, sending my pulse into overdrive. Just like the first time.

"I'm Riley. Owner of Wild Romance. It's a pleasure to meet you. Officially. Please." I gesture to the chair across from my desk. "Sit. Of course, you can still have the appointment."

Jackson nods and sits, placing his hat on the empty chair next to him. His knee bounces just as fast as the time we sat and shared lunch, and I pull over my notepad and pen to take notes, happy to have something to do with my hands.

"It's nice to meet you again, Riley." Jackson smiles with a small nod. "I'm sorry I wasn't at the park today. My friend Hunter owns a ranch. You might know it? Anyway, he had some bulls he needed help trailering. He used to do the breeding stuff at his place, but now he sends them out. Well, he's clearing them all out and—" Jackson closes his mouth so hard and fast his teeth clack.

"Jackson? Are you okay?"

He nods and stares at the ceiling tiles. His Adam's apple bobs as he swallows, and a vision of me licking his neck and tracing my tongue over that part of him is so vivid I need to shake my head to clear it.

"I'm okay. This is why I made the appointment. When I'm around attractive men, I babble. The smooth factor no longer exists." His lips tilt in a crooked smile. "I'm forty and still single because of my absolute inability to flirt. When I'm nervous, I blurt out the first thing that comes to mind. Like, did you know camels aren't born with humps? I don't do parties well and..."

His eyes meet mine. "I'm doing it again, right? Is any of this remotely interesting to you?"

"As someone you've hired to help you find romance, yes. It's extremely interesting."

Especially since you mentioned I'm attractive. Again.

Jackson pauses and stares in his lap before meeting my gaze again.

"Does this mean you aren't available for me to ask on a date? I've hired you to help me, so isn't that a breach of confidence or something? Can I date you if I'm paying you? Or...can I just ask you out?"

Oh, boy. I don't normally talk about my past with clients, or new friends, for that matter. It's one of those things in life that people can be weird about.

"Well, in my former profession, that's exactly what I did. I used to be an escort. Men paid me to attend functions with them." Among other things, but I don't think I need to voice that part. Why I'm even telling him this, I don't know. We aren't dating and we can't even call ourselves friends.

Yet I've just thrown this huge thing about me at him before we even get to know the basics of each other.

Jackson nods slowly, like he understands but yet he doesn't quite understand.

"How did you end up with this business, then? If you're running an escort service in Kissing Ridge, I'm sure I would've heard of it by now." He chuckles. "Cowboys gossip like you wouldn't believe."

With a sigh, I lean back in my chair, feeling inexplicably more than comfortable with him. Without his hat on and his boots out of sight, I can pretend he's just another guy with nothing in common with Chase. He's easy to talk to. There's just something about him that has me spilling more than I usually would.

"I don't run an escort service. I build romance. Sex workers have a negative stereotype." I notice Jackson hasn't sneered or shown anything other than an openness to listen. So I keep going. "The men who hired me weren't always just looking for sex. Some were, but most wanted someone to make them feel loved and cherished. To feel like they mattered to someone in a world that was far too quick to dismiss them. If it led to sex and they wanted that, then I provided it. But you'd be surprised at how many men simply wanted to feel good about themselves in a non-sexual way."

Jackson nods along, riveted by my words, and I should feel relieved that a man I'm interested in seems to not care about all that. Instead, he shifts forward with a genuine smile on his face.

"That's a kind thing to do, Riley. What is Wild Romance then, exactly?"

"Well, the simple answer is that I love fairy tales. This is me making them come to life for people. I plan wedding ceremonies and receptions, proposals, and romantic dates for those who want to surprise someone special. Anything to make a magical moment. I love romance and love."

Jackson's cheeks flush under his scruff, and he ducks his head. Something about his demeanour just sucks me in, and instead of keeping my walls up, I've poked a hole in one to allow a bit of light in.

"I just want to not trip over my words. To meet someone who doesn't mind staying home and cooking dinner together instead of going out. I like a simple life and it's hard to find that."

He raises his gaze again, and our eyes meet. Jackson's tongue pokes out, licking his lips before biting his lower lip.

"And you'd like me to coach you on how to do that? To find someone like that?"

Jackson remains silent for a few beats before he finally speaks.

"I'd like you to be more than my coach. Would you...I mean, I wanted to ask you on an actual date today, but I was late. You're very, um, I like how you look." Jackson wrinkles his nose and shakes his head. "I mean, you're the kind of guy I'd like to ask on a

date, but most of the time, I just say something weird and...yeah."
He snaps his mouth closed again and my heart dances in my rib
cage, unsure of what I'm potentially about to agree to. After all,
this is my mystery man from the park. I want to know more about
him for reasons I'm not ready to admit.

"It's weird, but I feel like...like we're already friends I guess."
Jackson's lips tip in a small smile. "We shared hummus, and I told
you I like Lady and the Tramp."

I can't fight the smile that brings to my lips.

"We did have hummus in the park together. I'd consider that a
start of new friends."

Jackson's smile is what dreams are made of, and I like that I put
that smile on his face.

"You're right. We're no longer strangers. So...Riley, would you
like to go out with me sometime?"

Of course I want to date this man. He didn't blink an eye when
he learned I used to be an escort. He's as hot as those Thai chilis my
aunt dared me to eat once and he likes hummus. Not that hummus
is on the checklist of boyfriend qualities, but it's a definite plus in
my book.

But... my gaze drifts to the cowboy hat on the seat next to him
and I freeze. The small hole I poked in my walls gets plastered over.

"I don't date cowboys."

Jackson stares as his smile slowly drops and my heart squeezes.

"I don't know who did you wrong Riley, but give me a chance.
Not all cowboys break hearts. I think it means something that
you're the same guy I messaged to help me after we already met
at the park."

"So you believe in fate?"

Jackson's gaze slides from mine back to his hands. He squeezes his hands together repeatedly before twiddling his thumbs.

"I believe things happen for a reason. Sometimes we don't know that reason right away." With a sigh, he lifts his gaze to mine again. "This is the first time I asked someone on a date without stumbling over my words. I think that's reason enough for me to believe we were meant to meet like this."

Shit! Why did he have to say that? Why does he have to be so open and... good? And ridiculously cute.

"That's great that you've already noticed improvement, then. You don't need my help to get someone into bed."

His eyes flash. "Have you even been listening? I want more than just a body between the sheets, Riley. I want romance too."

The air in the room feels impossibly charged right now. He doesn't need to confirm it, but I feel like Jackson just went beyond his comfort zone to say that.

"If I were to say yes." His eyes light up and the giant smile returns. Damn man is so attractive it should be illegal. "If I were to say yes, where would you take me on a first date?"

"Well... would you come to a hydroponic gardening seminar with me? It's not really a date event, but...I could use a friend to be there with me. It's this weekend in Smokey Valley and I really don't want to go alone."

I almost laugh out loud but stop myself. He's sincere. A date for a gardening show is what he really wants, and that's... oddly charming.

He reaches down into the chair and sets his hat back on his head.

Fuck. Despite not wanting anything to do with cowboys, Jackson looks far too good. But hydroponic gardening? My interest in this man is more than piqued.

"I'll check my schedule and let you know. Is that okay?"

Jackson nods and tips his hat.

"It's not a no, so I'll take it." He holds his phone up. "You have my number. Think about it and text me." He stands and, after a beat, says, "It was wonderful to talk to you today, Riley."

Jackson leaves my office, closing the door gently behind him, and I collapse back into my chair with a whoosh.

Am I seriously thinking about a date with this guy?

As I google the hydroponic gardening show, I realize I'm not thinking at all.

Six
Jackson

"Wait, wait, Jack."

Hunter drops the load of feed at his feet and spins to look at me. He pulls the bandana down that's covering his nose and mouth to reveal his lips pressed together in a severe, thin line. We've been unloading feed bags today into the horse barn. The usual delivery person screwed up and Hunter isn't pleased to be lugging feed himself when he has a perfectly good silo that needs topping up.

"So you're telling me you've *hired* this guy? To date?"

Dropping my feed bag on top of his, I cough with the cloud of dust.

"No. But I thought about it." We exit the dark barn back into the late morning sun. It makes sense to me. Riley is the one I want to be on a date with. Full stop. If he told me I had to hire him, like what he used to do, I would have done it.

I might fumble through my words sometimes and feel awkward as hell, but I know he felt something yesterday, too. I'm not sure what happened to him, but I wasn't ready to let it drop when he said he didn't date cowboys. Awkwardness be damned. I wanted him to know I wasn't like whoever mistreated him.

"I don't know about this, Jack. I thought you'd just have an appointment with him and get a confidence boost. This sounds...weird."

"But he's the guy from the park." I follow Hunter up to his house. It's far too big for just him and I wish he'd hire more help. Fill the place back up so it's not so empty and sad. "He's *the* guy, Hunter. I didn't fumble or anything this time when I asked him out and he already agreed to go to the hydroponic show this weekend with me if his schedule is clear."

Hunter stops in his tracks on his porch and I almost slam into his back. He looks at me like I just sprouted an extra head and spoke a new language.

"Oh my god. Jack...you didn't."

"What?"

"You invited the man that you really like to a hydroponic gardening show?"

"Um...yes?"

He shakes his head as we wipe our boots at the door and head into his kitchen. Hunter reaches into the fridge and pours me a glass of cold water from the pitcher.

"Anyone in their right mind would pass on that. But he said yes?"

Swallowing the cold water, I lean a hip against the cupboard.

"He did. Sort of. I asked if he could make that our first date and he's checking his schedule. I also told him I could use a friend. So it's in his court now."

Hunter drinks and swallows and cocks his head. "He must like you to agree to attend a fucking gardening seminar." He sets his glass down and rummages in the fridge. "Did you invite him because of Cameron? I thought the business was over, anyway?"

"We had our final meeting with the lawyer last week. It's over, but I still want to go to this." But also… part of me wants to show Cameron if he would've just been more flexible, our partnership would've worked. I'm committed to the project, and I'll continue on my own in another capacity.

Our business may have died, but my love of hydroponics is still alive and well.

Pulling out my phone, I check my texts again for anything from Riley and this time, Wild Romance pops up in my email inbox.

Good day, Jackson.

I checked my schedule and I can be free this weekend to attend the garden show with you.

My only request is that we keep this a platonic date. We go as friends and if you're okay with that, I'll see you on Saturday.

Sincerely,

Riley Benton

Wild Romance

My lips tilt in a goofy smile. He agreed to go out with me, but he already put me in the friend zone. Which I won't lie, it stings. But I'm astute enough to know there's a reason he did that. One I hope to fix.

As far as this goes, it's a win for me. I'll take the friend date.

"Hey, Hunter?" He turns from the stove where he's fixing us omelets for lunch. "He said yes, but as friends only."

"Okay. So what does that mean? You can't kiss?"

"I don't know too many friends who kiss, do you?"

Hunter sets our plates on the table and throws me a put-out look.

"So it's a date, but not an actual date. I fail to see how this will benefit you if he already friend zoned you."

Hunter shoves a forkful of food in his mouth, and I consider his words.

"It means I get a chance. He didn't say no right away." While chewing my food, I point my fork at Hunter. "I don't expect you to understand, but there's something there with Riley. I can feel it. He just needs to let it happen."

"If you start spewing off shit about soulmates and fairy tales, I will legit kick your ass as soon as you leave this table."

I throw my head back with a laugh. "One day, some guy is gonna swoop in and thaw your icy heart, man. When that day comes, I will gloat so hard."

Hunter snorts. "Whatever."

Hunter has already emptied his plate and I'm still staring at my food. Pushing back from the table, I hit *dial* on my phone and go outside. I can't eat until I talk to Riley. I want his verbal confirmation about the whole thing. Maybe I'm old-fashioned, but I don't want to arrange a date over email.

"Wild Romance, this is Riley. How can I make your dreams come true?"

Kiss me and go out with me for real.

"It's Jackson. So you said yes, but only as a friend?"

There's a long pause and I fear maybe I've offended him. But he finally responds.

"You got the email then. Is that okay?"

I want to scream no, but...this man is different. We connected that day in the park, and I want an actual date, not a friendly one. He didn't laugh at my random food facts, so that's saying something. Perhaps I need to be more patient.

"No. I guess not. It's disappointing, but I'll work with it."

"Good. Did you have any other questions for me?"

I like his voice in my ear and I want to keep him on the phone longer. This indescribable want to just learn about him gnaws at me from the inside. Does he have siblings? Did he go to college? When's his birthday?

"Did you know starfish don't have brains?"

And there it is. Glad to know I still can't be normal with phone conversations. Why didn't I ask him his favourite colour instead?

"Uh...no. I didn't know that."

"It's true. They're not even fish."

"Jackson... I meant, did you have any other questions about Saturday?"

Of course he did. Ugh.

"Yes. Are you a morning person?"

"Sometimes."

"You need to send me your address so I can pick you up on Saturday at 7 A.M. We have a two-hour drive, and I want to be there as early as possible."

"I'd prefer if I drove to your house, and we left from there together."

Damn. He's just blocking me from all sides. This might be harder than I thought.

"Okay, that makes sense. Can I text this number if something comes up?"

"Of course. This is my cell, and it's always with me. Text me your address and I'll be there at 7 on Saturday morning."

"I'll do that. And Riley?"

"Yes?"

"I can't wait to see you."

There's another pause, and I swear I hear the smile in his voice when he responds.

"Thank you, Jackson. Me too."

After ending the call, I lean on the porch rail to stare off at the now mostly empty fields on Hunter's ranch.

"Starfish aren't the only things without brains."

Hunter leans in the doorway behind me with a teasing grin on his lips.

"You heard that? It's not nice to eavesdrop, you know."

"I know. But it's my front porch, and I didn't want to interrupt the call you abandoned your lunch for." He steps forward and punches me in the shoulder. "I hope you know what you're doing, Jack."

Hunter trots down his steps towards the barn where we still need to finish dealing with all the feed.

I don't know what I'm doing and I'm one hundred percent happy to admit it.

But I'm not about to walk away from the first man I've felt a spark with in years.

With any luck, I can make that spark into something more.

Growing up on a farm with chores needing to be done before school conditioned me to early mornings. I had the chance to sleep later in college, but it wasn't something I enjoyed. The day is half over by 10 A.M if you're only getting up then.

Riley isn't due to arrive for another half hour and, as I adjust the row of tea bags on the counter, I wonder if I've gone overboard. We never had the chance to discuss if he prefers coffee, tea, or something else. The only thing I know about him is he loves the hummus at Avocadabra and I can't really offer him a container of it when he drives up.

Can I?

No. That would be super awkward even for me. Maybe the second friend-only date.

Tires crunching up my driveway sets off a wave of anxiety, dampening my palms with sweat and I inhale a deep breath.

"Manifest, Jackson. You can do this."

Standing in the middle of my kitchen, I continue to breathe deeply and visualize Riley as he comes to the door. My mind paints a vivid picture of what he's wearing... which is probably a bad thing because Riley is an attractive man with clothes on and likely wildly attractive without them.

And now I'm thinking of him naked. God dammit.

The knock on my door pulls me back to reality.

"Manifest, Jackson. Best non-date ever," I mumble to myself as I stop at the mirror in the hallway to check my teeth. After offering a thumbs-up to my reflection, I finally open the door.

And I can't breathe.

Riley stands at my doorstep with a warm smile on his face. He's dressed casually like me, and I don't know why, but I was expecting more business from him. He wears a pair of stylish jeans, ripped randomly down the front, teasing peeks of his smooth skin. His shirt is a simple white T-shirt, tucked on one side and more flowy than fitted, but it suits him perfectly. Riley also wears a gold chain around his neck. It glints in the early morning sun as he waits on my doorstep.

"Hi, Jackson. Am I too early?"

Riley's smile fades a little as I shake my head and wheeze in a gulp of air. Words seem to have vanished now that he's on my freaking doorstep and I'm about to invite him in.

"Jackson? Are you okay?"

"Did you know that all tea comes from the same plant? It's how they're processed that makes them different."

Dear lord. Why can't I just say 'hi, you look great?' At least I didn't pass out. So there's that.

Riley's smile returns as he nods. "I actually didn't know that. I love tea."

"Great! Because I have some!"

I sound like a damn TV game show host. Why? Why am I like this?

"Come in. Leave your shoes on and follow me for a minute."

Riley's amused smile at least stays as he wipes his adorable leopard-patterned running shoes on the carpet as he steps inside.

In the kitchen, I motion towards the chaos of beverage choices that I stayed up all night worrying over.

"I didn't know if you were a caffeine lover. Or if you prefer coffee or tea. I like to have a mug of something when I drive. Here, I got you a mug." Reaching for the box, I open it to remove the travel mug that was, to me, Riley in thermal form. It's a gorgeous pale blue with a touch of shimmer. But it was the pattern that sold it to me.

Riley takes the mug and sighs. "Oh, Jackson. This is so thoughtful and sweet. You remembered."

Riley runs his fingertips over the pattern on the mug. It's the mirror from Snow White and the caption reads, *Who's the fairest of them all? I am, bitch.*

"It just seemed like something you'd like with the fairy tales and whatnot." Wiping my slick hands on my jeans, I ignore how damn cute he looks as he inspects his gift. "But I didn't know if you're a coffee drinker or tea. Maybe matcha?" I gesture again to the slew of beverage choices on my kitchen counter. "I picked some of everything. So choose which one you like and I'll make us one before we leave."

Riley smiles again, his gaze soft on me before he turns to survey the entire row of hot beverages I bought at *Walmart* last night. Flavoured hot chocolates, six flavours of herbal teas, a box of flavoured coffees, decaf coffee, and regular tea in three brands because they all taste different.

"What's your favourite?" Riley asks as he surveys the choices.

"Normally, if I stay home, it's coffee. But if I'm on the road, it's tea."

Riley immediately steps to the tea. "Which one?"

"Um, today I'd pick an herbal one because I already had caffeine and if I have more, I'll probably embarrass myself and talk faster than a squirrel at a rave."

Riley chuckles, and plucks the herbal tea box from the pile and scans the flavours. "I'll take a peach one, please. And you haven't embarrassed yourself at all."

Flipping on the kettle, I toss a tea bag in my cup and wash out his new travel mug before dropping a bag inside his too.

"Well, I could've said '*Good morning, you look great*' and not some ramble about tea."

"True. But it's cute, and it's real. And now I know something about tea." He smiles my way, and I can't help but smile back. "Have you ever talked to someone about your nervousness? Is it because of social anxiety?"

The kettle boils and I flick it off to pour the water into our mugs and set the timer for it to steep.

"Do you take cream or sugar? I like a bit of sugar just to take the bitter off."

Riley grins. "Make mine the same, then."

As I level a teaspoon of sugar into the mugs, I answer his question.

"I've never talked to a professional. I just...I guess the only thing I'm never nervous about is rodeo. When I made the connection in high school, I knew I couldn't give rodeo up. I felt... normal? Accepted maybe?" Shrugging, I remove our tea bags and tighten the lid on the mugs. "Maybe it is social anxiety. But I'm forty years old and it's all I know. Until I met you, I figured it would be my life, you know? Awkward and perpetually single, talking about misshapen carrots."

Riley remains quiet as he takes the mug I hand him.

"For what it's worth, Jackson, you've already gone above and beyond for a first date. If it was a date, I mean. As a friend, it's amazing. This is very thoughtful of you. You remembered something I like." He smiles at the mug and raises it in a toast. "And you gave me choices here. The amount of thought and effort you've demonstrated is honestly impressive."

Riley's words of praise make me puff my chest. Maybe I'm not so bad at this after all.

"Thank you. Ready to learn about hydroponics?"

"I won't lie and say yes because I don't know if I am or not." He laughs, and it's light and carefree. "But I *am* ready to drink tea from my new mug and take a road trip with a friend."

Riley follows me out, and after locking the house, I motion to my truck.

"Your chariot awaits."

Opening the truck door for him, he murmurs a thank you, and I walk around to the driver's side.

Before opening my door, I allow myself a tiny butt wiggle of victory.

I impressed him and he said I'm cute!

Seven
Riley

If you told me my first date with the mystery man from the park would be at a hydroponic gardening seminar, I'd likely have just laughed in your face and told you to try again.

And if you told me the same mystery man would be a cowboy, a rodeo cowboy at that, I'd have asked you what alternate dimension you live in.

But our drive here was enjoyable. For a two-hour drive first thing in the morning, it doesn't feel like I've spent time with someone I barely know. Jackson makes me laugh. He's genuinely charming once he gets past the *'opening line jitters,'* as I call them. And he's a complete gentleman.

He even checked in several times to ask if I needed a rest stop. It's only a couple of hours in a vehicle, but the offer was appreciated.

I'm enjoying his company at this hydroponic thing far more than I expected. Despite going into this knowing it's a friend-only date, Jackson keeps treating me like a date. I'm still on the fence about how I feel about that.

Watching him weave through the crowd with a tray of food from the concession, my lips turn up as he approaches. Jackson requested I sit at a table and asked my permission to bring me food.

While he waited in line and worked through the crowds—there really was a shocking amount of people here—I relaxed.

"Okay, you said to surprise you since it seems like we have similar food tastes. How do you feel about sharing a few things?"

Jackson sets the tray of food on the table and seats himself across from me. His hopeful smile is hard to resist, and I grin back.

"If you don't double dip, I'm game."

Jackson scrunches his nose like a disgusted little rabbit.

"Eww. No." He removes the lid from the containers and passes me a set of cutlery as he explains what he chose for us. "I got us each a salad. Everything is grown with hydroponics, of course. I didn't know what kind of dressing you like, so I got you all three, but my favourite is the grapefruit vinaigrette."

Jackson points to his favourite, so I choose that one as he tells me about the other dish he brought for us to share. If I'd come across all this information on a television show, I'd have changed the channel or fallen asleep watching it.

But experiencing a hydroponic gardening conference with Jackson, who is obviously into it, is an entirely unique experience. It's like pausing a live TV show to ask the host questions.

"Hydroponics works well with our area. We have so many cattle out here and they need the room for grazing. When I first pitched the business idea to Cameron, he was so in and we had this passionate idea. It was like...we just dove in headfirst, ready to take it on." He chews a mouthful of salad and gestures to the other container. "Strawberries, Riley. In a big enough facility, we could produce strawberries like this all year around and not worry about the weeding or how much land we'd need to give up for a strawberry patch. Plus...no frost headaches."

Jackson speaks with no hesitation or shyness. His enthusiasm for the subject shines through in his words. He'd make a great salesman.

"You never told me what happened to the business. May I ask?"

Jackson pushes his salad around before sitting back with a huff.

"You don't have to tell me if it's uncomfortable."

"No, it's not like that. It's just...he made me feel like I wasn't good enough to partner with. We verbally agreed on how it would work, and he made me feel bad when I sometimes missed crucial things. But he *knew* I would. I didn't shirk my responsibilities. I wanted this to work. Still do really."

"I don't understand. He dragged you through dissolving a business because he thought you were lazy? That doesn't make any sense. From what I've learned today, this isn't a cheap setup. Surely you both invested loads of money into this?"

Jackson nods and pushes a giant tray of strawberry salad between us. His previous glow of enthusiasm fades as he pokes at a strawberry.

"The honey glaze on this is locally produced. Organic too. The goat cheese is some of the best around."

Jackson stabs at a strawberry like it offends him, and the tightness of his jaw removes all the earlier traces of his easygoing smile.

"Cameron thinks because I make more money at rodeo, I'm not as committed to the hydroponics business. He said the company wouldn't be taken seriously if a guy who wrestles steers grows sustainable produce." Jackson lays his fork down and leans across the table into my personal space. "They can co-exist Riley. We did it for four years. We never had people complain about what

I do. What the hell does my being a steer wrestler have to do with anything? I can't understand why he'd just shove me out like that."

Jackson leans back again, and the disappointment in his voice is palpable. "We invested lots, yes. He bought me out. When you met me in the park that day, I'd just come from the mediator appointment, and I hoped it would end differently. I laid on the grass because I felt like my friend sucker punched me."

"Jackson...I'm so sorry you had to go through that. For what it's worth, I think he's made a mistake. I know we don't know each other that well yet, but you're very passionate about this. It's hard to fake that."

"Thank you. I'm sorry for unloading all that."

"I asked, so don't apologize."

Jackson finishes eating, and even though he's clearly troubled about his business breakup, he wants to enjoy this odd hobby with me. I feel like this is a part of Jackson that he doesn't always show people, and I feel very privileged he chose me to share it with.

"So...ready to get wicked?"

His sinful grin and sultry tone make my mouth run dry as he makes a joke with the name of the process used to feed the plants nutrients. Which, if I hadn't been here, I wouldn't have understood. It's adorably nerdy and I can't help but grin back.

"Is that what you say to all the boys?" I tease. But my skin runs hot when his gaze caresses my body.

"Just the extra pretty ones."

Despite my frosty attitude over the whole cowboy thing, it's hard not to like his charm. Or his attention. It's genuine and while he's already expressed his attraction to me, there's more to Jackson, and I can't quite figure it out yet.

"That was pretty smooth, Jackson."

He stands from our table and scoops all the trash on the tray. I follow beside him as he dumps our tray, sorting all the recyclables and organics in the bins, and we leave the small cafeteria at the conference centre.

"I have my moments, Riley. Not very many, but I definitely feel comfortable with you," he murmurs.

I return his small smile because it *is* comfortable with him.

"I think you just wanted someone to keep you company today."

He pauses outside the next lecture hall that's filling for the afternoon talk.

"Can I make a confession?"

I step aside to allow others to enter the room. "As long as it's not a biblical confession. And no kneeling."

Jackson blinks for a moment, clearly not knowing how to handle my attempt at humour, before stepping over to the side with me.

"Um, no. Not that I wouldn't kneel for you if you asked. It's just not something I do? Um..." He closes his eyes and presses his lips together. "Not so smooth now, am I?"

A giggle slips out, and he raises an eyebrow while I slap a hand over my mouth.

"I'm sorry. I'm not laughing at you. You're just super cute when you get nervous."

"That's the second time today you called me cute." He inhales a deep breath. "You really think I'm cute?"

His soft gaze holds mine and I can't lie to him.

"I do. Immensely cute."

Jackson's smile is so bright I need to fish out my sunglasses.

"My confession was: yes, I asked you for company first. But I really wanted to prove to Cameron that I'm not the fuckup he seems to think I am if I have a boyfriend." He huffs a small laugh. "I know that sounds lame, but me being here during rodeo season and with a date makes me feel validated. Like I can still have rodeo and other things. A relationship and a business. So thank you for boosting my confidence."

Well... this Cameron guy sounds like a dick.

"Is Cameron here?"

"Yeah. I saw him earlier, and he's probably in this talk."

"Well then. Let's give him something to think about."

Taking Jackson's hand in mine, I pull us into the lecture building and ignore how much I like holding his hand.

"Where is he?" I whisper out of the corner of my mouth.

Jackson bends low and whispers near my ear. "Balding guy near the front in the orange shirt."

There's space in the row in front of Cameron, so I tug Jackson along by the hand and, once seated, I make a show of sitting close to him and leaning my head on his shoulder.

When Jackson drapes his arm across the back of my chair, I smile up at him. In my periphery, Cameron raises an eyebrow when he notices us, and I turn my gaze fully back to the front of the room.

"He noticed," I murmur low, and Jackson squeezes my shoulder.

As the talk begins, I expect Jackson to withdraw his arm and take notes or something, but he doesn't.

Tapping his knee for his attention, he tilts his head down.

"I just need to step out for a few minutes. I'll be back."

"Is everything okay?"

"Yeah, I just need to check on something."

Jackson's eyes bore into my soul, and I turn away without another word to shuffle out into the hall.

Once outside, I walk down the hall to the nearest exit, desperately in need of fresh air and to clear my mind of everything Jackson Sutherland.

I won't fall for another cowboy.

"I know you thought I'd be bored today, but I had a wonderful time."

Jackson smiles over at me before returning his attention to the road.

"For real? You were interested?"

"Yes! My aunt likes to tease me about my love of salads, but I love knowing more about food and how it's grown. It's why I love Avocadabra. They're not the usual burger and fries place. It's fresh and healthy, organic and local as much as they can be."

"Good, that makes me happy. Avocadabra was our first commercial customer. We sold them strawberries and spinach. Since we were local, they could call up in the morning and order if they needed to keep their stock fresh. I found their hummus by accident when they needed a taste tester. It was an experiment, and I said '*This needs to be on the menu, Hannah.*'"

Jackson chuckles, lost in the memory. The headlights of passing vehicles shine into the cab, illuminating his small smile as he's lost in thought. I imagine him encouraging Hannah with her recipes. He'd do that because it's who he is. I don't need to know him for longer than today to know that Jackson always wants his friends to succeed.

"I need to get healthier meals for my aunt. She lives alone, and she says she's fine, but I know she eats a lot of canned stuff. I read there were cases of scurvy on the rise with seniors. Did you know that?"

"What!? No! What the hell?"

Jackson's fingers grip the wheel, and his jaw tightens.

"Yeah. It's the isolated seniors or the ones who can't afford the fresh fruit and vegetables on their pensions. It's scary to know a disease like that is still around when we've come so far."

"That's very sad. But your aunt, is she okay?"

Laughing, I smile into the darkened truck cab. "Oh yeah. Stubborn as fuck, but she's okay."

Jackson nods and swallows. The click of his throat sounds over the low music from the radio.

"Can I ask you something?"

"Of course you can."

Jackson bites at his lip as Blondie croons softly from the radio set to 80s hits.

"When you left me in the seminar, you seemed very shaken up. Did I do something wrong?"

As great as the day has been, it was the tiny bump that he noticed. I should have known he would. He's far too observant.

"No." Sighing, I let my head rest on the window. "I just...sometimes I get stuck in my head and it was one of those times."

Jackson hums and I'm not sure if it's in understanding or something else.

"You'd tell me if I did something to make you uncomfortable, right? If pretending for Cameron was—"

"No. It's not that Jackson. You did nothing wrong. You've been great."

One nod with his gaze out the front is all he gives me, and I'm relieved he doesn't press it because I'm not sure how to voice what's going through my mind right now.

When he pulls into his driveway and stops alongside my car, I realize the night is about to end, and a hollowness sits in my chest.

"I had a nice day, Riley. Thank you for joining me and indulging my nerdiness."

"You're not nerdy. You're passionate."

The silence lingers as the cooling engine ticks.

"Um, for what it's worth, Jackson, I don't think your awkward mumbles when talking to someone you like are terrible. You seem to get more comfortable the longer we're together."

He does that hum again that I can't decipher.

"That's because it's you. You do that, Riley. I don't know if I'd be the same with a stranger." Before I can reply that we are still mostly strangers, despite all we've shared today, he fumbles with his seatbelt before exclaiming, "Oh! I have something for you inside! Don't forget your mug and I'll be right back."

Jackson bolts into his house and I grab the adorable mug from the truck console. No way am I leaving that behind. Stepping into the dark yard, I frown when the interior truck lights extinguish, plunging me into darkness. There's not even a streetlight out here and I reach out to touch my car while my eyes adjust to the dark.

The door of Jackson's house opens and light from inside spills out as he stalks back to me.

"I keep forgetting to change that damn light bulb. Sorry I left you out here in the dark. I, uh...I got this for you, but didn't want to give it to you earlier."

He holds what looks like a bouquet, but there aren't any stems to hold on to. Instead, there's a brightly patterned paper bowl and inside is...vegetables?

"What is it?"

"Um, this is lettuce from my garden. I have it all year around. There's a handful of strawberries. It was all I had left for now. The rest are still green. Anyway, it's for you."

This is new. Not unwelcome, but new.

"Wow. Thank you, Jackson. That's thoughtful and I don't think I've ever been gifted produce by a date before."

"I probably shouldn't do that with a real date, then? Stick with flowers?"

Right. We aren't really dating. We're just friends. I don't do cowboys and I'd do well to remember that.

Clearing away the lump in my throat, I paste a smile on again. "I'd wait until you're extremely comfortable with them before shoving a salad bowl in their hands."

"Heh, yeah. You're probably right."

His swallow clicks in the night silence.

"Can I take you out again? As a friend, I mean?"

"Yeah. I had fun. We could do something together."

Jackson opens the car door for me and wordlessly moves to the passenger side, setting my gift of produce on the seat before returning to the driver's side.

"Goodnight, Riley. Text me when you get home?"

"Goodnight, Jackson. I will."

His hand touches my arm briefly before he withdraws it and stuffs it in his pocket.

I climb into my car and when I've backed out of his driveway, he's still standing there, watching me leave.

Eight
Jackson

"**Y**ep!"

The steer shoots out with a moo and Hunter has the animal damn near under my horse before I can slide off and wrestle him to the ground.

"Let's give Jackson Sutherland another round of applause for the fastest time tonight of 3.3 seconds! He's a big guy who gets it done f-a-s-t fast, folks!"

The announcer has the crowd on their feet and I wave to them as I walk over to my horse, standing with Hunter.

"Fucking hell, Jack. You keep getting better and putting all the young pups to shame."

Laughing, I pull myself back up in Lady's saddle and pat her neck.

"I'm in the zone, Hunter. I don't know what it is this year but I feel like we can't be stopped. I'm winning this season. *We're* winning this season."

It's only our third event this year, but I've never done better. I feel like a superhero. No steer will get past me.

"The boys will want to celebrate tonight."

The crowd cheers, drowning out Hunter's voice, but I know what he's already saying.

There's only one person I want to celebrate with tonight and I won't be finding him in a bar six hours away from home.

"You go without me. I'll stay with the horses."

Hunter already knew I'd say that. Some rodeo stops require us to have a trailer and tie our horses outside. Hunter has a massive camper with the horse trailer built in, so at least if it's raining we can provide them shelter. But we never leave them alone.

The usual scenario is the boys hit whatever bar is closest and I stay at the campsite. It's worked for several years and I don't mind one bit.

Rodeo is something I live for. The adrenaline surge is real and rather than riding it the whole night, I crash in the evening and search for a quiet space. Sometimes, it's around the campfire with the guys, and other times, it's in my bunk with a book and an early bedtime.

Me and Hunter are the only ones in our group who travel with our horses. Jamieson and Griff travel together but will share a campsite with us. I know I'm the father figure of our friend group, too, but I really don't mind.

After my victory lap in the ring and securing the horses, me and Hunter head back to the chutes to wait for Jamieson's bull ride. We spot Griff in his bullfighter attire wearing a scowl so off-putting I'm almost afraid to say hello.

"Hey, Griff. You okay?" Hunter asks.

Griff, normally a more cheerful guy, growls when he stops in front of us. I don't think I've heard a man growl like that. It's creepy.

"Not really. That asshole isn't taking me seriously and I've got a bad feeling."

Hunter and I exchange a confused look. Griff isn't a ball of sunshine, but he's also never angry. Not like this. He states facts and goes with blunt honesty as a default setting.

"Who isn't taking you seriously? Jamieson?"

There's no way he means his best friend. Jamieson listens to Griff a hundred percent. Griff is like Hunter, but with bulls. He studies their patterns just like the bull riders themselves, and Griff has a knack for sniffing out trouble.

"Yes, Jamieson! He drew Homewrecker and doesn't want to listen to my advice! Says I should stick to my job and let him do his."

Both Hunter and I suck in a breath. Bullfighters have one of the most dangerous jobs in rodeo. Griff is one of the best and it's not like Jamieson to be rude to him. He's like a six-foot-tall stick of cotton candy.

"Do you want us to talk to him? I don't have an issue if he snaps at me," Hunter asks while I search the chutes for Jamieson. "Let him take out whatever is bothering him on me."

Spotting Jamieson, I put a hand on Hunter's chest.

"Let me talk to him. He doesn't need to be upset before he gets on the back of a bull."

Hunter shrugs and I study Griff for a beat.

"Are you okay doing *your* job tonight?"

Griff nods. "Yeah, I'll...I can shake it off. But...if he listens to you Jackson, tell him Homewrecker is behaving off. I don't think he'll be a straight bucker tonight. He's gonna spin and..." Griff throws his hands up with a huff. "It's just my gut, okay?"

"I get it. I'll talk to him."

Leaving the two of them, I walk down the chutes until I find Jamieson in his gear, pacing at the rear of the loading chutes.

Jamieson has the same ritual every time he rides. I don't know how to describe it other than being very animated. But he's not doing any of his usual stuff. He's currently pacing a groove in the ground with his hands curled into tight balls.

"Hey, J. Ready for the ride?"

He stops and whips his head up at the sound of my voice. Jamieson closes his eyes with a huff. "No. Yes? I don't know." His voice carries off in a whisper and I motion for him to follow me and step away from the chute area. There's less action outside the chutes on the grass and we can still hear the announcer from where I stop near a truck loaded with barrels for the barrel racers.

"Talk to me, J. I saw Griff, and he's worried."

At the mention of Griff's name, Jamieson drops his head.

"I was an asshole to him and…I don't know how to fix it." Jamieson swallows and looks up at the sky instead of me and crosses his arms as he leans on the truck.

"He said you drew Homewrecker. He usually throws up a great score."

Jamieson nods. "Yep. That bull is a straight bucker, but he gets air. He's a tricky one."

"Mhm, from what I hear, he might spin."

A faint smile appears on Jamieson's face. "Did Griff tell you that?"

"He did. He's a lot like Hunter that way. Hunter and Griff get gut feelings, and I always listen to Hunter."

Jamieson bites at his lip before turning to me. There's a swirl of emotion in his eyes I can't quite sort.

"I always listen to Griff too, but this isn't about not taking his advice, and I don't want to get into it with you right now."

"No problem. But if you change your mind, I'm always open to listening."

Jamieson nods, opening his mouth to say something, but closes it again. After a beat, he says, "Tell him I'll be ready for the spin. He doesn't need to worry."

"Okay." Clapping him on the back, I motion to the chutes. "Sounds like you'll be riding soon enough. Good luck tonight."

He nods and walks back to the waiting area, and I wander back to where I know Hunter will watch from the sidelines. He never likes to sit in the bleachers, instead staying inside the competitor zone and standing near the chutes.

Griff is in the ring, waiting for the bull riders to start. I wave and, once he sees me, I give him a thumbs-up and his entire body sags. He quickly brings his hands together in prayer and nods his thanks before focusing back on the riders.

"Is Jamieson all squared away, then? Did you give him the full dad talk?"

Laughing, I shove at Hunter. "Just a half one. He's fine. I bet there's more to their fight, but I'll let him come to me."

Hunter says nothing and we watch the bull riders. All the bulls are rank tonight, throwing riders hard, and few riders have stayed on for their eight seconds. The bull fighters are working extra hard to keep the riders safe.

We watch Jamieson mount his bull in the chutes. "Do you have a feeling about his bull?"

Hunter remains silent for a minute, watching the movement in the chute. "No, but I'd listen to Griff. It's his job, after all."

Homewrecker bursts from the chute with Jamieson on his back and, after two straight bucks, does something I've never actually seen before. The mammoth bull bucks and spins, but not how I would have expected. The bull seems to do both movements with all its feet off the ground. It's the most bizarre thing I've ever seen.

And Jamieson holds on. Even when the bull changes direction and lurches him the opposite way as his feet touch the earth before lifting away again. Jamieson makes it look easy, adjusting his tall frame to remain centred and in control, all with one arm in the air. When the buzzer sounds and Jamieson is still on the back of the bull, I hold my breath. The bullfighters hover nearby and Jamieson finally dismounts, stumbling along the sand and immediately swooped into the arms of Griff, who steers him towards the safety of the chutes while the others coax the bull to the exit.

"That was wild." Hunter breathes, and I release a long breath of relief.

"No kidding."

Jamieson's score flashes. A 92, which is epic and launches him to the top of the leaderboard.

Hunter claps me on the shoulder.

"Let's get back to the campsite. I think it might be a long night of celebrating."

"Are you sure you don't want to join us?"

Shaking my head with a laugh, I clap Jamieson on the shoulder.

"I'm not feeling the bar scene tonight. You guys go have fun."

"I get it. You're sneaking in a secret hottie." He mimes zipping his lips.

"Not quite, but let's go with that."

Jamieson cocks his head. "So you are keeping a secret? I promise I won't tell."

"Get out of here. Have a shot for me." Before he turns away, I touch his elbow and lower my voice. "You and Griff are okay, right?"

"Yeah. We're good." He hesitates like he wants to say more, but simply says, "Thanks."

Jamieson joins the group, and they meet the taxi at the park entrance for the trip into town. After getting a blanket from the camper and checking on the horses, I settle by the campfire and add another log.

Sadly, there's no secret hottie. There's a hottie, but if he was mine, I'd be showing him off every chance I get. But Hunter's words about being careful with a man who seems to have issues with cowboys sticks. As much as I wish Riley was more than just a friend, I have to wonder if he'll ever get past the cowboy part. It's not something I can change about myself.

That doesn't stop me from hitting video call on Riley's contact number though.

He answers on the second ring, but not with his face.

"Uh, Riley?"

"Hi, Jackson. I'm here. I just, it's a spa night and I have a mask on my face."

Spa night?

"Oh. I don't mind. Can I see your pretty eyes at least?"

With Riley, it's so easy for me to say stuff like that and before I can apologize for being so forward, he responds.

"Are you playing me?" I smile at the tease in his voice. "That's not what someone shy and awkward would say to their friend."

"Well, I'm not shy with you. Just awkward sometimes. But it's the truth. I like your eyes. Friends can compliment one another."

His phone moves and my screen goes dark. Like he covered it with something and I laugh. "If you won't let me see you, you'll at least talk to me, right?"

"Of course I will. But you can see me if you promise not to laugh."

"I'd never laugh at you."

The darkness moves away and the phone moves again. This time, Riley shows his face. But I don't laugh. Instead, my heart turns to mush.

"Oh my god, Riley. When you said a mask, I thought you meant, like, a mud mask or something. Are you a...polar bear?"

A sheet is stuck to his face, and it's all white. There's a black animal snout over his nose and eyeholes to show me his pretty blue eyes. A tiny pair of bear's ears sit on the mask at his forehead. It's the most fantastic and cutest thing I've ever seen.

"Yeah. It's a moisturizer, and it has an animal face. I bought a few on sale and they're not bad."

"It's fucking adorable."

Riley's small huff of a laugh sets me at ease.

"Thanks. So, um, how did your weekend go?"

"Amazing. I won again. I'm posting the best times of my life, which is great for overall points at the end of the season."

Riley smiles under his mask and the bear nose shifts to the side.

"That's so wonderful for you!"

"It is. It means I get an invitation to a big money rodeo in Big Rock. I don't always plan for that one because it's by invite only. Only the best go and I think after today I'll be getting the call."

Riley shifts and even under his polar bear mask, I know his brow dipped.

"I googled you," he says quietly and for a moment, I don't understand.

"My rodeo event?"

He nods. "Yeah. There are loads of *YouTube* videos with you out there. I know what steer wrestling is, I just...never paid attention."

"And what do you think?"

My heart slams hard, hoping he likes it.

"You're very good at it." He clears his throat. "It's, ah, you're...um..."

I laugh softly. "Now who's tongue-tied?" If he didn't have that mask on, I'd bet his cheeks were a cute shade of pink.

"You look good. Comfortable even. Well, as comfortable as one can be, diving off a running horse like that."

For a man who was against cowboys when we met, this feels like an enormous breakthrough for me. If Riley Benton took time out of his day to google me and my rodeo event... and liked it? I will hold that close and celebrate the breakthrough.

"Thank you for saying that. I know rodeos aren't your thing, so that means a lot."

Riley's polar bear face stares back at me, and his lips part before closing again. He clears his throat. "So how come you're all by yourself?"

Okay, he wants to change the topic and as much as I want to keep poking to find out more of what he thinks, I'll let it rest. One day, he'll tell me why he has barbed wire around his heart for any cowboy who gets close.

"Well, I don't like the bar scene and we have our horses here, so I stay behind and let the others go out." I pan my phone to the fire. "I like to sit by the fire and just be outside. Sometimes I have a book. Tonight I wanted your company."

Riley scratches his cheek, and his mask slips. "Damn it. Give me a minute. I'm going to take this off. You can keep talking while I do."

The phone moves as he walks and now my view appears to be the ceiling in the bathroom. Water runs and I figure I'll just keep talking like he said.

"Jamieson—he's a bull rider—was teasing me about staying behind. He said I must have a secret hottie. I just let Jamieson go along with it. He likes his friends happy, you know?"

"How are you going to meet someone and get over your awkwardness if you don't go out with your friends, Jackson?"

I still can't see Riley's face, and that's probably a good thing. He's the only one I'm interested in more with, and I was never good at hiding my facial expressions.

"I told you. I don't want to be with some guy I meet at the bar."

Riley's face reappears, all shiny and soft. He slicked his hair back, and his lips are shiny with a substance. Maybe lip gloss? He's stunningly beautiful, and all I can do is stare.

Riley's lips tilt in a small smile. "Jackson? Did you hear me?"

Shit.

"No, sorry. I was...um, you're really fucking pretty, Riley."

Dear lord, I sound out of breath as the words tumble out before I even register what I said.

His eyes grow wide, and for a minute, I think I've overstepped, maybe even shattered this tender new friendship with my limited ability to not just blurt out what I'm feeling. This is one instance in which weird animal facts would be less embarrassing.

Riley's face softens, and there's a longing in his voice that's new.

"You're making it really hard to stay away from cowboys, Jackson." With a sigh, the phone moves, and the rustle of blankets sounds. The screen shows Riley again, tucked under blankets with a pillow under his head.

"I think you deserve to know why I avoid cowboys. How much time do you have?"

"All night if you need it."

Riley nods, and he moves around again. Now I'm positioned to see him with both hands tucked under his cheek.

"Let me tell you about a guy named Chase and how he broke my heart."

Nine
Riley

"**Y**ou told him everything? Over the phone?"

"Over a video call, yep. Every single thing about Chase. Right from how he hired me as an escort first to how he kept coming back and I wouldn't accept his money. The charade I fell for and how I loved the whole cowboy bit he played."

It wasn't easy telling Jackson about Chase. But Jackson asked me twice why cowboys and rodeos were on my list of avoidances. I didn't owe him an explanation, really. But even as a friend, I felt like I should tell him. I confide in Gabe most days, and he's great, but Jackson lives here in Kissing Ridge, and it's nice to have that one person you can count on no matter what close by.

Even if I could maybe see myself dropping my walls for someone like Jackson.

Maybe.

"So, how did he take it?"

Leaning back in my office chair, I roll my eyes with a soft laugh.

"Like the fucking gentleman that he is, Gabe. He apologized *for* Chase. Doesn't even know the guy, and he apologized for his actions. Then he had to go on and tell me that even if we never date for real, he still wants to be my friend and show me not all cowboys are assholes like Chase."

"To be fair, Rye, can you even say Chase was a real cowboy? He entered a few rodeos here and there that we know of, and he had a failing beef farm. Hardly a cowboy. Not like this Jackson guy who sounds like he has more chivalry in his pinky than Chase's entire body."

Ouch. That's too close for comfort.

"Don't bring logic into this. I judged him and placed him into a do-not-go category. Is it the right one? Probably not, but there it is."

Gabe hums under his breath, and I want his opinion. It's why I called, but I don't want to hear it now. Because Gabe has a way of picking apart all my insecurities and making me face them. Which is what makes him an amazing lawyer, a phenomenal friend, and an annoying ass all at the same time.

"Don't do the hum thing. Say it."

"Since you called," he drawls, and I shake my head. "Here are my thoughts on this. You don't hate cowboys. It's a convenient excuse to avoid this guy who makes you feel things. You think if you let anyone else in, they'll break your heart. A cowboy was just easy for you to dislike. You love romance, Rye. Why do you keep making it for others and not yourself?"

Okay, valid question.

"Because I don't want to get hurt again. I don't know, Gabe. I always rush in and fall hard and when the breakup comes, I just...it feels like it's not for me and I should enjoy romance from afar. You know, watch all the *Disney* movies and create the moments for others I won't have myself. Avoid the pain."

Gabe laughs. A full-on belly laugh, and my mouth drops open.

"You're fucking laughing at me? What the hell, Gabe!?"

"Riley, for one minute, listen to yourself. How the hell do people pay you money and trust you to plan weddings and shit when you're like this? You plan these amazing things for them and what? Think they're going to fail?"

"Of course not! I want them all to have beautiful lives together. It's just not something I'll ever have. It doesn't affect my job. I can have romance and be a part of it without a breakup is all." There's zero chance of having my heart crushed if I'm an observer. "It fulfills me." I add lamely.

Gabe sighs. "Give him a chance, Rye. He sounds like a good one and you like him. I can do a background check if you want."

"Really? Wait, no. That would be such a gross thing for me to do. I trust him. Mostly."

There's a knock at my door and a silver-haired man pokes his head in. I motion for him to come in.

"I'll think about it and call you later. My client is here. Thanks, Gabe."

"Anytime."

Ending the call, I apologize to the man in front of me.

"I'm so sorry, Carlos. I lost track of time."

He laughs and smiles and I love how happy he always is. He and his wife are turning seventy this year and celebrating fifty years of marriage. Carlos wants to go big for his wife and I'm here for it.

"That's okay, Riley. I know how it is. You're a busy guy. All the ladies at the bridge club are talking about how you staged the proposal for Linda's grandson. The one who wanted a flat-bottom boat and peaches under the moon?"

"Ah, yes. I remember. That was a swoon worthy proposal and went off without a hitch. Although having a harpist in the wilderness at dark was a challenge, but we did it." It cost a fortune, but I delivered. "You said you wanted to meet today but didn't tell me what you needed. Is there a change to our plans?"

"Yes. A small one if you can help me." Carlos pulls a wrinkled and folded piece of paper from his pocket. "When we were married, Jackie had a woman bake us the most amazing strawberry shortcake. Jackie still talks about it."

"It was that good, was it?"

He passes me the paper, and it's a recipe for the cake. Written in a shaky handwriting that tells a story on its own, I smooth the paper and read it over with a smile.

"I finally tracked down the actual recipe. I don't know what's special about this one, but Jackie insists there was something different about it for it taste so good. I need your help to have one made for her from this recipe, but you can't use the baker in town. He's the brother-in-law to Jackie's cousin's son's girlfriend and they gossip like you wouldn't believe. I don't want her finding out about it."

My mind gives up trying to map that family connection because, honestly, it doesn't matter anyway. He wants it discreet, so I'll figure it out.

"Not a problem. Even if I have to make it myself, it will remain a secret. When do you want it? At the surprise renewal ceremony? It would be nice to have a piece right after you say your vows. Oh! I could arrange for a small tent if you want to rearrange or let me check if the atrium room is available at the Holiday Inn. That would be stunning, Carlos. And the cake could stay air-conditioned, too."

"That's what I like about you, Riley. You're always thinking of things."

"Well, you're the one who kept track of what his wife loves for fifty years. I'm just putting it all together for you."

"Speaking of that, how did you make out with the dress?"

Carlos and Jackie were first married at a courthouse in a quick ceremony with cake and lemonade in a friend's backyard as the reception afterward. He always wanted to give her the big wedding she had dreamed of. Young, newly married with a kid on the way, their finances were tight, and they skipped it. Even when the kids were grown and gone, and they settled into their lives, Jackie insisted the expense wasn't worth it. Carlos, though, a romantic at heart, disagrees.

"Very well! Look at these." I slide two photos over to him. "I have these two dresses and a seamstress ready to arrive on the morning of your ceremony. They'll probably be too big, but they can easily alter either and meet our time expectations."

"Oh, these are perfect. Riley, you have such a great knack for this." He runs his fingers over the dress with mostly lace and a shine forms in his eyes. "I hope she chooses this one. She'll be so beautiful in lace."

"I like that one too. Classic lace can't be beaten."

"So the cake is doable? I know it's short notice, but she mentioned it again the other day and it will be so special for her."

"If I can't make it work, I'll let you know."

Carlos stands, we shake hands, and I walk him out. After he's gone, I pick up the phone to make venue changes first. When that's done, I take a photo of the cake recipe and hit the grocery store.

This might be a mistake.

I shouldn't have asked Jackson here. But friends help each other in times of need, don't they? And right now, I need a friend.

Right on time, my security buzzer goes off and for a minute, I consider not answering. I can make up an excuse. Maybe call an ambulance to get out of here before making another great big, stupid cowboy-sized mistake.

But I can't do that to Jackson. Instead, I press the button on the intercom.

"Jackson?"

"Hi! Fancy place here. What's your apartment number?"

"Uh, just take the elevator to the top. It's a security thing. I'll meet you."

Living in this town's first luxury condominium project has been a learning experience. When I found out they hadn't finished the entire top floor, I used all my savings and bought it. The mortgage payments weren't as hefty as I thought they'd be with my down payment, and I'm thankful that being a tight saver, and smart investor paid off.

But right now, I'm self-conscious about how it might look to Jackson.

Simple, farm-boy Jackson, who likes to sit by the campfire and read books about gardening. Welcome to my super fancy penthouse!

He's going to hate this.

The elevator opens into my private foyer and Jackson steps out. Fuck. In a pair of tailored dress pants and a short-sleeved button-down shirt, he's a dream. His lips tilt in an easy smile as he takes the few steps towards me at my front door.

"An apron? You're cooking for us?"

"Well, *we're* cooking. I never fully explained the task to you."

Jackson's smile falters. "Did I overdress? When you said you wanted to invite me over for fine dining, I thought it sounded like more than jeans and a T-shirt were needed."

"No. You're perfect. I mean...what you're wearing is."

Jackson smiles wide as he raises the bag in his hand.

"You can't take that back. You said I'm perfect." He winks and my mouth goes dry. "I brought something for you."

Closing the door after he's inside, I notice the way Jackson focuses on me. He's not once done the gawking around thing or commented on how the entire top floor is mine. It's like I'm all he cares about and that's a dangerous thought for me to have.

"Oh? You didn't have to bring me anything."

I open the bag, and for a moment, I'm confused, but a bubble of laughter bursts out.

"You brought me baby carrots?"

"It's kind of our thing."

Jackson shrugs like it's not a sweet gesture, and I gawk at him like he's a prize pig at the fair.

"Rye?"

"Oh, yeah, let me just...put them in the fridge?"

Jackson nods as I turn to the kitchen, clutching a bag of baby carrots to my chest like it's my favourite teddy bear.

"You can have a seat at the kitchen island." Behind the open fridge door I duck my head, hoping the cool air takes away the flush I'm positive sits on my cheeks right now. "I'm sorry to have called you on such short notice. When you mentioned you had a long stretch of rodeo travel coming, I thought..."

Honestly, I just wanted to see him after I spilled about Chase over the phone. It's gnawed at me all week. Making a cake is just a convenient excuse to invite him here. To maybe see if what Gabe said was right.

"No! It works great. You're right. I'll be away for almost three weeks. Then you have a few events you're busy with, so if we didn't meet up tonight, it might be awhile before we could again."

"Wow, three weeks is a long time to be away from home." Holding up a bottle of wine, I offer him a glass. "Do you drink wine? If not, I have herbal tea. The same kind you had at your house."

Jackson laughs softly. "Maybe I should have brought you that, too. Sure, I'll have a glass if you are."

After pouring us each wine, I settle on the stool next to Jackson.

"When I told you about Chase the other night, I hope you understand why I said I don't date cowboys."

Jackson sips his wine and his knee touches mine as he bounces it. Even with my nerves, it makes me smile that he's still nervous around me.

"I do and I'm sorry you had to meet someone like that. We're not all bad though, you know." Jackson shifts his gaze and his warm brown eyes lock with mine. "Sometimes we don't acknowledge the signs in people because we truly are blind. Other times, we don't believe we deserve better. But you deserve more than what he did to you, Riley."

Jackson means it. I know he does, and it's difficult for me to accept his words as truth.

"Thank you. I know I do, but my best friend Gabe kindly pointed out to me that I like to find excuses to hide away and I'm trying to fix that."

"I think that's a brave thing to do." Jackson gestures to the ingredients on my island. "Are we baking tonight?"

Grateful for the change of topic, I grin.

"Yes! So, I'm in a bit of a crunch to make one of my clients happy. He's the sweetest man, and he wants a cake for his surprise wedding reception, but I can't use anyone in town because of gossip."

Jackson laughs, and the sound is just like that first day. Deep and uninhibited. So warm and friendly.

"Don't I know it! The gossip vine is crazy here. When we first set up our hydroponics on my property, all the ladies at the hair salon said I was growing illegal marijuana and had a dog fighting ring."

My hand flies up to cover my mouth. "Oh my god! I can see how marijuana might be assumed, but dog fighting? You'd never do that. Don't they even know you?"

Jackson's gaze finds mine again. "Apparently not." He lifts his glass to his lips and swallows. "But you do."

Good grief, I want to crawl in his lap and have him call me baby. I want him to be the one to press all my pieces back together. He can't be this good...can he?

Clearing my throat, I tear myself away from his gaze.

"Well, can you bake?"

"I guess it depends on what we're making."

"Strawberry shortcake." I tap at my *iPad* on the stand. "Specifically, this recipe. If we can make it well enough, I'll do it myself for Carlos. No gossip, and I don't have to worry about a delivery getting lost or a cake that's subpar."

"We? So I'm part of this event now?" He smiles as he pulls the iPad closer and knocks his knee into mine. "When is it?"

"Oh, I didn't mean that you had to help me with the event or anything. I just—"

"I'm kidding Riley. I'd love to help you bake it and if I can help you pull it off, I will."

Jackson pushes the iPad back in place.

"Do you have another apron? Let's do this."

Ten
Jackson

I've never baked before.

But I have to admit it's been fun. Riley isn't too good at it either, but on our second attempt, we do a decent job of making a cake. I always thought shortcake was like shortbread. Turns out I was wrong and the cake part is quite spongy. Still tastes amazing, and it's kind of cool that we made it.

My stomach growls when Riley pulls the second cake from the oven. I don't want to be rude and ask if he has food, because I thought maybe he might cook for us and we'd stay in, but I didn't eat and I'm starving.

"I heard that from over here, Jackson. I'm going to feed you."

Laughing, I feel the heat on my neck as Riley looks my way. Lord, what I wouldn't give for him to not mean food right now. Who knew baking with someone you wish was yours could be the most torturous form of unreciprocated foreplay.

"Sorry. I thought you were planning a gourmet feast by the way you sounded on the phone."

He dusts his hands on his apron and opens the fridge.

"Sort of. I wanted to bake the cake before we ate. But I cheated and I have some dishes from Avocadabra for dinner. I do like to cook simple stuff sometimes, but since I know you love their food, I figured why make it hard?"

Riley pulls several takeout containers from the fridge and I step forward to help him. "Oh, that's a lot. I can give you some money for my half."

He pauses before turning to me. "Can this one just be me repaying you for helping me bake?"

"If that's what you want. But I don't mind paying you for it."

Riley's shoulders stiffen, and he turns away from me. "No."

There's a definite shift in our playful energy from a minute ago, and I don't know why. He flips lids of containers as the silence grows and I replay my words.

Oh.

Stepping closer, I touch his arm and force him to look at me.

"I wasn't trying to be mean about your past, Rye. That comment was just me wanting to pitch in like a friend would."

Because you keep putting me in the friend category.

"Sorry. I know what you meant. It's...it caught me off guard, is all."

No, it was more than off guard. If he had an invisible shield, it just went up to the heavens, and I hate it. Being bold, I cup his cheek with my palm and he closes his eyes.

"If you give me the chance, Rye, I won't hurt you." My voice scratches in my throat, but I have to be sure he knows I'm nothing like the man who broke him. "You're not a dollar amount or anything less than a beautiful human being who I'd love to know better. I'm not him."

He swallows and keeps his eyes closed. "You aren't awkward at all, Jackson. You say all the right things."

"Because I like you, Riley. I have since the first time I saw you. I'm more comfortable with you than anyone else." Shrugging a shoulder, I don't know how else to describe it. "It feels easier with you."

His slender fingers wrap around my hand, and he pulls it from his cheek. His lips part and moments pass before he releases my hand and turns back to the food.

"How do you feel about eating on the couch and watching Disney shows?"

Okay, message received. Still friends.

"Like it's the perfect evening."

Riley breaks out in honest-to-god laughter and he's gorgeous like this. Comfortable in his space and free to be himself. He passes me a stack of napkins with a beaming smile.

"Jackson, I swear to god you don't even know how adorable you are." He nudges me towards the living room while he carries two containers of food. "Your eyes lit up when I said Disney."

After settling the food between us, Riley turns the television to a streaming service I've never heard of and there it is... Lady and the Tramp.

"Oh my god, Riley! It's even the original version!"

Riley sits with a smug smile. "Of course it's the original. It's a classic. Even if bits don't age well, I still prefer watching the original."

"I haven't watched this in...lord, twenty years at least."

As we pick at the food he bought us, including our favourite hummus, I'm transported in time to the worn sofa in my parents' living room. How many times did I watch this on weekends when my chores were done?

"I drove my mom nuts with the number of times I watched this as a kid. But I remember when the Tramp came out to defend Lady the first time. With the conviction only a seven-year-old could have, I thought, I want to be like that dog."

Riley's sweet laughter fills the room and I smile over at him.

"You wanted to be like a dog?"

"Yeah. He just went for the cocker spaniel, you know? He was tough and not all spoiled like her, but yet he stepped up when needed and fell in love with her. Partly because she was pretty in dog terms, but also, I think, because they complemented each other so well. I wanted to make someone feel like Lady did when she realized how awesome the Tramp was." Huffing a small laugh at how silly it sounds to speak it out loud, I shake my head. "I wanted to be brave like Tramp and shoot my shot, no matter how out of my league I felt. One day I wanted to do that."

Riley's gaze is soft before he turns back to the movie, and I study his profile. His little button nose is the cutest thing. He doesn't have dimples, but when he smiles, it sort of lights up his entire face. Like he has this inner bulb that glows when he's happy and brightens all his best features.

But I can't be like Tramp. Not if Riley doesn't want it.

"Okay, truth. Do you find the spaghetti scene romantic?"

Riley turns to me after he sets the nearly empty food containers on the coffee table.

"I feel like this is a trick question."

He shakes his head with a smile. "No trick. I just want to know your thoughts."

"Okay." He asked for the truth, so I'll give it. "I think sharing food with someone, off the same plate as they did, is an intimate activity. More so because they have no cutlery, but they're dogs, so it had to go that way. But I think it's very romantic, yes. It gave that first push for them to mean more to each other. To own their feelings."

Riley wrinkles his nose. "Really? Even the slurping spaghetti and knowing they share drool? That's still romantic to you?"

"With all politeness, Rye, people do a lot more than share drool when they get together." Riley's gaze drops and I reach over to lift his chin with my finger. "I love it when they touch noses. It's the most adorable thing ever. Seven-year-old me loved it and forty-year-old me still loves it."

Riley says nothing for a few moments, and the movie plays on in the background, but it no longer holds my attention.

"When do you leave for the big rodeo tour?" Riley breaks the moment and moves to take our dishes back to the kitchen. His movements are shaky, so I don't help immediately. I may be awkward with my words sometimes, but I know when someone is uncomfortable. Right now, Riley is throwing me all kinds of mixed signals and I should probably take the opening to leave before I say something wrong.

"Two days. Hunter and I will take his trailer and the horses. It's a two-day drive to the first event. We have two days to rest, then a three-day rodeo before a full day's drive to the next rodeo. We dip into the United States for a few rodeos there before heading back. The whole thing is almost three weeks of living out of his trailer on campgrounds."

Riley leans on the kitchen island and grips the edge of the countertop with his hands.

"That's a long time to be gone."

Nodding, I shove my hands in my pockets to keep from reaching for him.

"It is. It's the longest one of the season, but it's worth it for us. We earn a lot of money at those events when we do well."

"Will you have cell service while you're away?"

Riley bites at his lip and keeps his gaze down. I wish he wouldn't.

"I will. I make sure I have US roaming off when we go, and I get a package for travel. I learned that lesson the hard way."

When he says nothing for a moment, an awkward tension grows between us, and I don't know what to say. Well, I do. I want to tell him I'll call every night if he's available and I want to see what other animal face masks he has.

I want to tell him I'll miss him, and that tonight was one of the best nights I've had in a while.

"Did you know bats have thumbs?"

Ah, there it is. Heaven forbid I say what I'm actually thinking.

Riley's lips twitch, and at least he turns his beautiful eyes on me.

"I didn't know that."

"Yeah, they have this weird claw thing on it for climbing. It's kind of cool."

Riley raises his thumb and wiggles it. "I suppose a claw thumb could be useful." He trails off and shoves his hands in his pockets. "Thanks for helping me out tonight. I'll send you pictures when I make the whole thing for the event."

"I'm glad I could help. This was fun."

"Call me when you get to your first rodeo stop?"

"Yeah, I can do that." With a nod, I turn to the door and once my hand turns the knob, Riley calls out.

"Good luck, Jackson."

"Thanks, Rye."

Slipping out the door before I can say something else stupid, I punch the elevator button, which opens immediately, and I step on.

Before the doors close, I catch Riley at his door watching me, and like a loser, I give him a thumbs-up. But he laughs as he turns away into his apartment.

I'll take it.

"Jack!"

Jamieson bellows across the campsite as he runs over to me, and I brace myself for his incoming affection.

"Careful, J, you're—*oof*."

Jamieson reaches me and pulls me into a firm hug before letting go.

"You're a rock star. Did you hear? You're already guaranteed to win this season with points after tonight. Do you know how amazing that is?"

"I don't want to assume anything yet. I still have two more events on this circuit before Kissing Ridge's big rodeo. Anything can happen."

Jamieson shakes his head while he throws an arm around me and guides me to a camp chair. After he plops in one and I do the same, he continues.

"Nuh-uh. Brody Coutts just got injured. He was your closest competitor. You can lose every event and still take the title. Not that you'll lose because this is the best season of your life, but it's locked up, man."

"What? Is Brody okay?"

Pulling out my phone, I scroll to my contacts and find Brody. He's a younger steer wrestler and has heaps of promise. I watched him when he was still on the college circuit and he was incredible. I'd hate for his injury to be something serious.

"Yeah, I think it's a torn biceps, though. He'll need some intense healing if he wants a future."

My fingers rapidly type a message and hit send. Then I switch to the standings and see the ticker across the top that Brody really is out, and it's projected I'll win the season. Running a hand down my face, I sit back with a sigh.

"Shit. I want to be happy, but Brody is a good guy. This sucks for him."

Jamieson nods. "I guess that makes sense. I'm sorry. I didn't think about Brody. When I saw you were going to take the title, I just got excited."

"It's okay. I understand and I *am* excited. It's just a lot to digest right now."

My phone vibrates with a text from Brody, confirming that he tore his biceps and is out for the rest of the season. He congratulates me and teases me about not getting too comfortable at the top because he'll be back next year to knock me down. Hearing him remain upbeat while he must be devastated makes me feel a little better.

"So, still staying behind tonight then, gramps?"

Laughing, I reach over and swat at Jamieson.

"Yeah. Maybe after the next one we can go out. I just want some quiet time tonight."

"I'll hold you to that Jackson. You need to go out sometimes. You're a big deal, and it's okay to celebrate." Jamieson rises from the chair and claps my shoulder. "Maybe one day you'll tell us about whoever it is you text all the time that makes you smile."

My cheeks heat as Jamieson laughs.

"I may be slow sometimes, Jack, but I notice when my friend smiles at his phone more than the friends in front of him. Don't stay up too late."

He saunters off to the trailer he shares with Griff, and I lean my head back with a sigh. I've only been away for ten days with two rodeos done. There are still ten more days and three rodeos to go before I'm back home.

Before I can have another friend-only date with Riley.

Riley makes it super hard to stick to the only friends part. A condition I'm now very suspicious of only being created out of fear.

"Yo! Jackson!"

Hunter calls, and I turn to find him ready to leave for the bar with Jamieson and Griff for the night.

"It might be a late night. Don't worry if I don't come back. I'll text you."

I raise an eyebrow. "You're planning an entire night away with someone and not a bathroom quickie? Impressive."

"Meh. I'll see what happens, but I could go for more than a BJ tonight."

"Have fun with that."

He laughs and waves and the three of them head off in Jamieson's truck with Griff driving. Since our campground is a fair bit away from town, they all did rock, paper, scissors to see who would be the driver tonight, and Griff lost.

As far as I'm concerned, he won. The drinking and partying Jamieson and Hunter can get up to are not for me.

The campfire crackles and glows in front of me and Lady huffs in the background with Hunter's horse. It's a clear night with stars out and for the first time in what feels like forever, a wave of loneliness washes over me.

I've always been happy with my life. Yes, I've tried to date occasionally, and I've had a few fun flings. But those were fleeting and nothing of substance. Nothing that made me want to hang on to them forever, but they filled the gap at the time.

They weren't Riley, though.

Just like rodeo, Riley has this way about him that makes me think I can have it all. Do it all. Sure, we've only just started to know each other better, but I know we could be so good together if he'd just give us a chance.

My phone pings and lights up with a message.

> **Riley:** I was just sitting here with my pizza and thinking how nice it would be to have company. Are you free to talk?

If that's not a sign he's meant for me, I don't know what is.

Eleven
Riley

With my feet up on the table and the spinach and mushroom pizza next to me on the couch, the most natural thing in the world to me was to invite a friend over.

The problem with that is I didn't have many.

Okay, I had none outside of clients and clients don't count. Jackson is a friend, though. Of that I'm sure. He's been very transparent that he'd like more, but even if the attraction wasn't mutual, I'm positive he'd be a good friend to me.

Before I could overthink it, I texted him. There was a very high chance he would be off celebrating tonight. I may have googled the rodeo results already and saw he won another event. Even for a greenhorn like me, that's a big deal. Racking up points for the season is critical.

But I sent a text, mildly hoping he'd pick up.

Wiping my hand on the napkin and setting my pizza slice down, I reply not with words but with a photo of the pizza and send it off.

Laughing out loud in my empty condo, I chew and swallow as I send another reply.

> **Riley:** I wasn't aware you'd enjoy a food pic that much. Next time I'll send something different.

When Jackson doesn't reply right away, I start to panic and send another text.

> **Riley:** That was very unprofessional of me. I'm sorry.

> **Jackson:** You don't need to be professional, Rye. We're friends. Friends tease each other. This isn't work.

Right, I can't use that excuse with him. Good to know that he's up for teasing, though. I'm not sure if I am or not. The heat burning low in my groin says I am, but I'm shutting that train down now before it jumps the track.

> **Riley:** How come you're not out celebrating?

> **Jackson:** I'll go out next time. I wasn't feeling it tonight. How's your week been? Make any more cakes yet?

> **Riley:** I did! One more trial of the whole thing and I brought it to my aunt for the official taste. She loved it. Carlos said it's great too. So I think I'm ready.

Jackson: I know you can do it. You're amazing.

Riley: So, have you tried speaking to any new hot cowboys yet? Meet anyone you need some advice about?

I cringe after sending the text. It's not like me to be so intrusive. I shouldn't have asked that. Part of me wants him to say yes to prove that he's working on overcoming what he thinks is some sort of social flaw. In reality, it's what makes Jackson, well, real. The other half of me wants him to say no because I don't want to hear about who he's met.

It's a new kind of fucked up for me to wish for a friend to fail.

Jackson: Cowboys aren't really my type.

Riley: Okay, some cute buckle bunny then?

Fuck, I need to stop this. It's not fair to him. Either I let him in, or I don't, and stop fishing for information. From personal experience, I already know that mind games never end well.

Jackson: Nah. My heart isn't in it yet.

An enormous weight loosens as I chew on my pizza, elated Jackson isn't doing what he originally asked me for help with.

Jackson: Can I ask you something?

My heart leaps into my throat and I push my pizza away.

Riley: Of course.

> **Jackson:** Why did you become an escort? You said you loved making men feel good about themselves when you were doing it. But why did you start?

Well, that's not what I was expecting. While yes, I told him that, I never really revealed the why. Most people fall into sex work out of desperation. They fall on hard times or, sadly, get hooked into the addiction cycle.

I don't have a sad story to tell about it. I chose it willingly, with eyes wide open. Making huge coin was a draw, but money wasn't the primary motivator.

> **Riley:** It's hard to put into a text, but the short answer is because I wanted to belong. To be picked by someone else. Romance wasn't in the picture yet. I was happy to just be with people.

> **Jackson:** Did you not have people before that?

> **Riley:** Not really. My parents wanted to send me away when I was very young and it's a lot to tell you in a message. But the escort business made me feel like I was a person to be desired no matter what anyone else told me.

Very few people know about my conservative family and the need to distance themselves from '*the gay boy*.' The pretty boy who always seemed to make family gatherings awkward. Aunt Agnes was the only one who ever looked out for me. When I told her about the escort gig, she implored me to stay safe and to do what my heart said.

She never judged me for anything.

The people who hired me also never judged me. They were often seeking validation themselves. Some were men in the closet and didn't know any other avenue they could take and remain discreet. Others were simply wanting someone to care.

Being an escort made me feel like I wasn't alone. That people could like me for me. And as corny as it sounds, I could make a difference to the men who also felt untethered and unsure of their place. Sure, Chase fucking exploded my self-esteem, and I developed an awful case of distrust, but I became a real person. I found myself.

Yes, I was paid for it, but they *wanted* me.

The wetness on my cheeks is new and I brush it away, relieved Jackson can't see it.

> **Jackson:** Thank you for being honest. You matter to me. I just want you to know that. I already told you how rodeo was something similar for me. All my differentness disappeared when I was in the ring. I wasn't the kid who had the lowest math score or the kid who never partied. I was the bad-ass steer wrestler winning championships and representing my school. So don't ever feel like I'd judge you about your former life. When something saves you, you cherish it.

Bloody fucking Christ, why does he say all the right things?

Riley: I appreciate that.

Suddenly emotionally drained, I send him a text that I have an early morning and thank him for the company. Then I power my phone off, which I never do, and toss it on the table.

Until I met Jackson, I never considered myself a complicated person. But here I sit, wondering if maybe I am. I love creating romance for others, but not for me. Escort work was enjoyable. I loved it for the way I could make others feel seen like I never was. It provided a closeness sometimes I couldn't find in bars.

And in a twist of self-discovery tonight... I was never alone. Sitting here with my pizza and texting Jackson made me realize how much time I now spend by myself, and I don't like it.

Then I quit escorting when I fell for Chase's lies because I needed the distance from the one thing that made me happiest. He tainted it. I hated cowboys and rodeo because it was an easy target. Where should I place the hate of having the best thing in my life taken from me if not on the very platform Chase based his lies on?

It certainly made sense to me then.

Walking my pizza to the fridge, I slide it inside and see the bag of baby carrots still sitting that Jackson brought me. Fresh wetness pricks behind my eyes. Over a stupid bag of carrots!

"I'm such a fucking mess."

But how do I fix this?

The remaining wine in the bottle seems like the best answer. After drinking a half bottle of wine and feeling somewhat mellow, I collapse into bed.

Holding that fucking bag of carrots.

"So, you want me to help with a goat wedding?"

There's a first for everything, I suppose.

"Yes! See, Gerber was a rescue, and we already had Daisy."

"It's a perfect match!" the woman cries with a clap, and I do my best to smile.

The couple laughs together, and I mean, goats are cute, but a wedding?

"I'll be honest. I have zero knowledge about goats, and I'd be going into this blind."

"That's okay. Delilah from the nail salon said you were amazing at arranging the bachelor party for her nephew. That's the one who wanted strippers, and you had them all dressed as rodeo men like that Down Under show." She fans herself and my eyes dart to the man, who still grins like a fool. "Then they all left lipstick marks on his cheek and took pictures for the fiancée. She loved it."

Delilah's nephew was openly bisexual and married a straight woman who was the loveliest person I'd ever met. She knew he had a thing for cowboys, and it was her idea for him to have this huge erotic party, and I have to admit I was jealous of that one. I saw the strippers, and they needed firemen nearby. They were that hot.

A goat wedding is not the type of referral I'd expect to get from a bachelor party, but goat matrimony money is still money.

"Tell me what your vision is, then."

The couple launches into their idea of a barnyard ceremony in the pumpkin patch this fall. The goats love pumpkins, so they want to let them loose to eat or smash them after they say I do… or whatever a goat would say.

I scribble notes as they speak and, as odd as it is, ideas come to mind, and I write them down as they do.

"And we need you to find us goat tuxedos. We had pyjamas lined up, but they look terrible."

"Ah, okay, and do you have measurements?"

The woman opens her purse and slides a worn recipe card over.

"Gerber needs the tux and Daisy needs a dress that will stay on."

"Or a pantsuit," the husband supplies. "We don't need gender conformities unless we have to."

"Of course not. I just want to be upfront that my fees are the same as if this was a human event before we go any further."

"Of course it is. They're our babies and just like humans, so we treat them like that."

"Okay. I'll email you a contract and spend some time putting a cost list together. We can review and go from there."

"Thank you so much, Riley! I'm looking forward to it."

After the couple leaves, I fill in my standard contract with the details I already know. Then I look into seamstresses who can sew animal clothing and what do you know? I have one on my contact list, which was better than I expected.

When my phone rings and I see my aunt's name on the screen, I immediately reach for it, shocked at how much time has passed.

"Auntie, I'm so sorry. I lost track of time. I'm still coming over."

"Is everything okay, Riley? It's not like you to not call. I was worried."

"Yeah, it's...I'll tell you when I get there? What do you want to eat tonight?"

"I've already started the sauce for my lasagna. Just bring your sweet smile and laughter. Oh, and your wallet. I'm whipping your ass in scrabble tonight."

Snorting a laugh, I save my work and sign out of my laptop before shoving it in my bag to take home.

"I'll be there in half an hour, and I have a whole jar of coins for you, woman."

"Bills, Riley. Leave the kiddie coin at home."

Smiling bigger than I have in days, I end the call with my aunt and head over to her place, hoping like hell that I draw some good letters tonight.

"Ha!" Aunt Agnes finishes placing her letters and sends a smug smile my way.

"Dick? You're happy you made the word dick?"

Shaking my head and reaching for my wine, I can't stop the laugh from bubbling out.

"I'm perfectly pleased with myself. Especially to draw that kind of laugh from you." She leans back in her chair and swirls the rest of her glass of wine. One glass on game nights is what she allows herself. Since she loves it, I don't nag her over it. Alcohol is one thing she shouldn't have with her meds, but as she likes to say, don't steal all the fun from me.

I have to admit the laugh felt good. Enough that I need to get something off my chest with her.

"Auntie...I think I made a mistake."

"Is it like the time you shaved your eyebrows off? Or is it more like when you shopped online while high and then had a living room full of toy cars because you thought they were real and too much of a bargain to turn down?"

"That was one time!" I laugh again at the memory before finally pushing aside my insecurities and laying it out for my aunt.

"There's this guy—"

She leans forward, interrupting. "I've been waiting so long for this! Tell me about him." My aunt shakes her head. "Wait. A mistake with a guy? That's not what I've been waiting for at all. What happened?"

"I met him at the park. It was kind of blind and very romantic. We met and had lunch, and I liked him. We just had this sort of instant connection, and I was excited to get to know him."

"That sounds so fairy tale. Meeting in a park must have been nice. Then what happened?"

"Well, turns out he's a cowboy...and wanted to be a client."

Aunt Agnes knows very well my issues with cowboys since Chase and she frowns.

"What kind of client? Are you escorting again?"

"No. Nothing like that. He wanted to hire me to help him with his social awkwardness around men he's attracted to. I didn't know his name until he showed up in my office." My thoughts flash to the look on Jackson's face when he entered my office. His shock morphed to happiness to see me while I went from shocked to an immediate asshole because of the hat in his hand.

"So, what did you do?"

With a wry laugh, I drain my wine glass. "Well," I begin as I reach for the bottle and refill the glass. "First, I was a bit of an asshole. Then he was kind and forgiving. Then I debated internally about what to do." With my glass now full, I take a long swallow. "Then I accepted his offer of a date, but only as a friend because I couldn't say no."

"Oh, Riley. Why didn't you just go out with him for real? Not everyone is like Chase, sweetheart. I know a lot of good men in this town who are cowboys."

"That's the million-dollar question. We've had two non-dates or whatever, and we've texted and called each other while he's on the road with rodeos. He's not Chase. I know that, but...it's really difficult to convince myself it's okay to ask for more."

"Is he still interested in you?"

Snorting, I run a hand down my face. "Yeah. He's...awkward but not subtle. He very much would like to be more than friends."

"I'm so confused, sweetheart. What's the mistake then? Sounds like you made the friends only condition to keep your heart safe. Which isn't wrong, but you're fighting yourself on it. Why?"

A question I've rolled over far too many times in the past few weeks.

"The mistake is I like him. A lot. But I don't know if I can handle his lifestyle. He's away so much for rodeo. He wants to build a business. And what if he *is* just like Chase?" Swallowing hard, I look at my aunt's concerned face. "I'm afraid he'll hurt me, and I can't go through that again."

Gabe had messaged me this week to update me on my testimony for Chase's alibi. I can do it by a video conference at the local courthouse. But the whole thing is yet another stressor on my plate. I'm working on moving on, but until this thing with Chase is finished, it's holding me back. More than I care to admit.

"But if you don't take a risk, Riley, you'll never know. Nor will you be happy."

She reaches over to squeeze my hand and I squeeze back, grateful for her support as always.

"I know. It's just...he makes me want to let him in. He really does. But then I don't and he's so understanding. I don't want him to give up on me, but I'm also sort of wanting him to."

My aunt laughs, but in a kind way as she pats my hand and sits back.

"Hearts lead us astray. But hearts also lead us home. I don't have any advice for you except to not miss an opportunity because you're afraid. Be brave, Riley."

I really want to. But I can't survive another broken heart. Jackson wouldn't just break me, he'd shatter me forever.

Aunt Agnes sips her wine and studies her remaining scrabble tiles.

"If we end the game now, I win with dick."

Sputtering around my wine, I laugh out loud.

"Everybody does, Auntie. Everybody does. Let me get my wallet."

Twelve
Jackson

Rubbing at my eyes, I roll over to grab my phone that's rattling away on the nightstand. We got home at 3 A.M. and I instantly crashed. As much as I love the events we attend, this stretch is a killer, and I'm exhausted.

"Hello?"

"Jackson? I'm so sorry. Did I wake you?"

My body perks at the sound of Riley's panic-laced voice.

"Riley? Yes, but it's okay. Are you all right?"

"Not really. I...I need your help."

In an instant, I'm sitting up and searching for clothes.

"What do you need, and when?"

"I hate asking you this, but since you helped me with the cake before, I'm hoping you could again?"

"Of course. When do you need me and where? I just need to get dressed and I can be there in a half hour."

There's a long pause on the line, but his ragged breaths are still there and I stand in my bedroom, acutely aware that something big has its hooks in Riley.

"Rye? Tell me what you need. I'll be right there."

"I need...could you, um. I'm going to text you a code for my condo. All the stuff to make the cake is there. There's been...I needed to be at the courthouse five minutes ago. I'll explain later, but I needed to make Carlos' cake and..."

He stops again with a shaky breath, and while he told me he may need to provide testimony for something soon, I thought he was prepared for it. Clearly not.

"If you need me with you—"

"No! I'll text you the code and see you later. Please."

His voice cracks and I hate how he sounds so...defeated.

"Whatever you need, Rye."

"Thank you."

He ends the call and a code for his condo comes through almost immediately. After finding fresh clothes, I throw a hat on my bedhead and rush out the door. A shower will have to wait.

Riley said he wouldn't be gone long, but I've already baked and cooled the cake without hearing another word from him.

I don't know if I should leave or wait for him. He sounded so upset, though. I'd hate to leave and have him come back to an empty apartment. That wouldn't be right.

While trying to decide what to do next, I run the sink full of water and clean up the mess from baking. I hit play on my favourite country music play list and hum along as I lose myself to the mundane task of washing dishes.

The scent of a freshly baked cake, the soft sounds of music I love, and my hands plunged into a sink of soapy, lemon-scented water, shouldn't embed themselves into me this much. The only thing that would make this perfect is for Riley to walk through that door and greet me like a boyfriend.

To let me kiss him deeply and ask him how his day was. Maybe even sit at the table before supper and eat dessert first. We'd have a dog and it would lie at our feet while we ate before we walked it to the nearby dog park. I'd throw a ball and Riley would laugh every time the dog brought it back to him instead of me.

It's perfect.

So perfect, I don't hear Riley come in until his hand is on my shoulder, and a very surprised squeak leaves my lips before I spin around.

"Shit, Riley. You...." Riley's normally glowing face is pale, and his red-rimmed eyes stand out like beacons. Without a second thought, I pull him against me in a tight hug. "Rye, what happened?"

His hands clutch at my sides, bunching the fabric of my shirt in his fingers. He doesn't pull away though, and I smooth a hand up and down his back.

"They made me feel like I was trash, Jackson. Complete untrustworthy trash."

Anger. The primal need to rip something apart flares and I hold him tighter.

"Give me names and I'll make sure they never make you feel less than ever again." The words growl out of my mouth and Riley hitches a breath against my chest before pulling away.

"Chase and the other lawyer! Gabe said it would just be a sworn statement to provide an alibi for him. It would be five minutes tops." He rubs his eyes with the heels of his hands and sobs. "It wasn't! My reputation was dragged through the mud because I was a '*sex worker*!' I was doing the right thing, you know. Gabe told me to confirm Chase was with me on that night and he was. I even have the transaction to prove it."

Riley paces to the large window in his living room that looks over the town.

"His wife's attorney tore me apart and made even me doubt my story." He huffs a humourless laugh. "Because why should my word be taken at face value when I worked for sex? And that's..." He sighs and turns back to me. "Sometimes I wish I'd stayed invisible."

"Rye...no, don't say that."

He ignores me and walks back to the kitchen. He glances at the cooling cakes, the kitchen sink full of soapy water, and then takes in my still-wet hands.

"Were you doing my dishes?"

"Well, yeah. What else was I supposed to do? You weren't back, and the cake was baked. So I cleaned up."

Riley nods like I've just stated the weather and stands in place.

"Rye? You're scaring me. Are you okay?"

"I need to lie down."

He spins on his heel and walks down the hall towards where I assume his bedroom is. Part of me wants to go to him, but the other part says to stay put. Deciding he needs time to gather himself in private, I return to the dishes and finish washing. Then I dry them and put away the few where I know their places and leave the rest on the counter.

Riley hasn't come out yet and I don't just want to leave, but I also don't want to wander through his place uninvited. But my concern for Riley wins, and I walk softly down the hall where he disappeared until I find him in his bedroom. Asleep.

"Oh, baby," I whisper as I pad into the room. Riley is curled on his side, hands tucked under his head, much like the night he told me all about Chase. A soft blanket sits draped over a chair in the room. I grab it and gently cover him with it while watching his chest rise and fall with deep, steady breaths.

How much stress has this caused him to crash this hard? How hard has he been working at this all alone with no help? Not knowing what else to do, I quietly leave the room.

Once back in his kitchen, I grab a pen and tear a piece of paper towel from the roll to leave him a note. After placing it by the cake, I let myself out of his apartment, careful to lock the door behind me.

The weights clang and bang as I settle them back into the holder.

"Really, Jackson? You're going to cross a friend line when he clearly said he wanted to be friends?"

Hunter and I walk over to the treadmills for our cooldown after an intense weight training session where I relayed in bits and pieces what happened yesterday with Riley.

"I think I need to, Hunter. You didn't see the look on his face. He looked so lost and alone as he just...he just clutched at me like I was the only good thing in his life. He asked me to bake a cake, gave me his code for the elevator up to his place and then hugged me like it would make everything better."

"Yeah, but I gave you a key to the ranch gate too, and I don't want your tongue down my throat."

I punch him in the shoulder with a scowl. "That's different and you know it. He's asked me directly for help, but he's also asked me indirectly and if I didn't know any better, I'd think he's hoping I make the first move."

"I thought you said this Chase guy totally fucked him up? You really think he wants someone to make a move? Sounds an awful lot like someone afraid to trust."

Hunter punches buttons on his machine as I narrow my eyes.

"Sounds like some personal experiences you might want to share?"

"Nope. This is about you, Jack. But think about it. Chase was a cowboy, sort of, and so are you. He had a meltdown at some court thing and came back home to find you. The guy has to be all kinds of mixed up and not knowing what he should do about anything."

My treadmill kicks in and I fall into the brisk walk while I turn his words over in my head. Maybe he's right and I shouldn't do anything, but Riley knows I'm interested. I told him the first day we met in his office that I wanted to ask him out.

Maybe I just have to accept that Riley isn't interested in more and just wants to be friends. I'd hate for him to think I was another asshole, like Chase.

"Okay, so if I don't try to move things along, should I still be friends?"

"Are you happy as friends?"

"Yeah, we have a lot in common. I enjoy talking to him and spending time with him. He's funny."

Hunter shrugs. "Then stay friends Jack."

It's not that easy, though. Is it?

"Yeah, maybe you're right. I don't want to ruin a good thing. We do have fun together. Maybe I'll finally join you guys after the Big Rock event and see if I can find someone to move on with."

Even as the words leave my mouth, I cringe. I don't want to move on.

Hunter laughs. "You can easily find someone to get under you, Jackson. Trust me."

"Yeah, maybe."

My words lack any desire for that, though.

Hunter pops his earbuds in, effectively ending the conversation, but I choose to go without and run with my thoughts instead.

I want Riley, but I can't figure him out. My gut says he's just hurt and if that's the case, maybe he needs more time to let us become more. He's followed my rodeo for the last six weeks. He knows my stats, and he's kept track of things. That's not a sign of someone who hates cowboys.

Surely, I can't just be imagining there's more to us.

But Hunter has a point. If Riley has been hurt and is distrustful, he wouldn't want me barging in and insisting we become more.

Maybe I'll be patient a little longer and just keep being there for him.

The sky is perfectly clear, and my truck idles at the curb while I wait for Riley.

When he shows up with sleep lines on his face and bedhead, my hands itch to pull him to me and kiss the ever-loving fuck out of him.

"This better be good, Jackson. It's 1 A.M. and I have a wedding to take care of today. Not to mention you have a long drive ahead of you."

"I know, but...you need to see this. *We* need to. I promise it will be worth it."

Riley sits quietly, still in his pyjamas, as I drive us out to the country and into an open field. After parking the truck, I tell Riley to sit and wait as I quickly throw the patio chair cushions and blankets into the truck bed.

When I'm done, I hurry around to Riley's side and open the door. He almost falls into my arms since he was propped against the door snoozing. After internally sighing at how damn cute he looks hitching his pyjama pants up after stepping onto the tailgate with his old man slippers, I bounce up beside him and lead him down onto the bed I'd made in the truck bed.

"When I was a kid, I was fascinated with astronomy. I still have a telescope and I get these daily emails about star reports and phenomena and..." Riley's unimpressed stare has me break off. "So, anyway, look up and watch for shooting stars. There's a meteor shower happening and the next hour is prime time to see it."

Riley's surly face softens as he leans back and pulls the blanket up to his chin.

"Really? I've never seen a shooting star or anything like that."

We lie together on the cushions, snuggled under the blankets, our eyes roaming the sky. It's still and quiet out here in the field, just down from Hunter's ranch. It's actually part of his ranch and was once filled with cattle, but not anymore.

"Oh my god, there's one!"

Riley, suddenly wide awake, struggles to get his hand out from under the blanket and point to the sky.

"I saw it! Oh, there's more!" Riley gasps as three orbs streak across the sky in quick succession. "Jackson...this is so...fucking cool."

Grinning to myself, I sneak a peek sideways and catch his profile in the darkness. Eyes wide and lips parted in wonder like a child who just discovered the magic of Christmas. What I wouldn't do to put that look on his face every day. I'm just happy it worked out that I could do this before I have to leave again.

He points out a few more meteors, but I miss them because the view beside me is far more breathtaking. Riley twists his head to find me watching him.

He remains silent, but our gazes lock and we're so close we share the breath between us.

"You're missing the stars," he whispers.

"No, I'm not. The brightest one is right here."

Riley's eyes drop to my mouth before he turns his head back to the night sky. After a beat, I do the same.

I know we shouldn't be out here. He has a big wedding event tomorrow and I need to drive to the Big Rock rodeo. I got the invitation, and it's a quick turnaround for me and Hunter, but I needed to show Riley something I always enjoyed. Hopefully, it lightens his spirit like it does mine.

I've always wanted to share this with someone I cared about. If I can't have him in the way I want, I can share these kinds of moments with him instead as a friend, because that's what friends do. I'd do just about anything to make him smile and realize there's more to life than living in fear.

It might make me want him more after sharing this with him, but I'm willing to feel the pain if it brings him joy.

"Jackson?"

"Yeah?"

Riley is silent for a long beat, and I fear he may have fallen asleep mid-thought.

"Thank you."

Swallowing hard, I can only reply in the way my parents taught me.

"You're welcome."

Thirteen
Riley

The Big Rock fairgrounds are alive this evening with the laughter and screams from midway rides. The mouth-watering aroma of freshly spun cotton candy and deep fried dough teases me, but for now, I have to ignore it.

My guts are a mess without it.

After my butterfly release ceremony went off without a hitch at the wedding, I rushed back home to pack a bag, then hit the road to drive three hours to Big Rock for the invite-only rodeo Jackson is competing at tonight.

Since he picked me up in the middle of the night to watch the meteor shower, my thoughts have been in a state of constant chaos. It was such an intimate outing, but he kept himself contained and made it more about an attempt to lift my spirits after what happened at the courthouse. When Jackson called to invite me, he said astronomy was something that soothed him. He wanted me to find peace with what happened, and I felt like he wanted to say more and didn't.

I didn't trust myself to say anything either. Instead, I thanked him for the experience and tucked it away as one of the most thoughtful things anyone has ever done for me. Jackson was knocking down all my walls with barely any effort. We both had our lives to handle and whatever this was between us had to wait until I could wrap my mind around what exactly I was doing and what I wanted.

I wanted Jackson. I always have, but I needed to process and get over the cowboy thing. Jackson won't do me dirty like Chase. I knew it like I knew the sun set in the west and to never trust gas station sushi.

Which is why I came to the rodeo.

After driving as fast as I safely could, I still had time to spare before the rodeo started. I paid the admission, then I had a chat with a volunteer about the rodeo schedule and learned Jackson's event happens in the first half near the end.

Scanning the stands, I found a seat midway up the bleachers and sat next to a group of older men and in front of a large crowd of women. Nodding hello, I turn my focus on the event ring. Various riders on horseback ride in circles. Some have a lasso they swing but don't release and others have their horses respond to commands. No sign of Jackson, though.

I didn't tell him I was coming because it was spontaneous. When I woke up after the disaster of a court visit to find the note he left me near the cake, I opened a bottle of wine and gave myself a long, hard talking to.

Then I called Gabe and told him what happened. Since he had vouched for the other guy and assured me that the lawyer would just need a statement, I felt he deserved to know how wrong he was about the man. Gabe was plenty pissed to hear about it, and after apologizing profusely, he talked me off my wine-induced cliff to say something I needed to hear.

Again.

Was I willing to let a good man walk away because of a singular trait he shared with Chase? By doing so, I was allowing Chase to win, and that didn't sit well with me.

So not only did I swear off cowboys and paint them all with one brush because it was easy to do… I moved back to a town where half the male population was some kind of cowboy. I'd doomed myself to unhappiness.

And I was possibly shoving away one of the sweetest men I'd ever met simply because he wore a cowboy hat and made a living with rodeo.

After wallowing in the wine, I chose not to be a loser. First, I wrote a letter to Jackson. Then I threw it out. Then I composed a long text only to delete it. In the end, I felt an in-person delivery would be the best. When he invited me to the meteor shower thing, I almost said what was on my mind, but I held back and blamed it on not being fully awake.

Now I'm here and hoping like heck to catch Jackson after his event and celebrate with him. To throw away this notion that all cowboys are the same and to give us a chance at something real. Something more than friends.

Music blasts through the speakers and a voice booms over the audio system, announcing the start of tonight's event. The crowd cheers and claps and after a short rundown of what will happen, along with the cowboy prayer, I settle in to watch.

Saddle bronc is up first, followed by bare back bronc. Both look extremely painful. Next comes tie down roping, which actually has me on the edge of my seat. Who knew watching a man tie a calf's feet together could be so enthralling?

After a quick drag of the ring and some crowd interactions, the barrel racers come out. Each one seems faster than the last, and I laugh and cheer them on with the crowd. Most importantly, though, I'm enjoying myself immensely.

I've not had this much fun at a rodeo since I was a kid. I've missed it. Maybe it's the laughter floating over from the midway or maybe it's the smiles on all the faces in the stands as they cheer on their favourite cowboys. Whatever it is, I'm loving it.

When the announcer states that it's time for the steer wrestlers, my heart rate speeds up listening to the announcer describe the event. My eyes scan the area and when I finally find Jackson on his horse, my belly hits the ground. Smiling and confident and incredibly sexy on top of his chestnut-brown horse, he's the poster child for what all cowboys should look like. He chats with a serious guy next to him and I wonder if that's his partner. His hazer, I learned when I googled Jackson the first time.

The first two wrestlers are out quickly, with the second one being so fast and smooth that my jaw drops. They just fall off their horses and thump this animal to its side effortlessly. I know it takes skill and loads of technique and effort, but all these men make it look like anyone can just step up and do it. I'm hooked.

Jackson and his partner move towards the chutes and the announcer's voice has drifted away as I focus entirely on Jackson. His horse prances for a moment and then everything settles for the barest of moments. Jackson nods and his "yep!" carries across the ring. The steer bursts out with Jackson and his partner right after it.

I hold my breath as Jackson leans over, only just leaving the gate, and slides off his horse onto the steer. He scoops one arm under the steer's horn and grabs the other horn before he slaps the beast to the ground. It all seems to happen in the blink of an eye.

The crowd is in a frenzy as the steer hops up and trots away. Jackson's bright smile and wave to the crowd as he dusts himself off take my breath away.

There's no hiding how much fun he has out there and how much he loves this. The time displayed is one-tenth higher than his usual, but it'll be enough to land him in the money, which is what he came here for.

He mounts his horse again and exits to the back of the ring and I sit there, stunned. When Jackson told me rodeo made him feel more confident and it was where he felt like he most belonged, I didn't really understand until now. Jackson was made for this.

I bet if an attractive man approached him while he was in the ring, he'd have no problem asking for a date. His quirky facts wouldn't spew forth over his nervousness. This is his domain, his living room.

The rest of the rodeo happens while I sit in a fog. One thing I never asked Jackson about was what happens after his event? Is he here or does he leave right away? Other than staying with the horses at the campground most nights, I don't know what happens in between.

"Are you going to the Silverado tonight? All the rodeo guys go there after."

Two women behind me speak to each other and I boldly turn to ask them about it.

"Where's the Silverado?"

Pink, glossy lips smile at me. "About four blocks from here." She points over the trees dotting the edge of the rodeo grounds. "If you go that way, you can't miss it."

"And the cowboys all go there?"

The friend leans forward like she needs to share a secret.

"Yep! And they never leave alone, if you know what I mean."

Touching a finger to my nose, I nod. "I know. Thanks for the tip."

Turning forward, I watch the rest of the rodeo, but I'm already planning how to surprise Jackson at the Silverado.

When the rodeo ended, I bolted from my seat to get to my car before I got stuck in the mass of people leaving. Turns out I had nothing to worry about because a lot of the rodeo goers stayed for a music performance after.

Once I found a hotel and checked in, I risked messaging Jackson to see how he was.

Riley: I hope you had a great showing today.

Jackson: We did! A little slow, but still good. Did you know I'm already guaranteed to win the overall points competition? That's why I got the invite to this one.

Riley: I didn't know that! Congrats! Sounds like something to celebrate. Will you be going out tonight?

Holding my breath, I wait for his answer while I perch on the edge of the hotel bed.

Jackson: I promised Jamieson I'd celebrate and I can't go back on my word.

Riley: Aww, that's nice. So you'll go with everyone?

Jackson: Yeah! A few of the barrel racers are staying near us and they said they'd check on the horses. So there's no backing out. I'll go for a while and then come back.

Riley: I think you deserve to celebrate for once. You might enjoy it.

Jackson: Maybe. How was the event you had today? The butterfly ceremony, right?

Why do my insides warm that he remembered that?

Riley: It was great. Went off without a hitch, and it's another happily married couple.

Jackson: Aww. I bet they appreciated all your hard work, too.

My heart races. I want to run to him and tell him I'll celebrate with him, but I don't.

> **Riley:** I'll let you go. Have fun tonight. I hope you meet someone special.

> **Jackson:** Thanks, Rye. I already have. I'll talk to you soon.

Was that a comment meant for me? Or did he actually meet someone already after I specifically told him to?

Tossing the phone on the bed, I cradle my head in my hands.

I'm telling him how I feel, even if he's met someone else. I drove all this way to do that, so I'm doing it. Even if I might have missed my chance because I spent too much time being stubborn.

A grand display of my feelings is what I want. To show Jackson he won me over. A brilliant plan to tell this tender man that he convinced me not all cowboys will break my heart, and I'll date him.

But for the first time ever, my mind is blank for a romantic way to do it. It's literally my job and I'm fresh out of ideas.

Ignoring the ball of nerves that sits in my gut, I grab my shave kit and head to the bathroom.

Tonight, I'm telling Jackson I want more than his friendship.

It might be eloquent, or it might not.

But it's happening tonight.

Fourteen
Jackson

The country music is on point tonight and I sway to the tunes more than usual. For once, I don't mind being out at the bar with the guys. Still not my favourite thing, though.

Hunter tips his chin at a pair of younger guys *not* discreetly eyeballing us from the corner.

"I like the taller guy." He turns to me. "Want to come with?"

The other one in the pair is attractive, and I know just by how he's been whipping his head around the bar tonight, he clearly wants to bag a belt buckle. Which is fine. I might be the one to do it. Maybe.

"What if I don't like him and what he wants?"

Hunter raises an eyebrow with a smirk. "Then I'll take both of them."

Coughing into my fist, I shake my head at Hunter's bold statement.

"If that's what you want."

He downs the rest of his drink and places it on a table behind us.

"Oh, I want. Come on."

The crowd parts for us as we approach the two younger men, and I have to laugh a little. Only in rodeo country are we treated like gods and rock stars because we wear hats and belt buckles. I'd prefer to leave the hat at home, but the guys tell me it's a babe magnet.

When we stop in front of the pair, Hunter nods and turns the charm dial up to a hundred.

"Good evening, gentlemen. My friend and I couldn't help but notice you're here alone. Would you have room for some company?"

The tall one immediately pats his lap with a sultry grin.

"My lap has room, sugar." He taps his thigh, and Hunter raises an eyebrow again.

"Since I'm bigger, why don't we trade places, and you can sit in my lap instead?"

"How big?" the man breathes and I'm almost embarrassed for him.

Hunter chuckles as the man scrambles off this seat and motions for Hunter to take it. Hunter does, but on his way down, he grabs the man and pulls him into his lap.

"Oh! Hello, Daddy," the man purrs, and Hunter laughs again.

"Just call me Hunter."

"Sam."

The two of them fly past any form of flirting and head straight into kissing as Hunter holds the man's head still with his hand around his jaw.

Jesus Christ.

Clearing my throat, I attempt a smile at the friend and hold out my hand for a proper introduction.

"Hi. I'm Jackson."

The man takes my hand with a smile. "Blake. Nice to meet you."

"I'm, uh, not really like my friend. Thought I should put that out there in case you were hoping for..." I wave my hand toward Hunter and Sam still canoodling and being far more intimate in a bar than I'd be comfortable with. "That."

Blake smiles, and I like the way he laughs.

"The only thing straight about Sam is his method of just going for what he wants. Sometimes I envy that."

Blake moves over and I squeeze into the seat next to him.

"I understand completely. I need time to work up to asking someone out and I don't kiss people right away."

Blake swirls his drink with a sigh.

"So, no chance with you tonight, then?"

His words take me off guard. I'm not stupid. I know what he and Sam are after, but his question leaves me reaching for words.

"To be honest, no. And it's not because you're not attractive or anything like that."

Blake turns towards me, and his soul-filled eyes remind me of Riley so much it pains my heart. "You're a proper gentleman, Jackson. I feel like you're not a regular at the bar scene."

Sam and Hunter have finally come up for air and join the conversation.

"My friend is a true romantic. This is the first time he's been to the bar with us all season." Hunter reaches for his beer while Sam remains cozy as a cat by the fire on this lap with Hunter's palm firmly on his ass.

"That's really sweet." Blake gazes longingly at me and I stare into my ginger ale. "I'm disappointed, but it's good to know you're comfortable with that. Not a lot of men wouldn't admit they don't like casual sex."

"It's not that I don't like it. I've had it. It's just..." I trail off, wondering why I'm considering pouring my heart out to a complete stranger while my best friend makes out with another stranger across from me.

Sam leans forward. "There's someone else, isn't there?"

My eyes snap to his and he shrugs. "You're an easy guy to read." He lifts his drink and settles back against Hunter.

"My friend has a heart of gold, but he's been friend-zoned. It's killing him."

Blake sighs again. "You're pining for someone who doesn't want you that way?" He brings a hand to his chest. "God, Jackson. That's something out of a romance book. Is he still your friend too?" I press my lips together and both he and Sam gasp.

"We aren't here to talk about me."

"Okay then." Hunter places his beer on the table and nudges Sam. "Let's dance, sweetheart."

Without another word, they leave me with Blake, and my tongue grows thick. I don't want to make small talk with him or cockblock him. I should just go.

"I had an impossible crush on my straight friend for years. I know how you feel to not have him return the attraction."

"How did you deal with that?"

Blake shrugs and draws a finger through the condensation on his glass. "I avoided him for a long time after I told him how I felt. I knew he wasn't into me that way. But I wished for it so hard because I loved him."

"Are you still friends?"

Blake genuinely smiles and nods.

"Oh yeah. I still love him because he's one of my closest friends, but I've accepted it's a different love, you know? I still have him, but I don't yearn for him that way anymore. He married a lovely woman, who I consider a close friend, too. But at one time I couldn't entertain being with anyone else because I was so into him it was all I could think about."

That's how I feel too. Blake is a gorgeous man. He seems kind, and he's easy to talk to. He's obviously attracted to me, but I can't go there with him.

"His name is Riley," I blurt and feel the heat rush to my cheeks. "He's a friend, and he told me that before we had our first non-date. I went into it with my eyes open. I just hoped I could change his mind."

"Are you sure he hasn't?"

"I guess I don't know."

"You don't know?" Blake places a hand on my arm and I turn my gaze to his. "Is there something that makes you think he's changed his mind, Jackson?"

"Um…maybe? I just…we connect and I don't want to give up on him because I think he's the most perfect person I've ever met."

"Does he know how you feel?"

Biting my lip, I shrug. "I'm pretty sure I've made it clear. Short of kissing him like I need it to live, I don't know what else to do."

Blake punches me in the shoulder. Hard.

"What was that for?" I whine as I rub the spot. For a small guy, he sure hits hard.

"Listen, I speak from experience. Go tell him all this. No hints or subtlety. You go and fucking tell him, Jackson, that he's the one for you. Kiss him like you want to if he consents, of course. Put it all on the table. Until you do, you'll never be able to move on." Blake shoves at me again. "Pick up your phone and make the call. Go."

He's stronger than he looks, and I stumble out of the booth. Blake slides out after me. "I'm going to dance with your friend. Don't worry about me. You're a diamond, Jackson. Truly. He'll be stupid to turn you away."

Without another word, he elbows his way through the crowd over to Hunter and Sam. They open their dance to invite him, and Hunter's eyes find mine. I nod and he tips his hat as I make my way to the exit with Blake's words in my mind.

With my phone gripped in my hand, I have every intention of calling Riley outside and confessing everything in my heart.

But a group of men near the bar catch my eye. A larger man has a smaller one caged against the wall with a leer on his face that I don't like. The smaller man keeps trying to pull his arms away or duck under them and my feet change course.

"Excuse me. The man doesn't seem to be interested. Let him go."

The man turns over his shoulder and eyes me with a smirk.

"He's plenty interested if the dollar amount is right. Ain't that right, sweet thing?"

Peering over the man, my eyes meet the terrified gaze of Riley.

"Riley? What are you doing here?"

His mouth moves, but he says nothing, and I just... react. My hand curls into the back of the bigger guy's shirt and I yank him away with a strength I reserve only for the most difficult steers.

"Get the fuck away from him." Reaching for Riley, I sense the punch before it actually hits me, and I stagger sideways when a fist catches my jaw. A pair of hands land on my shoulders and turn me to face the man who punched me.

"You fucking cowboys always come into this town and think you're hot shit. You don't get to walk in here and ruin my chance because of your shiny belt buckle."

"Ruin your chance? He's not interested."

I'm not interested in a bar fight either. I just want to make sure Riley is okay. And what the hell is he doing here, anyway? But the man has other ideas, and this time, I'm not blindsided. Ducking his punch, I throw one of my own and send him staggering as he clutches his jaw. We've drawn a crowd, and it's about to get ugly.

Before he can recover and start fighting again, I spot Riley pressed up against the wall with his hand over his mouth. Rushing to him, I take his hand and drag him to the exit.

"Rye, trust me?"

He nods and grips my hand tighter. Together, we run like the devil is on our heels, and I only stop when he pulls me into a park area and leads me to a bench.

After collapsing and catching our breath, I ask the only thing that I need to know right this very second.

"Are you okay?"

Riley nods. His throat bobs as he swallows and his hands shake on his thighs. I reach for the hand closest to me and squeeze it.

"When I saw it was you he was threatening, I just...I sort of lost my temper. I don't do that kind of thing normally. I...fuck, Riley. What are you doing here?"

"It's a long story, Jackson." His gaze meets mine and his eyes shine as he moves a hand to touch my face. My breath hitches, but not because of the low throb on my cheek. It's the tender way Riley dusts his fingertips across the fresh bruise forming and leans closer. "He hurt you."

"I'd rather it be me than you." My voice is rough and gravelly as I gently take his hand and press my lips to his palm. "I'd gladly carry the pain so you don't have to, Rye."

Riley inhales, his chest expanding as he bites at his lip.

"I don't deserve you, Jackson."

I don't like those words. Nor do I like how unsure and scared he looks right now.

"I can't always say what's on my mind. Sometimes it's easier to show you."

Riley has leaned closer, and I still hold his hand against my chest. "Riley." I rub my lips across his knuckles and he releases a stuttering breath. "Can I show you?"

His gaze finds mine again, and my heart races because, if I'm not mistaken, there's a need as strong as mine there. He nods. Just once and slowly.

Sliding my palm across his cheek, he closes his eyes with a swallow. "Jackson..." a hoarse whisper before I press my lips to his. His fingers bury into my shirt as he clutches at me. Riley sobs but opens and I deepen the kiss, trying desperately to convey he's the one I want. That he deserves the world and then some. He's not a piece of flesh to fight over, but a beating heart who breathes happiness and hope into my life.

His body trembles against mine and I break the kiss, pulling him against me.

"I hope you understand what I meant by that kiss."

"Maybe?" He pulls away from me and traces my lips with a fingertip. "I think we have a lot to sort out. There's an all-night diner I saw earlier today. Would you like to join me for...coffee?" He chuckles and some of the normal Riley returns. "Maybe they'll have baby carrots or something."

"Yeah, Rye. Lead the way."

And he does.

Without dropping my hand that he only holds tighter.

Fifteen
Riley

Sitting in a diner decorated in a 1950s style, complete with waitstaff in poodle skirts, is not the place I envisioned having this conversation with Jackson.

But here we are in the middle of Doo-Wop heaven with a poster for *Brylcreem* on the wall next to us as we giggle at the names of food on the menu.

"I'll be honest," I say as I close my menu. "I can't bring myself to eat a cheeseburger named the Chubby Checker Special. I just can't."

Jackson snort-laughs.

"Okay. I sort of agree, because even though some greasy comfort food would be great, I can't eat Ritchie Valens Ritz Dip."

We both giggle and snort as the waitstaff delivers our drinks. Jackson went with a root beer float, and I chose a strawberry milkshake. We agree to share a plate of fries which have no weird name and after ordering, an awkward silence settles between us, and I clear my throat.

"I guess I'll start with the biggest question and tell you why I'm here." Jackson brings his gaze to mine as he scoops a spoonful of float into his mouth. The memory of our earlier kiss replays in technicolour as I track the way his tongue moves across the spoon and a ball of heat burns low in my gut.

"I only went out with the guys tonight because I promised Jamieson I would," Jackson states before I even get any words out. "That and you said I'd never meet anyone unless I went out there and tried."

My entire skeleton freezes in my body. I can't be too late. He kissed me. But had I not shown up tonight…

"Did you meet someone tonight?" The words are like shards of glass across my tongue.

Jackson pokes at his float and watches the ice cream fizz in the root beer.

"I wanted to. He was a nice guy. Checked a lot of my boxes."

"But?"

"I told him the guy I liked friend-zoned me and I wasn't ready to give up on him yet."

I don't know whether I should throw up or climb into his lap. His gaze meets mine. Naked and honest. Hopeful.

"I came here for a few reasons. I had a heart-to-heart talk with Gabe about you."

Our waitress delivers the mountain of steaming fries and both Jackson and I laugh at how big the heap of potato product is.

"You can't say you don't get your money's worth at this place, can you? I think this plate of fries has three pounds of potatoes." Jackson raises the ketchup bottle. "Do you dunk?"

"Is there any other way?"

"Only if you're a chaos creator and like ketchup everywhere."

We quietly eat a few fries before Jackson breaks the silence again.

"So, what did Gabe tell you?"

"Something I both didn't want to hear and something I needed to hear." Jackson dips a fry in the remainder of the ice cream in his floats and eats it. "Eww, what did you just do?"

"I've always seen people do that at the fast-food places. Figured I should try it."

"And?"

"If I wanted potato-flavoured ice cream, I'd order it."

A laugh bursts from the bottom of my toes at Jackson's dry delivery. But he's not laughing. There's a small smile on his lips, but his serious face pulls me back to why we're here.

"I kept you at a distance because I was scared you'd be another Chase. By doing that, I was letting him win. Gabe kindly made me see I was making myself miserable out of a misplaced...dislike."

"The whole '*I don't date cowboys*' thing?"

"Yeah. It made sense at one time, but the longer I thought about it, the more I realized I needed to change my thinking."

"And you came here to tell me in person?"

It's so much more than that. I wanted to see him in his element. Jackson, in the job that puffs his chest with confidence and makes him who he is.

"I watched you tonight."

Jackson pauses with a fry at his mouth. "Did you like it? Not just me, but the rodeo?"

"I really did." Jackson's shoulders relax and I move a fry through the ketchup. "When I was small, my parents took me to the Kissing Ridge rodeo a few times. Before I came out to them." Listening to my dad go on and on about what real men do eroded my heart in ways that took me years to realize. But I always enjoyed watching the men do their thing. It's an artful sport when you understand the history of it. "When I met Chase, as horrible as he was, he encouraged me to attend rodeos to watch him. He wasn't that good, but being there and remembering rodeo is a part of where I come from sparked some good, you know? When he revealed his true colours, I slapped it all up and packed it away again because that was easier."

Until now, I didn't realize I'd always taken the easy way in my relationships. If it was too hard, I fabricated excuses, and the time to stop that is now.

"I'm sorry I pushed you away without giving you a chance, Jackson."

"I understand mostly, Rye. It just hurt at first and spending so much time with you..." He sighs before slumping back in his seat. "It just proved to me my gut was right."

"About?"

"You."

Swallowing, I stare down at the pile of fries and Jackson's hand, palm up, slides across the table. Closing my eyes, I slide my hand in his.

"I was hoping to surprise you at the bar. I had this big thing planned where I'd find you and probably say something cheesy just to see your face light up when you saw me."

"Well, you definitely surprised me." Jackson rubs at his bruising face with his free hand. "Not in the best way, but I'm so glad I found you. If he had hurt you, I'd have never forgiven myself."

Jackson's genuine concern for my safety makes my chest tighten, so I do what I came here to do. Letting go of his hand, I walk around to his side of the booth and slide in next to him.

His gaze tracks every single movement and once I'm next to him, I angle towards him.

"Jackson, I came here to watch you and by doing so, I learned a lot about you. But I also came here to tell you I saved your note and read it obsessively." He'd taken care of me in more ways than I thought he would. Then I woke up to find his note on a paper towel next to the cooled cake he'd made when I asked for his help.

'Whatever you need. Call me. Anytime.'

"This is me telling you instead of calling you. I need you in my life and I'd like to try being more than friends."

Jackson's sharp inhale is loud in the quiet restaurant. He turns his face away as his throat bobs and I place my hand on his thigh to get his attention.

"Jackson?"

"Octopuses have three hearts," he blurts, before pressing his lips together with a sigh. "Sorry."

"Don't be. I love your facts."

"My heart is big enough to love you like an octopus. Not that I'm telling you I love you. I mean, one day, I will. But not like this. Something romantic with less talk of octopuses."

"I bet octopuses are very romantic, having three hearts and all."

Jackson huffs a laugh. "That's what I like about you. You just take all my facts in stride. I don't even know where I get them from."

"Can we get out of here?"

"That's a great idea."

After flagging down our waitress, Jackson pays our tab with a stern look my way to not argue. So I give him that victory. He wants to take care of me, and I understand because I want to do the same for him.

We exit the diner and he reaches for my hand like it's the most natural thing to do. I take it as we walk back towards my hotel.

"Did you drive here?"

"Yeah. My hotel is a few blocks away."

"Can you drive us somewhere if I give you directions? I want to show you something."

Since he was familiar with the area, it was easier if I let Jackson drive my car. After a thirty-minute drive outside the town limits, he brings us down a small unlit road that opens to marshland.

As soon as he kills the engine, he holds up a finger. "Listen. Tell me if you hear it."

I strain to pick up what he can hear and shake my head.

"I'm sorry. I can't."

"Then we get out."

I follow his lead and step out. He leans on the hood of my car with his hands behind him and the most adorable smile on his face. Then I hear it.

"Bullfrogs?"

"Yes! Isn't it cool? This is a protected marshland, and in the daylight, you can walk all the floating boardwalks. Turtles, frogs of all kinds, fish, muskrats...so much wildlife in a small spot. But I love to listen to the bullfrogs."

"How did you find this place?"

"The campground we stay at had a pamphlet when we checked in once. Since I usually stay behind, I figured I'd find this place to kill some time while the guys went out. I must have got here at the perfect time because the bullfrogs were so loud you could hear them inside the truck."

First meteors and now bullfrogs. Jackson finds joy in the simplest things and I love that about him.

"I love that you're so into these things, Jackson. You make it so easy to push aside all the shit and to just live in the moment and hear bullfrogs."

"Life is too short to not enjoy the little things, Riley."

Jackson ditched the hat in my car, and I study his profile in the moonlight. He's so strong in his features; the sharp jaw and hard body, but he's also soft. His eyes are always kind and his smile is just... perfect. But it's the organ inside that nobody sees that's both the softest and fiercest part of him.

Jackson's heart is his most attractive feature, and I've pushed it aside the last few months over my own fears. I don't want to be afraid anymore.

Stepping in front of him, I kick his legs gently to allow me to step inside his stance. He remains reclined on the car's hood as he watches me from beneath hooded eyes. Sliding my hand up his chest, I lean closer and gather his shirt in my fist.

"Jackson...I came here to find you and kiss you."

He sits up and grips my hips, pulling me against him.

"I'm not stopping you, Rye."

Leaning in, I press my lips to his and a gentle kiss turns deep and hungry in a matter of seconds. A palm kneads my ass and his other hand dives into my hair.

"Riley…I've waited for this," he murmurs between kisses. "God, I've waited for this."

"I'm so stupid," I breathe as my hand drifts to his belt buckle.

Jackson slides his hand around and grips my wrist, pulling my hand away. "Not here, love. You deserve more than being on your knees in the dirt."

Swallowing, I stare into his kind eyes that mean every word he says.

"I mean it, Riley. I've wanted you since I first saw you in that park, and I don't want this to be cheap and rushed." He cups a hand to my cheek. "I don't go halfway. I'm all in, Riley. With everything. If you want me, it's all of me."

Jackson kisses my forehead. Then my eyelids. My nose, before finally kissing my lips again.

"Will you spend the night with me?" I whisper across his lips before pulling away.

He wipes a hand down his face, but a small smile forms on his lips.

"You're making it awfully hard to go slow and do this right, Riley."

"We can go as slow as you need to, Jackson. Don't worry about doing right by me. I know you will." I trace his lower lip with my fingertip. "It's been too long since I've allowed myself to feel again. To open up to someone. You've made it easier, but I…I want the promise of wild romance I sell to my clients."

"I'll give you that and more, Rye." He holds my face in his hands as he kisses me so thoroughly my toes curl into my shoes. "I'll give you everything."

My grin breaks through against his lips. With the bullfrogs and peepers making their song and this man in the moonlight with me, I can't help but smile.

"Then take me home. Take us home, Jack."

With a nod, he places a kiss on my hand and leads me to the passenger door. After opening the door, he only closes it after stealing another kiss and a goofy laugh bubbles past my lips.

"Are you always like this?"

"I only know how to be me, Rye. So I guess the answer is yes."

He closes the door gently and rounds the front to the driver's side. After he starts the car and buckles himself in, he hums softly.

If I'm not mistaken, it's the song from Lady and the Tramp when they share their spaghetti dinner.

'Bella Notte.'

Beautiful night indeed.

Sixteen

Jackson

Riley opens the door to his hotel room and after we're both inside, the reality of tonight slams into me like the ground when I miss a steer.

He wants this.

It feels like forever since the day I first met him in the park, to the day I finally asked him out and he said he doesn't date cowboys.

"Hey." His soft voice brings me back to the present. "If this makes you uncomfortable, Jackson, don't stay."

"No, it's not that. It's just...did you know rodents can't vomit? I kind of wish I was a rodent right now."

Oh, for god's sake.

"Do you not feel well? What can I do?"

Riley's face is a mask of concern as he takes my hand in his.

"I'm fine. I'm just..." With a swallow, I kiss the back of Riley's hand. "I'm overwhelmed in all the best ways to be here with you, but I also sort of feel sick. Not about you! I like you. Probably more than a honeybee likes pollen to be fair. But what if, I mean, what if you're with me and you change your mind? What if I don't meet your expectations?"

As much as I've wished for this day, I know he has more experience than me. I'm no blushing virgin by any means but...

"No disrespect, Rye, but you have far more experience than me here."

"Is this about the escort thing?"

I nod, and when his smile falls, I wish it wasn't because of me.

"That was just sex, Jackson. It's not like this. Those men didn't get all of me. With you...I want more than that. I want what nobody has ever given me from you."

"What's that?"

"Romance. Love. Friendship. Hope for a future. Someone to share my deepest fears with."

"Riley..."

Reaching for him, I cup his face in my hands and kiss him, soft and slow, as I walk us backwards towards the bed. When his legs hit the edge of the bed, I pull away from his lips. "You're safe with me. I promise."

"And you with me, Jackson. Don't let what I did in the past affect how you feel when we're together. Please."

I can't possibly feel anything other than a desire to please him in every way I can. To prove to him I'm the one and it's forever.

"I've always wanted you. But you know I don't like casual. I was just, I guess I'm worried I might not be good enough."

Knowing Riley was an escort never bothered me. Like he said, it's just sex. But he's had far more sex than I have because once I cross the line and sleep with someone, my feelings always get involved. It's why I can't do casual relationships. It's too hard for me to separate the two. If we get naked, my heart gets involved no matter how hard I try to keep it out of it.

We've never talked about it because I wasn't about to bring it up if I never had a shot with him. Is this the best time to mention it?

Probably not, but I can't get physically naked with him until I'm naked with my intentions.

"You're already the best man I've ever allowed this close to me. Believe me, I'm just as worried as you that I won't measure up."

"What? Why?"

"Because you're so kind and pure, Jackson. You're real and I fucking love that about you. You've been nothing but honest with me right from the day we met."

Fuck, he's my person. I know it. Sliding my hands under his shirt, his warm skin under my fingers pulls a sigh from my lips. "I want to feel you against me. Every inch of you pressed against me." Dropping my mouth to his neck, I graze the skin with my teeth. Riley's moans tear the rest of my resolve away.

"Yes," he sighs and sags against me. "Please, Jackson."

With the tender care he deserves, I pull his shirt over his head before unzipping his jeans and pushing them to the floor. The bright red lace boyshort-style underwear is a surprise. Not unwelcome, but still a surprise.

Riley watches me as he steps out of his jeans while I kneel at his feet. His hard cock presses against the fabric and I lean forward to press a kiss through the lace.

"Red is a good colour on you." My voice is thick as I stand and Riley's hands immediately fly to the buttons on my shirt.

"Thank you. I bet it looks even better on the floor."

Despite my nervousness, I laugh. Riley rewards me with a smile before sliding my shirt off my shoulders and running his hands down my chest. "Good lord, Jackson. You've been hiding all this under clothes." His fingers dust down my abs before reaching for my belt buckle. "You're incredibly fit."

"Must be the hummus."

Riley snorts as he releases my belt. "Or all those baby carrots."

With my pants falling under the weight of my belt, Riley moves to lower himself to his knees, but I grab his arm. "I don't want you to do that. Let me."

His brows knit together as I step away and shuck my jeans aside before pulling him back against me. "One day, yeah. I want to see what you look like on your knees, but tonight it's about you."

"You really are a romantic, aren't you?"

"More than you know."

Riley isn't small. He's roughly the same height as me and while he's thinner, he has a sleek and toned body. But I wrestle four-hundred-pound steers for a living. I know I can scoop him up easily for what I want to do next.

He squeaks when I sweep him into my arms bridal style and lay him down on the bed before blanketing myself over him.

"That's hot. And unexpected."

Riley's arms wrap around my neck, and he pulls me down to his lips.

"Everything about this is unexpected, Rye."

I've never felt so keyed up before to have a lover touch me. Every soft touch and kiss is like gasoline to a fire. I want to bottle every moan and sigh so I can listen whenever I'm away from him.

"I haven't had a make-out session like this since I was a teenager," Riley gasps and I go for the little space along his collarbone that he seems to enjoy having kissed.

"Get used to it. It's one of my favourite things to do." My hand skims up his side and he shivers.

"But you're gonna let me come, right? This isn't—oh, hell Jackson, don't stop." He arches into my palm once I slide my hand over his cock in his now very sticky, lacy shorts.

"Isn't what, Rye?"

"Isn't going to end in frustration like when the parents come home and we have to pretend we were only watching a movie."

Slipping my hand under the band of his shorts, I grip his length as I whisper near his ear. "No frustration. I want to see how beautiful you really are when you come because of me. Show me how good you feel right now."

Riley's hand grips the back of my neck as he presses his lips to mine. His other hand plunges into my boxers like he's desperate to touch me. Maybe he is.

"We should have got completely naked," he breathes as he wraps his fingers around my length. My breath hitches as I press my forehead against his.

"God, Riley..."

I give myself over to him instead of making myself wait like I planned. I just wanted to see him come undone under me and make a mess of his usually put-together self. Riley kisses me with heat I feel to the soles of my feet, and in one white flash of a moment, my body uncoils, and I come in his hand.

Fuck, I've never come that fast in my life, and I should be embarrassed, but Riley... lord. He jacks his hips up into my fist and I get back into the game. Stroking across the tip of his dick, I'm in awe at how he gives his body to me for his pleasure.

"Yessss, I'm so close, Jack. Make me..." With my free hand, I cup his balls with a small squeeze. His mouth quivers with an O as his gaze locks on mine. "God...Jackson..."

He's already twitching and shivering and I stroke him through his orgasm with his hand still holding my softening cock.

"Why did I keep you away for so long?" he breathes as I lean closer to kiss his swollen lips.

"Because you were just as scared as I was, I imagine."

"Will you stay with me tonight?"

"I'd love to. But I have to ride to the next rodeo with Hunter tomorrow. It's early, if that's still okay?"

"Of course. I don't want to upset your routine." He finally lets go of my spent dick and removes his cum-covered hand. "I can't believe I jerked you off like that. Seriously. That was..." Riley's eyes search my face, and he whispers, "That was extremely intimate, Jackson."

"It was. And was it...okay?"

I feel like a kid seeking approval. Asking a partner if they were satisfied is something I've never done before, but it's Riley. I don't want to disappoint him. Ever.

"More than okay." He leans in and kisses me softly. "You turned me into a spineless jellyfish. A+, cowboy."

"They don't have spines because they contract their whole bodies to move themselves forward."

Riley snorts. "Of course you would know that." He kisses me again. "Don't change. I love that about you. Now let's get cleaned up so I can fall asleep wrapped in your arms."

Riley heads to the bathroom, and before I follow him, I pinch myself.

"Yep. Still awake. That happened. Holy shit."

"You coming?" Riley's voice calls over the sound of running water.

"Be right there!"

Am I coming? If I had bells, I'd be wearing them.

I don't want to leave this bed or let go of Riley, but I need to meet Hunter early to start our drive. When I messaged him last night to tell him what happened, his compromise was that I'd drive today since he didn't plan on sleeping. He also added that since he had to feed and load the horses first, it was a generous deal for me.

I guess Sam and his friend gave Hunter what he wanted last night if he hadn't planned on sleeping.

Riley stirred immediately when I shifted to leave the bed and mumbled something that sounded like, '*I love your carrots*,' but I could be wrong. His hair is sleep-rumpled, and in the dim light filtering through the hotel curtains, he's stunning.

My heart skips triple time just watching him sleep.

"Staring is creepy, Jackson."

Riley's voice is thick and rumbling, but it carries a hint of a smile.

"Sorry. You're so beautiful asleep like that. I couldn't look away."

Riley still hasn't opened his eyes, but a grin spreads across his face. "How did I ever resist your sweet talk?"

"Stubbornness, if I had to guess."

He laughs and cracks an eye open. "You're probably right. Kiss me before you leave?"

"Of course. I stayed here with you as long as I could. Hunter will be by shortly and I have to meet him on the corner. The trailer is too big for this parking lot."

"It's okay. I understand."

I kiss him softly before rolling out of bed and finding my clothes still all over his floor. After we showered, there was a lot of talking and touching long into the early morning hours. I couldn't get enough of everything Riley. His kisses, his secret smiles, and his hands on me.

Even the way he had a snore that sounded like a broken kazoo.

"I'll miss you. Maybe more than I did before." Leaning down, I kiss him as I button my shirt.

"One more stop before you're home?"

I cup his cheek with my palm. "Yeah. It's a last-minute thing. We weren't going to, but Hunter wants one more for practice before the big Kissing Ridge rodeo. I'll be home in three more days."

Riley turns his head to kiss the palm of my hand.

"Call me when you get there?"

"Absolutely I will. Drive home safe, Rye."

Fuck if I don't want to tell him I love him already. It's too soon and I don't want to freak him out. But it's true. I know it as sure as I know Hunter will be over-sharing about his threesome as soon as I'm in the truck.

After pulling on my clothes and going commando for the first time in my life—there was no way I was wearing cum-crusted underwear for a few hours—I turn back to find Riley still snuggled under the covers watching me with a sleepy gaze. He's like a cute little burrito with eyes.

My phone buzzes with a text that Hunter is waiting and after making sure I have my hat, I drop to the floor next to Riley in bed.

"One more for the road?"

He laughs softly and puckers his lips in jest, but I grip his chin and kiss him until he's breathless.

"Fuck...I could get used to that every morning."

"Good. Because I want to kiss you like this every damn day of my life."

He swallows hard.

"Don't keep Hunter waiting."

Standing before I change my mind and get back into bed, I walk to the door.

"Jackson?"

Turning to look over my shoulder, Riley hasn't moved from his burrito.

"I want that too."

I blow him a last kiss and step out into the quiet hallway of the hotel. Once outside, I jog to the end of the street where Hunter sits in the truck waiting for me. When I'm close enough, he steps out from behind the wheel.

"So...when's the wedding?"

"Fuck off and get in. Did you make us coffee?"

"You know I did. I can't be in a truck for three hours with you not properly caffeinated."

"You're gonna sleep the whole way?" I take a gulp of the campfire-made coffee and adjust the truck's mirrors before pulling us away and heading back to the highway.

"After I tell you how fucking epic it was to have those two blow me at the same time, I will."

Hunter launches into his sex-capades, and I listen. I make the appropriate nods and exclamations as needed, but my mind is back on Riley and how my entire life is about to change.

"...and that's why I need to stop at a pharmacy for more condoms."

"At least you're safe. I'm glad you've paid attention to all those safe sex talks we've had."

"Are you even gonna spill a little about what happened with you last night? How did Riley get here? I have so many questions."

Hunter yawns and covers his mouth.

"The only thing I'll say is that he's everything I hoped he would be, and it's going to be a very long three days."

Hunter groans and leans his head against the window.

"You and your damn romance."

My smile is so wide it hurts my face.

"Me and my damn romance found the man of my dreams. Get some sleep or I won't find a place to stop so you can get condoms."

With a mutter, he pulls his hat down over his eyes and leaves me to the hum of the tires and the low country music on the radio.

And thoughts of Riley.

Seventeen
Riley

Through the grace of caffeine, I made it home safely.

As soon as I parked in my space in the covered parking, I immediately messaged Jackson to let him know I was home safely. His reply came as soon as I stepped out of the elevator towards my condo.

He sent a heart emoji and a promise to call as soon as he was done settling the horses. With a yawn, I let myself into my condo and headed straight for the shower. After sleeping late at the hotel, I jammed all my things into my suitcase and left without showering, choosing to hit a takeout window and head straight home.

I don't smell like sex, but my suitcase sure does. Jackson left his boxers behind and maybe it's obsessive, but I wrapped them in my dirty laundry and brought them home to wash. Never being one to handwash delicates, I dropped them in with my lace boy-shorts and favourite T-shirt on a gentle cycle in the washing machine.

I don't know why, really, but seeing his underwear mixed up with mine in a washing machine at my home causes all kinds of weird emotions.

"Get a grip, Riley. It's underwear, not a wedding ring."

Closing the lid of the washer, I turn on the shower and walk in. Of course, my mind can't stop replaying everything that happened in the last twenty-four hours. I know I made the right decision about letting Jackson in, but I'm a little overwhelmed.

Sure, I knew he was a romantic. He's shown me plenty of times since we've met, but I wasn't prepared for how much. Or how vulnerable he felt with me because of my escort background. I'd never fully considered that might be an issue for him.

My body shivers, remembering how he reacted when he saw it was me being cornered in the bar. Shock followed immediately by a softness, then pure rage as he took on the brute who felt I owed him something because he paid for my services in the past.

I've never been rescued because I always—always—took care of myself. Now that I'm home, the possible what-if scenarios race through my mind because I've become complacent. I left the city and no longer looked over my shoulder or told people where I was going and who I was with. No more emergency call plans and check-ins. I'd let all the personal safety go because here in Kissing Ridge, I felt safe. It's my home.

But what if Jackson hadn't seen me?

Shutting off the shower, I towel myself dry and for the first time in twenty-four hours, I no longer feel confident about being involved with Jackson. If he'd been hurt because of me, I'd never forgive myself.

Slipping into my most comfortable pyjamas, even though it's barely 3 P.M., I call my best friend.

"Hey, doll." Gabe's voice answers with the sound of traffic in the background. "I hope you're calling to tell me all the good things. How did it go?"

"You sound chipper. Did you finally get out of the office at a decent time?"

"I did. But before you deflect and ask about me, what happened?"

"Everything, Gabe. Fucking everything." My voice wavers and I clear my throat. "I went there and found him. I watched him at the rodeo first, then overheard a few women talking about where the cowboys go after."

"Did he know you were there?"

"The smart thing to do would have been to give him a heads up on that. He didn't know until he saw me being harassed in the bar by a former client."

Gabe growls and I know he's clenched a fist as he listens.

"Jesus, Riley. Are you okay? Do I need to get involved? Tell me the whole damn story right now."

So I do. I tell him how determined I was to watch Jackson in the ring and how I wanted to be romantic and surprise him at the bar that I was confident he would be in.

"But I wasn't counting on some drunk asshole recognizing me and harassing me. You know the type. Just give me a freebie, baby, and I'll leave you alone. I was stupid. If Jackson hadn't seen me..."

I trail off as Gabe's angry growl sounds over the line.

"If the bar has a security camera, I can track him down, Rye. Just say the word."

"No. It's a reminder that I need to be more careful about the people I let into my life. This kind of confrontation is rare but not nonexistent."

"How did Jackson take it?"

"Perfect, Gabe. He was amazing. He took a punch and threw one back, then grabbed me and we ran. And then I finally kissed him."

"Ah, see. I can hear how your voice changed, Riley. You don't regret it, do you?"

Not in a million years could I ever regret a moment of last night with Jackson. Even if he woke up this morning and said he couldn't do it. I'd hold the memory of last night in my heart forever.

"No. To be the object of Jackson's affection is...unreal. But I never thought about him jumping into a fight like that. What if he got hurt because of me?"

"He throws himself on top of moving cattle. I don't think he's afraid of getting hurt, Riley. What other excuses do you have? Tell me. I'll rip them all apart for you with a smile on my face."

"He told me he was nervous, that he'd not measure up with my experience. He's incredibly sweet, Gabe, and I really fucking like him. So much, but..."

"Riley, listen to me. Don't go there. He likes you. He shared his fears with you, and without sharing intimate details, I know you set him at ease. Stop with the what-ifs and excuses and just enjoy having a man who loves every part of you. Unconditionally, it sounds like."

"Why am I like this?" I laugh without humour. "I think I want to believe he's the one so badly that I'm missing something important."

"The only thing you're missing is allowing yourself to believe it's real, Riley. We've been over this. Chase had a great story. You didn't miss anything, he was just good at acting. Jackson lives in the public eye and the whole town can vouch for him. There isn't a single reason to believe you're missing something."

My phone beeps with an incoming call.

"Thanks for being a great friend, Gabe. I mean it, but I've got a call coming that I need to take. I'll talk to you later."

Gabe chuckles. "I know you're dumping me for the hot cowboy. We'll chat later."

Without looking at the display, I accept the call with a smile.

"Hi. Sorry. I was just chatting with Gabe, and before I lose my nerve, I wanted to tell you I know I'm a lot sometimes, and I'm sorry for what happened at the bar. Just be patient with me."

Silence. "Uh, is this Riley Benton?"

Shit. That's not Jackson.

"I'm sorry. Yes, it is. I didn't look at the display. How can I help you?"

"This is Dr. Morgan at the Kissing Ridge General Hospital. Your Aunt Agnes has you listed as next of kin, and we need you to come as soon as possible."

My guts drop to the floor. "Is she okay? What happened?"

"She's stable, but I'd like to speak to you in person."

"I'll be there in 15 minutes."

"I'll still be here. Just ask reception to direct you to the surgical waiting area."

"Thank you. I'm on my way."

Oh god. Aunt Agnes, what have you done?

Please be okay. Please be okay.

Without changing my clothes, I slide my feet into my sneakers, grab my phone and wallet, and take the stairs in record time down to the car.

The entire drive to the hospital feels like I'm in a movie. Like it's not really happening to me. We just had a Scrabble night last week, and we had our usual noon-day call. I told her I was going to see Jackson. She was fine!

My hands shake as I place the car in park in the hospital visitor's lot. The doctor just said surgery. He didn't say she was unconscious or anything.

Think positive, Riley!

Finally inside, I ask for directions to the surgical waiting area, and after making a wrong turn to a dead end, I retrace my steps and notice the giant red sign pointing to the surgical waiting room.

"May I help you?"

"Ah, Dr. Morgan is expecting me. Riley Benton."

"Oh, yes. Right this way."

She leads me down a corridor filled with hospital rooms and stops outside of Room 8. After knocking, she pokes her head in. "Riley is here. Can I let him in?"

My aunt's voice is faint, but it lifts some of the unease. "As long as he doesn't make a fuss."

The nurse steps aside, and I enter the room. The man, who I assume is Dr. Morgan, leans against the wall with his arms crossed and a fond smile on his face as he watches my aunt. My aunt, who looks like she stepped into a boxing ring with the reigning heavyweight champion.

"Auntie. Oh god...what happened?"

"I told you not to fuss."

"I'm not."

Aunt Agnes's face is swollen and purple. Her left eye is so swollen it looks like a failed attempt at a wink. A temporary cast secures her left arm, and a urine collection bag sticks out from under the covers. My gaze finds Dr. Morgan as he smiles and pulls up a chair next to me.

"Your aunt is quite stubborn."

"Pfft. Tell me about it."

"Don't forget who raised you, kiddo."

Despite the slur to her words, she's still sharp, but I glance back at the doctor. "Is she on pain pills?"

"Oh, yes. As much as I can give her for the next few hours. But she has a long road of healing ahead of her."

"Tell me what happened first."

"I fell. Boom. My face stopped the fall."

Aunt Agnes tries to laugh but groans softly and tears prick my eyes.

"Not fucking funny, Auntie."

"She tripped outside on the sidewalk. A neighbour saw and helped her. They called an ambulance because she was unconscious. She likely has a mild concussion, but I'm more concerned about the broken bones."

"As in, more than one bone is broken?"

Dr. Morgan nods. "Her left arm has a compound fracture that we'll need to set properly, but the worst is her hip. She needs a hip replacement. How long has she been having mobility issues?"

"Um, a few years now. She's been asking for one every time I take her to the doctor, but she keeps getting turned away by the specialist." A snore sounds from Aunt Agnes. I guess she finally let the pain pills take over. "How serious is all this? Will she make it through the surgery?"

"There's a risk with any procedure and anesthetic. My biggest concern is the concussion right now. We can keep her comfortable for a few days and monitor that before surgery, but three days max before we take her to the OR. The longer we wait, the greater the possibility for infection to set in. She might have a urine infection as well."

"I just talked to her. We talk every day, actually. She was fine. She never complained." Swallowing hard, I take in my now dozing aunt's frail body. Maybe I chose not to see it because she's all I have left. "What are the odds of complications with this?"

"There are some because of the time we need to wait. It increases with her age. Her heart is strong and her lungs sound good. I can't give you any definite numbers, but it's a risk she needs to take. We'll make it as safe as we can."

"And after? What sort of care will she need?"

"She'll need to stay in a rehab facility for as long as needed until we're satisfied she can be mobile safely on her own. Once she returns home, it would be wise to make sure she has no stairs and an accessible bathroom and that sort of thing. Hip replacement patients are usually fine on their own once at home."

Dr. Morgan stands and places the chair back. "Do you have any more questions for me?"

"When do you hope to do the surgery?"

"Tuesday afternoon. We'll assess every day and keep her comfortable, but I don't want to wait longer than that. I'll be here between 7-8 A.M. each morning if you'd like to be here for an update each day."

"Thank you. I'll be here."

Dr. Morgan sees himself out and I adjust to take my aunt's other hand gently in mine. "You'll be okay, Auntie. There's no other option here, okay? You need to meet Jackson. I haven't told you how it went yesterday, so you better wake up tomorrow so I can tell you."

It's not until my bladder forces me out of the chair that I notice I've been sitting here watching my aunt sleep for three hours. When I exit the bathroom, a nurse is checking her vitals and smiles my way.

"You're more than welcome to stay, but I think she'll be doing a lot of sleeping."

"Is she okay?"

"Everything is as okay as it can be. We'll give her more pain meds as needed and keep her comfortable."

I want to stay by her side so she's not alone, but I also know I have a crap load of stuff to organize to prepare for her to come home. Contractors and plumbers are needed, and I'll clear some of my schedule to help. I should probably answer all the emails I put off yesterday as well.

It's a lot and overwhelming.

"Thank you. Can I leave you my number in case anything changes overnight?"

"Of course you can. And call the nurses' station, too. We can update you over the phone if you're worried, but right now, she's okay."

Lingering a little longer, I kiss my aunt on the forehead and return home.

Eighteen
Jackson

Our drive to the unplanned rodeo stop took far longer than expected because of a traffic accident that needed to reroute traffic.

Hunter dozed for most of it, and I daydreamed.

About life with Riley. Getting the dog I've always wanted. Maybe one big enough to protect him when I'm away. Or maybe he'd want to travel with me sometimes, and he'd prefer a smaller dog?

I thought of showing up with lunch while he worked and growing his favourite vegetables at my greenhouse. When I thought of life after rodeo, Riley was in it. I know in my heart that man was made to be mine.

"Would you stop smiling like that? It's creepy." Hunter tosses a hay bale down from on top of the trailer before climbing back down himself.

"I'm pretty sure I'm in love, Hunter. It's not creepy."

"You need to work on your dreamy lovey look, then. You have the whole zombie-ate-my-brains look, and it's not attractive."

"Oh, fuck off." I throw my empty water bottle at him, and he catches it with a laugh.

"You know I'm teasing you, Jack. If you want to have some privacy and call him in the camper, I'll stay outside for a while."

"Thanks. I tried to call him earlier, but it went straight to voicemail. I'll give it a little longer and try again."

Instead of hanging out, we take a ride into town and scope out the rodeo grounds quickly. We stop at a local diner and have an early dinner before heading back to the campground for an early night. On the road since 5 A.M. and up most of the night with Riley is catching up with me.

I still haven't heard from him since his text saying he got home, and it's hard not to let my mind wonder if another man like the one from the bar showed up again or something worse. There's so much we still need to talk about and I want to do it all now. The timing is all crap. If we'd have done this at a different time, I'd have been home today, too, and at his place. I could be holding him while he sleeps and kissing the back of his neck in the night just because I can.

"He probably had something come up at work, Jack. He's not ghosting you."

We skipped the campfire tonight, and after showering, we've both been quiet while lounging in the camper; Hunter doing crosswords and me reading a birding magazine. Barn owls are super cool.

"Yeah, I know. You're probably right."

"Trust me. A guy doesn't drive 300 kilometres to tell a guy he likes him and then disappear. He might have his phone on silent. Maybe the battery died. Don't obsess. We have a rodeo tomorrow and then you'll be home."

"You're sounding like you have some experience in all this again, Hunter. Anything you want to talk about?"

He's silent for a long time, and I figure it's his sign he doesn't want to talk and I'm about to turn off my light to sleep when he surprises me.

"I might lose the ranch." Hunter keeps his eyes down on his crossword. "When my grandfather died, he left all his assets in a complicated trust."

Hunter lifts his gaze, and it's the first time in years I've seen him look so scared and vulnerable. I knew something must be going on. Why would he be selling off all the rodeo stock unless he needed the money?

"How come you never said anything?"

"It's nobody else's business." He shrugs as he scribbles down another word. "Anyway, I just wanted to tell you that for perspective. You still don't know each other that well, and maybe there's something big he's trying to work through without dragging you into it."

"Hunter, you're my friend. If I can do anything —"

"You can't. Helping me with labour when I needed it was enough. Right now it's in a lawyer's hands."

When Hunter's grandfather died two years ago, I assumed he had inherited everything since he still lived on the ranch. The man had no other heirs, and while he was an absolute homophobe, I didn't think he'd leave his only grandson out of his will.

"Fuck, I'm sorry Hunter. But you know if you need anything, you better fucking ask me. You're like the brother I never had. I'm here for you."

He sucks in a breath and nods. "Thank you. I appreciate that." He folds the crossword book away with the pencil inside. "That's enough being up in the feels for me tonight. Let's get some sleep."

After we both brush our teeth and turn the lights out, I reach for my phone one last time. My message to Riley still sits unread, but I send another one, anyway.

Jackson: I'm sorry we didn't get to talk today. I'll see you soon and hope your night was okay.

Hunter is likely right. He's not ghosting me, but I still wish he'd pick up his phone and tell me he's okay.

"Yep!"

The steer bolts out of the chute, and Hunter guides the animal exactly where I need it. Sliding off Lady, I grab the steer like I do every single time, and the damn thing doesn't budge. I plant my feet harder and twist him, giving the stubborn animal an extra bump with my hip. He finally hits the dirt with a muffled moo and points his feet in the air.

I don't even have to look to know that time is too slow for a good money showing here. It will bring money, just not the amount we wanted.

4.4 seconds. That's way off the mark and it's frustrating since we had such an amazing rodeo a few days ago.

"It was a stubborn steer. I told you he'd fight you."

"You did."

Hunter doesn't show his disappointment, but I sure as hell hear it.

"It's not a broken barrier, at least. We still get money for it."

Hunter leaves with his horse as I watch the next steer wrestler out throw down a faster time than me. I know where Hunter is going. He's packing up and we won't stay to collect in person. He gets like this whenever we can't have a top-three finish. It's been over a year since we've had this low of a showing, but his behaviour hasn't changed.

Stopping at the official timekeeper's hut, I give the woman our information. They'll send me a form asking for banking information once the results are official and will transfer our winnings then. Which is more progressive than some of these rodeos who still mail paper cheques.

By the time I catch up to Hunter, he has his horse unsaddled, and he's brushing her while she eats.

"Do you want to head home tonight?"

Hunter glances my way. "Yeah. You're gonna be all mopey if you don't get back, anyway."

Disappointment drips from his words, and it's hard not to take it personally.

"I can't be perfect every time, Hunter. Cut me some slack."

He opens his mouth and snaps it shut before opening it again. With a heavy breath, he hangs his head. "I'm sorry, Jack. That was unfair. I'm just...the shit with the ranch is weighing on me and the extra money would help."

"Hunter...I can loan you—"

"No." His eyes flash like it's the most offensive thing I could offer. "I'm sorry I snapped but I still want to get home if you're good with it."

"Yeah, man. Let's go home."

Hunter pulls into his ranch yard at 2 A.M. We unload the horses and get them into their stalls for the night before he heads for the ranch house and I hop in my truck with a promise to be back in the morning.

The drive to my place is short. I'm barely ten minutes away from Hunter's, but I drive past my place and straight into town to Riley's. I shouldn't be doing this. It's probably weird and stalker-ish, but I have the elevator code to his floor and he gave me the entry combo for his place.

I won't be able to relax until I know he's okay, and he hasn't changed his mind about us. Yeah, that's kind of selfish, but I only just got to kiss him. That can't be the only chance I get.

After parking in the visitor space, I'm relieved to see his car in its spot, and without stopping, I take the elevator to his floor. My hands itch to hold him and my gut keeps telling me something is definitely not okay. Pausing at his door, I knock softly. When there's no answer, I knock louder before entering the code and stepping into his condo.

A soft glow from the kitchen lights up enough of the open floor plan for me to notice he's not out here.

"Riley? Are you home?"

His laptop is on the kitchen island, so he has to be here. He takes that thing everywhere. I pad softly down the hall towards his room and let my eyes adjust to the darkness. There's a form under the covers and a smile finds its way to my face.

"Hey, Rye. Sweetheart, it's me." Leaning down to kiss him on the cheek, I pause. This cheek isn't Riley's. It's a short beard and Riley is clean-shaven. What the actual fuck?

Not caring anymore if I wake anyone up, I reach back and flick on the lamp next to the bed. Riley is here all right...with another man.

I don't know what to say or do. Riley stirs as the strange man rubs his eyes.

"Don't fly off the handle, buddy. It's not what you think."

"Jackson?" Riley lifts his head. "Jackson!" He flings the blankets back and throws himself at me, clinging so hard I can barely breathe.

"You're not supposed to be home until tomorrow."

"We came back early because we were both in shitty moods and had a bad time."

Riley steps back and the sleep lines on his face are too adorable. But his eyes aren't right. My gaze flicks to the other man, who now sits up and places a pair of glasses on his face.

"This isn't how I should be meeting you, but I'm Gabe. Riley's best friend, so please don't throw a punch."

Riley reaches up to dust his fingers across the bruise on my face.

"How come you had a bad score? Your face?"

"No. Because I didn't hear from you after you got home. You didn't answer my texts or calls. I thought...I thought you might have had a change of heart."

Riley's lips part with an inhale as he shakes his head.

"Oh, Jackson. No. I'm already shit at this. No change of heart." He runs a hand up my chest, leaving it to rest in the centre. "I didn't want to bother you. I assumed as an athlete, outside distractions should be minimized. My problems shouldn't become yours."

My gaze once again drifts to Gabe, who watches us. His eyes meet mine while his lips tick up in a small smile. "For what it's worth, I told him to call you. When he said the same thing to me about bothering you, I came because he needed someone." He grabs his phone from the nightstand and shoves his feet into a pair of slippers. "I'll go sleep on the couch."

Gabe grabs a pillow and a throw blanket from the bed and squeezes Riley's shoulder on the way past before closing the bedroom door softly behind him.

"You will never be a bother to me, Riley. Ever. Promise me you'll come to me next time, no matter what. I spent almost two full days thinking I'd never have you to myself again. It was...horrible."

That's probably melodramatic, but Hunter was right that I let it get to my head. I'm so into this man, and the thought of having him out of my life after only one night didn't sit well with me. He always answered me before, so my head went right to the worst-case scenario.

Riley takes my hand and leads me to the edge of the bed. After I sit, he wordlessly climbs into my lap and buries his face in my neck. My hands smooth up his back before wrapping tight around his waist and kissing his neck.

"My aunt fell and is in the hospital. She needs a hip replacement, and she looked so terrible. I thought I'd lose her. There's so much to take care of for when she returns home. I have events still on the go and I called Gabe because...."

Riley sits back with shining eyes. "I've known him since forever and he's like a brother to me. I didn't want to drag you into all this when we'd only just started something."

"Have I ever given you a reason to think I wouldn't be there for you? Just because I'm at a rodeo doesn't mean I can't help. It caused me more stress not hearing from you, sweetheart. I *needed* to hear from you."

"I'm sorry."

"When I left you that note to call anytime with anything, I meant it, Rye. I will come running and that's not an exaggeration."

I should be more angry at arriving here to find him in bed with another man. But my heart never led me astray that badly before. After the jolt of realizing there was another man here, I knew Riley wasn't like that. Of course, it helped that Gabe spoke when he did and maintained the same calm demeanour I had.

If he hadn't, I might have done something less... civil. Like punch him.

"You're right, I should've called you. I just...I didn't want to throw you off your game."

Squeezing him tighter, I kiss his cheek.

"You're forgiven, but please don't keep things from me again. I told you I was in this all the way, didn't I?" Riley nods and I sweep the hair back off his forehead. "I mean what I say. Always."

Riley swallows and rests his head on my shoulder. "I should have known that, Jackson. Will you...will you stay?"

"I have no intention of going home alone, Rye."

He nods and slides off me. Standing between my legs, he unbuttons my shirt. When I stand, he deftly takes care of the belt and unzips my pants, letting them puddle around my feet. He says nothing the entire time, but he doesn't have to. Riley thinks he needs to make it up to me, that I need to be shown proof of his regret.

"Riley." My voice is hoarse as he turns those gorgeous ocean blues on me. "I'm going to hold you all night and never let go. I've got you, beautiful. Let me help you."

"Okay." He exhales a shaky breath. "What did I do to deserve someone like you? If you were —"

"I'm not him, Riley. I promise you, this is how you deserve to be treated. Now get in bed and let me hold you until I have to leave for morning chores."

"Are you always this bossy?"

"Not at all. I'm as laid back as they come, but something tells me I'll need to speak up more with you to get my point across."

We settle under the covers, and I pull him to my chest. Just like the night in his hotel, he fits like a missing piece, and for the first time since that night, I feel settled. Like everything will be right with the world if I have Riley in my arms.

"I'm glad you're here," he whispers, and I squeeze him closer.

"Me too."

After kissing him on the cheek, I lie there until his breath evens out and he's back asleep.

Then I do the same.

Nineteen
Riley

The aroma of freshly brewed coffee and voices drifting down the hall wake me, but the time on my phone propels me from bed like I'd been shot in the ass.

Rushing down the hall towards the voices, I find Gabe and Jackson at my kitchen island with their heads together, looking at my laptop. Jackson obviously went home and got new clothes because he wasn't wearing that tight T-shirt last night.

And he looks so comfortable here with my best friend. In my kitchen. Like he belongs here. Jackson sips from his mug before glancing up and noticing me.

"Hey, sweetheart. I hope you slept well."

"I'm late for the goats!" I blurt. Both men look at each other and laugh. "No, no, you don't understand! I have a goat wedding soon and they had to come today to pick up the outfits. We have to finalize the arrangements because it's only a month away! I-I, we need to—"

"Rye, take a breath." Jackson's deep voice has my jaw snapping close. "It's taken care of."

"What? How?"

"I checked your calendar, and thankfully, you leave very thorough notes," Gabe says from behind my laptop. "I met with them this morning and they send you good wishes. They love the goat suits and signed off on the rest. Everything is fine."

"Oh."

"I also reached out to the woman you had in your contacts marked as *possible assistant*. You'll be meeting her at 2 P.M. in your office. If you like her, I'll take care of the setup for salary and such."

"Um…"

Gabe pushes away from the counter. "Agnes will be in surgery and you need to stay occupied. Jackson and I are here. Let us help. It's why you called me."

Jackson places his mug down and strides towards me.

"Riley, baby, look at me, please?" His powerful hands grip my shoulders and I meet his eyes. "I'm sorry if I've overstepped here, but you can't do this alone. I won't let you."

Years of fighting for my independence make the automatic response to shake him off rush to the surface. At first, I do, and step away from him, but Gabe calls me out.

"Riley. Don't. I know you think you need to prove something and do it all yourself, but you really don't. Let him help you. If he had me up at 5 A.M. without an argument to meet goats, he's a keeper. So put the lame arguments away and kiss him or something."

Jackson stands and waits, a patient and hopeful smile on his handsome face. Gabe mutters about taking a shower and leaves us alone.

"Did you sleep well?" I ask because the shift of the energy between us is so overwhelming I'm not sure what to say.

"Never better."

"So you got my suit-wearing lawyer friend to meet goats. That's impressive."

Jackson laughs softly. "Not really. He'd do anything for you, Rye. He loves you."

"And what about you, Jack?"

"Are you asking me how I feel about you, sweetheart?"

Swallowing, I nod because my mouth just ran dry. I can't believe I asked him that. How very unromantic. I'm not even dressed. I literally just rolled out of bed and I'm asking this man who I have growing feelings for to tell me his first.

Most men might change the subject, but not Jackson.

He reaches for my hand and kisses my knuckles. "Well, my first response is to tell you that graham crackers were invented to prevent sexual urges. Some reverends felt that a bland diet was a way to curb sex drives. Which I find interesting." He tugs me closer and kisses my forehead. "But then I took a breath and told myself, now isn't the time for nervous facts. Riley needs me to be direct." Jackson kisses my cheek and then my neck while my heart races like a *NASCAR* engine. "Riley, I can't tell you how I feel about you yet because I don't know the words to describe it. When I'm with you, I feel like I belong. You make me think I can have a future like I've always wanted."

Jackson cups my cheeks and forces me to meet his gaze.

"My feelings for you are mighty big, Riley. I'd do anything to see you smile and hear you laugh." He runs his thumb over my lips. "All I ever want to do is kiss you when we're in the same room."

"Jeez...Jackson..."

"Can I kiss you?"

I don't answer with words. Instead, I grab his hips and pull him against me, smashing my lips to his. Jackson remains gentle, but firm. It's a kiss, not just with attraction. It's an unspoken promise. He won't let me down and he's here for me in every way. There's probably more he wants to tell me, but I won't let my mind go there. Not yet.

Pulling away, I stay close enough that my lips brush his when I speak.

"You sure can kiss for a cowboy."

"You don't think cowboys can kiss?"

"Not with feeling. Not like you." I kiss him again, with a tenderness I can't hold back for this man who I'm falling for so hard that it might hurt once the words leave my mouth. "You make me feel like I can have a happily ever after."

His smile is so big I laugh. It's adorable and real. So fucking real it makes my heart ache for what I might have let slip away if I hadn't gone to him to take a chance.

"Yeah?"

"Yeah."

He wraps his arms around my waist and lifts me off the ground before spinning us in a circle with a celebratory whoop.

"Stick with me, sweetheart, and you'll get your fairy tale. I promise."

Gabe returns with damp hair and is now more casually dressed.

"Save sex for later. Like when I'm out of the condo, okay? We have a lot to do today." Gabe's words may be snarky, but the tone of his voice is kind as he looks at me.

"He's right Riley. Get in the shower and get dressed. I'll make you breakfast and we have to get to the hospital if you want to see Agnes before her surgery."

The mention of my aunt has all the sadness and anxiety rushing back. But only briefly, as Jackson kisses me once before turning me back towards my bedroom. With a smack on my ass, he leans in close. "I'm not letting you out of my sight today. Or tonight."

I shiver as I practically run to the shower.

"So your aunt raised you then?" Jackson asks as he parks us in the visitor lot at the hospital. I'd filled him in on how my parents weren't really all that accepting of their gay son.

"Yeah. She stepped in when I was fourteen and my parents wanted to send me to some fancy private school in the States. It wasn't really a school, you know? It was more like we can pray the gay away kind of thing and Aunt Agnes immediately said no and took me. She even had a lawyer do up legal guardian stuff and my parents were like, oh well, that saves us the financial trouble all around."

Parents who view children only as a financial liability are a low I can't wrap my head around. I thought being gay disappointed them enough, but to also not want me because they had to feed and clothe me? Yeah, that was kind of the last straw for me. And, thankfully, Aunt Agnes.

"I'm so sorry Riley. It's their loss."

"I know. Don't worry. It's why I'm out of sorts with Auntie falling and all this stuff. She's all I have, you know?" My eyes well up, thinking of losing her, and he stretches his hand over the console to grab mine.

"I know. But now you have me. My family will love you."

After unbuckling, he takes my hand as we walk to the hospital. So many people know him and nod to say hello. He greets them all by name and doesn't once let go of my hand.

"So, um, where is your family, anyway?"

Our shoes squeak on the shiny hospital floor as we head to Aunt Agnes's room.

"Well, they moved to Arizona because of the winters here about ten years ago now. It's just my mom and dad. I'm an only child. But they come every year to the Kissing Ridge rodeo to watch me."

"So they'll be here soon?"

Jackson looks at his phone. "In less than 24 hours, yep."

"Oh, I didn't know that. Don't let me take you from—"

In the middle of the hospital hallway, Jackson stops and pushes me up against the wall before laying the most toe-curling kiss on my lips. "You aren't taking anything from me. Don't assume you're not my priority, Riley. Understand?"

My fingertips touch my still-tingling lips. "Y-yeah. Okay."

"Good. Now let's see Agnes before she's too drugged up."

He confidently walks alongside me into my aunt's room, who positively beams when she sees our hands still locked.

"Well, well. Jackson Sutherland, as I live and breathe. It's been far too long since I've seen you."

Jackson leans in for an awkward hug with my aunt while I stand with my jaw on the floor.

"Sorry, Agnes. I got busy with the garden and rodeo. You said you had help."

"Back the fuck up. How do you two already know each other?" I point to Jackson. "And why didn't you say anything?"

Despite being in pain and about to head into a major surgery, my aunt still gives me shit like the 16-year-old punk I once was.

"I have friends you aren't aware of, young man, and don't be taking it out on Jackson. He used to come and clear the snow for me."

"And then you'd feed me brownies." Jackson smiles so warmly at my aunt that I almost can't look away.

"Well, someone needed to eat it when I baked. My nephew wasn't always around to enjoy it."

Pulling up the chair next to my aunt's bed, I plop into it in shock.

"Are you telling me Jackson has been this close to me for...what? Years? And I didn't even know?"

Jackson smiles at me. More than happiness lives in that smile. "It's fate, baby. I told you."

"Is this the man you thought you made a mistake with, Riley? The one you told me about over Scrabble when I won with *dick*." She snort-laughs and winces, and I ignore the heavy stare from Jackson.

"Yeah. The same one. I guess I don't need to introduce him and hope you approve."

"Nope! Jackson is a good boy. He brought me strawberries one day in February. Right off the plant, he said. Your first batch, right?"

"Yes, ma'am. You were my test subject." He chuckles as he places his hands on my shoulders. "I'll bring you more once they spring you from here. We'll catch up."

"That would be lovely, Jackson."

Jackson leans down and brushes a kiss across my cheek. "I'll just be down the hall. I'll give you two some privacy," he whispers before wishing my aunt well and leaving us.

"Well, that's Jackson. Who you already know and he's...probably the man I'll spend the rest of my life with."

My aunt reaches her good hand to me, and I gently take it.

"He's a good man, Riley. His dad used to own the tractor dealership on the highway. He helped me out a time or two when you were still in high school. He cleaned the driveway in the winter and always made sure we were okay. By the time Jackson started helping me, you'd moved away, and he usually stopped by after snowstorms. He'd borrow someone's tractor and do the lane before shovelling all my steps. He even cleared paths to the gas meter and cleared away the vents."

This isn't shocking for him to do, because I know Jackson is indeed a kind soul. But damn. My aunt has known him for years and I never once met him. Maybe there's something to this fate thing after all.

"I went to see him at his last rodeo. I told him I'd been wrong and..." Puffing out a breath, I find my aunt's glassy eyes. "He's the most amazing man I've ever met and I can't believe I almost lost him because I was stupid enough to say I don't date cowboys."

"But it's fixed now? You're together?"

"I think so. He's amazing. Gabe is here too, but you already knew that. He came yesterday."

She smiles. "Yes, Gabe was here. Lovely man. He needs to work less."

"I'm working on that, but you know how he is."

The nurse arrives to announce that it's time to move to the operating room and my aunt squeezes my hand. "Stop worrying, Riley. I'll be fine and we'll figure it all out. I love you."

"I love you, too. I'll be here when you wake up."

The nurses wheel her away, and in a daze, I walk down the hallway to the waiting area to find Jackson at the nurse's station. Pausing, I watch him as he talks to one of the nurses and signs an autograph. His cheeks turn a shade of pink when an older nurse asks for a photo.

He smiles and I listen to bits of their conversation over the bustle of the hospital.

"My nephew loves watching you. Will you be doing any mentor stuff this winter? He really wants to try steer wrestling."

"I was thinking about it. It's been a while since I've done kid clinics. The hydroponic gardening took up a lot of my free time."

"Oh, I loved the strawberries you had a few years ago. I'm sorry it didn't work out."

There's more, but it all drifts off as I stare at the man I tried to keep at arm's length. He must feel my attention on him because he turns my way and winks before holding a hand out in my direction.

"If you'll excuse me, ladies, I have a man to take care of."

My cheeks heat with the chorus of *'awws'* from the nursing station as he kisses my cheek and takes my hand.

"You have my number, but I'll be back when she wakes up. Suppertime right?"

"Yes, Riley. She should be out of recovery by then. She might not be up to a conversation, but she'll be out of surgery."

Jackson leads me out of the hospital, and I pull him to a stop once we're outside.

"I can't believe out of all the people in this small town, you know my aunt. How is it possible we never crossed paths?"

"Well, I'm a few years older than you. I was away at college while you were in high school. You moved away and came to visit in the summers when I was on the rodeo tour."

"But, like...it's my aunt, Jackson. It's just so bizarre."

He pulls me into him and hugs me tight. "And yet we never met through her, but at a park. Over hummus." He kisses the top of my head. "Speaking of, you need to eat and then you have to interview the person who will become your assistant before we come back here."

We walk again, and words are hard to find. Even at his best, Chase was never this attentive and yet I thought he hung the moon. Now that I've let Jackson in and actually opened my eyes to who he really is, I know acutely that I unfairly judged him. If he wasn't so persistent, I might have missed out on him forever.

The world moves in ways I don't understand, but I don't have to understand it to be grateful for it delivering me a second chance at happiness.

Twenty
Jackson

"You're sure it's okay for us to stay in your space like this, Jack?"

"Mom, it's fine. I'll stay at Riley's."

My mom and dad always stay at my place when they visit. I usually sleep on the pull-out sofa, but this time I have a better place to lay my head, and I can't wait for them to meet Riley.

Mom smiles warmly and opens her arms for a hug. "I'm so happy for you, honey. Doesn't he look glowy, dear?" She's talking to my dad who's already poking his head out the door to check the outside light that I still haven't changed.

"Glowy? Is that what we're calling it now?" Dad smirks, pleased with his quip, and I release my mom from the hug. "Where's your ladder, Jackson? Let's fix this right now."

Dad can never sit still, and I don't even bother to argue. "Give me a minute and I'll get it." Kissing my mother's cheek, I whisper, "Thanks Mom. I'll fill you in after we change the lightbulb that Dad clearly needs to fix right this minute."

"I'll make some tea."

She pats my arm, and I follow Dad to the old barn in the back. When I bought this place ten years ago, I thought I'd turn the barn into an indoor practice facility of sorts. But then I got into hydroponics and it's now my greenhouse. Practice happens at Hunter's place instead.

"I'm sorry it didn't work out with the business, son. It's a shame Cameron left you like that."

"Thanks, Dad. I'm still working on something. Just not with Cameron. I can do it myself on a smaller scale."

Dad pokes around my hydroponics setup with a smile on his face. He's always supported everything I've done; from building a complicated *LEGO* to gardening to steer wrestling—he's been there.

"Um, so Dad. About Riley. His aunt is Agnes Benton."

"Small town, right?" Dad chuckles and follows along as I carry the ladder back to the house.

"Minuscule. We're far enough apart in ages that our paths never crossed. We're still really new and everything, but Dad." My throat squeezes and tears prick my eyes. "He's the one."

My dad stops walking and turns towards me. "Really?" The absolute hope and joy on his face tears me apart. Mostly because when my parents are happy, I'm happy. But also a little sad because Riley never had this kind of support from his parents. "Yeah. I mean, I haven't told him that yet. Well, not really, but yeah. I don't want to spend a minute away from him, you know?"

"I know, Jack. Very well. Have you told your mother?"

Shaking my head, I lean the ladder against the house. "Not yet. You were in a hurry to change my lightbulb, and I couldn't wait another minute to talk about him."

Dad shrugs as he hands me the lightbulb and holds the ladder for me. "Safety lighting is important. I raised you better than that."

He's right. Riley was here in the dark once, and I could tell it spooked him. When I opened the door and the house lights flooded into the blackness, he visibly sagged in relief.

After taking care of the bulb and putting the ladder back, we join Mom inside for tea. She's already made a giant pitcher of it to chill. Since my parents moved to Arizona, they're into iced tea like it's the answer to all life's problems. Not sweet tea either. Plain iced tea.

"I'm sure you guys are tired from your trip, but there's something I'd like to talk to you about."

Mom and Dad sit on the sofa together, and I sit in the oversized chair by the window.

"I've already told you a little about Riley. You'll meet him tomorrow. His aunt just had a hip replacement, and she's all the family he has. He's...upset about it, of course, and I've been helping him as much as possible." Leaning forward, I meet my mom's gaze. "He's the one, Mom."

Her eyes get all shiny and she carefully places her glass on the coaster. "Really?"

"Yeah, Mom. I'm madly in love with him and...yeah."

I don't know what else to say about Riley that could be better than admitting he's taken my heart in every way. I don't want to rush into marriage or anything. Riley deserves to be wooed for longer than a week before I confess how much I want him. Not to mention he makes a living delivering romance for people. I need to make sure I do all this right for him.

My mom takes the two steps over to me and hugs me tight. She's wanted me to get married since, well, since I was old enough to voice my vision of a future.

"I can't wait to meet him, honey. I love him already."

After an hour of talking about the rodeo this week and me staying with Riley and all things in between, I excuse myself and leave my parents to rest. We normally have dinner the first night they get here, but with all the hospital stuff and taking care of Riley, we left it until tomorrow, with Mom insisting she'll make her prime rib and Yorkshire dinner to welcome him.

My mom locks the door after I leave them even though it's barely 7 P.M. Gabe left Riley with his aunt a few hours ago and I'm about to pick him up and get him fed. Gabe graciously offered to stay at a hotel and while I didn't want to let him do that, he shook off my weak attempts to get him to stay at the condo. I'm grateful for the alone time, but a little guilty for kicking the guy out since he came for Riley.

After parking the truck at the hospital. I head towards Agnes's ward. She's in a regular room now that surgery is complete and she's recovering. Following the signs, I finally find her room, with Riley dozing in the chair next to her.

Agnes hears me first, even though I'm trying to be quiet. She smiles and lifts her heavy eyelids briefly. "Good. You're here to take my nephew home. He doesn't need to hover. I'll be back to playing Scrabble in no time."

Smiling, I pat her good arm. "He loves you and being here makes him feel better. I'd never tell him to stay away."

Agnes blinks slowly. "Thank you for being there for him. You're what he needs."

Riley stirs and sits up, rubbing at his eyes. "Jackson, hi. How long have you been here?"

Leaning down, I press a kiss to his cheek. "Hey, Sleeping Beauty. I just got here. You need to eat and sleep in your own bed. Those chairs are a disaster."

Riley nods, and the deep circles under his eyes break me. He's been trying to do so much the last few days.

"I've got dinner and I'm taking you home." He nods, and after grabbing his sweater, he leans down to kiss his aunt.

"I'll be back tomorrow, Auntie."

"Don't rush, Riley. The staff here know what they're doing."

"I know but—"

"Let Jackson take care of you. Do it for me, please?"

Riley's face twists into a pout, and I want to laugh at how adorable he looks.

"That's mean, Auntie. But I'll wait since you asked me to."

Riley seems just as frail as Agnes right now. He's almost clinging to her and even through the haze of pain drugs, she still comforts him.

"You need to take care of yourself, too, Riley. I need you just as much."

"I love you." He goes in for a gentle hug and Agnes smiles as she sinks back into her pillows.

Riley takes my hand as we leave the room and leans heavily into me.

"You okay?"

"Yeah. You're right about those chairs, but it just didn't feel right not to be there."

"I understand, Rye. It's hard when someone you love is not well and you want to help but can't. Agnes knows you love her, but she wants you to take care of yourself, too."

"I know. It's just...like I feel so damn guilty going home to have dinner and sleep in a bed without monitors and such." Riley sighs as we reach my truck, and I open the door for him. "What are we having for dinner, anyway?"

He climbs in and raises an eyebrow when all I do is smile at him.

"It's a surprise, but I know you'll like it."

Riley's soft smile is my reward as I round the truck and drive him home. I picked up the groceries before I went to the hospital and I'm glad I did. Riley's exhaustion is clear as he leans his head back and closes his eyes.

"Gabe said he already set up an account at the hardware store so we could renovate the house for Aunt Agnes. Six months with no payments."

"He told me. We have a plan in the works for that."

The truck is silent and when I sneak a peek at Riley, a single tear slides down his cheek. I want to pull over and wipe it away, but instead, I wait. Something about the way he's silently holding himself makes me back off a little.

Once I've parked in a visitor space and turned the truck off, Riley keeps his eyes closed and more silent tears streak his face. This time I can't ignore it and reach for his hand over the console.

"Riley..." I whisper and stroke the back of his hand with my thumb. His fingers curl around mine as he sucks in a breath.

"I'm sorry." He swipes at his cheeks before finally turning to me. "I'm not used to all this. I...it feels like some kind of dream and nightmare all at once."

"There's nothing to be sorry about. It's a tough time for you and bound to be overwhelming." He nods and gulps while he wipes at his cheeks more. "Let's go inside, okay?"

Riley nods and exits the truck while I grab the grocery bags from the back. We walk in silence to his condo and he enters all the codes. It's not until we exit the elevator and cross the door into his place that I reach for him.

"Rye." Setting the bags down quickly, I take his hand and gently pull him into my chest. He wraps his arms around my waist and squeezes while he rests his head on my chest. "The first thing I want you to do is relax in a shower or the tub. What do you prefer?"

"God, I haven't had a long soak in ages. The tub sounds amazing."

His voice is muffled against my chest, but he sounds a little lighter.

"Good. Let's get you in then."

Grabbing the bag from the pharmacy, I lead him to his bathroom as he cocks his head in question. I say nothing until I've started the water and put the stopper in his bathtub.

"Bubble bath or bath bomb?" I ask, and he finally smiles.

"Bath bomb."

Reaching in the bag, I pull out the soothing one the lady at the counter said is great for muscle aches and stress. She said it was amazing when she was pregnant, and that was all the endorsement I needed to buy it. After unwrapping the bath bomb, I set it on a dry cloth while the tub fills.

"Take your clothes off, Riley. Unless you prefer soaking in them?" When he doesn't move, I step over to him. "Do you want me to do it for you? Trust me, I don't mind."

He takes my hands and places them on his hips. "I don't mind either."

His red-rimmed eyes break my heart, and I lean down for a soft kiss before my hands sneak under his shirt to pull it over his head. When I kneel before him to remove his loose-fitting pants, he gasps and brushes his hand through my hair.

Tapping his leg for him to step out of his pants, he does so and steadies himself on my shoulder. His underwear comes next, and I kiss his hip bone before standing to turn off the water.

"Sweetheart, step in and relax, okay? Drop the fizzy thing in there and just shut it all out. I got you this pillow thing, too? The woman at the pharmacy said all bathtubs need one."

Rummaging in the bag, I pull out the bath pillow, which is in the shape of a peach, and I suction it to the place I think he'll put his head. "Do you want me to bring you wine? Maybe tea?"

"You're not gonna join me?"

"Not this time. This is for you. I'll make dinner and you stay here as long as you like."

Riley nods as he exhales a shaky breath. He lowers himself into the tub with a low groan and immediately rests his head back on the little fuzzy peach pillow.

"God, this feels so good. Drop the bomb thing in for me, please?"

I do as he asks, and he cracks one eye open. "Thank you, Jackson. This is perfect."

"You're welcome."

Before leaving him to relax, I turn the lights down low and close the door.

With my heart slamming in my chest, I retreat to the kitchen to make dinner.

Twenty-One
Riley

Jackson only checked on me in the tub once. And that was to make sure I was still okay and to tell me supper was almost ready.

He handed me a warm fluffy towel I didn't recognize, and I suspect he warmed it in the oven somehow since the laundry machines were in the bathroom with me.

Once dry, I stepped into my bedroom and pulled on a fresh T-shirt and lounge pants before padding to the kitchen.

Jackson had changed at some point, too. He's barefoot and wearing a pair of navy sweatpants with a tight-fitting white T-shirt that says, *Born to be a Cowboy*, on it. He pulls a pizza from the oven and smiles when he sees me.

"Perfect timing. Are you feeling better?"

He slides the pizza onto a cutting board and reaches for fresh spinach. It's then I realize what he's making.

"I am. You were right. I needed to decompress." Sliding up to him, I rest a hand on his back as he slices the pizza. "Jackson...are you making my favourite mushroom and spinach pizza?"

The cutest little flush appears on his neck, and he focuses on the food with a dip of his head.

"I am. It's not from Avocadabra, but it's easy enough to make."

Jackson turns and smiles my way before pressing a kiss to my forehead. "Sit and eat. I'll get you a glass of wine. Unless you prefer something else?"

"Uh, no. Wine is great, thanks."

He'd already placed plates on the kitchen island, and when he returns to set my wineglass in front of me, he places a small napkin with a pattern of horseshoes and cowboy hats on it under the glass.

We eat quietly, and whenever Jackson isn't using both his hands, he rests one on my thigh. Sometimes with a squeeze and sometimes just smoothing his thumb along in an imaginary pattern.

"This is amazing, Jackson. Better than the one I order in."

"Yeah?" His lips tilt in a pleased grin and I nod.

"Really. It's great. Thank you so much for this. For everything."

"Don't ever feel you need to thank me for taking care of you, Riley. When you care about someone, it comes with the territory."

"I'm sorry. This is just all so new to me. Since I left Aunt Agnes's house to be on my own, I've always had to take care of myself. I've never..." With a sigh, I reach out to slide my palm across his cheek. Jackson's lips part, and he places his hand over mine. "Nobody has ever made me feel like you do," I whisper.

I'm overwhelmed by all the new feelings percolating in my head and heart. Yes, I like Jackson as more than a friend, but I'm still afraid of being hurt. Even though there's no way he could be anything like Chase, the fear still pokes at me like the little plastic bit under a clothing tag that you didn't quite remove entirely.

And yet, we complement each other so well. He makes me feel safe and cares for me in a way no one has ever done. I want him. I want us, and I want to rip that damn remnant of plastic tag off and burn it because this man deserves all of me.

Jackson's gentle gaze is what it should feel like coming home. It's the welcoming arms of a loving partner who wants to give everything he has.

Not once has he taken from me. Not even at the hotel. I'm always first, and it's just the way he is.

"I can say the same thing about you, Riley. With you, I feel like I can conquer the world."

Sliding off my stool, I lean into him in the space between his legs. He rests his hands on my hips and his lips part when I slide my hands up his chest.

"Jackson...I want...you."

His entire face softens as he brings a hand up to stroke my cheek. "You can have me, Rye. I don't know what else to do to show you. You've had me since I rambled about baby carrots in the park."

Leaning in, I kiss him softly, but his hand grips the back of my neck, and he kisses me back. It's a kiss that leaves me breathless. It's tender yet passionate and so spine tingling it makes my knees shake. When he finally lets me breathe, I see him. I *really* see him. A man who gives everything for whatever it is he's doing. Be it steer wrestling, hydroponic gardening, or caring for someone special, Jackson doesn't do it halfway.

He's all in just like he said he would be and for the second time tonight, I'm a little overwhelmed that all his attention is on me. That this amazing man is here solely for me.

"Tell me what you want, sweetheart," he rasps as he runs a knuckle across my cheek.

"I...jeez, Jackson." Huffing a laugh, I rest my forehead against his. "I can't list it off because I want it all."

"Then we'll just check all the things off as we go." His lips on my neck and hands on my hips squeeze before he pulls away, and I try to chase after his kisses. "But you're exhausted, Rye. Let me clean up the kitchen and I'll meet you in bed. If you fall asleep before I get there, it's okay. If you're still awake..." He grins before turning back to the kitchen.

I huff a very annoyed breath, knowing I won't win, but I *can* play dirty.

Jackson runs the water at the kitchen sink and while his back is to me, I wrap my arms around him from behind, sliding my hands under his shirt.

"I'll let you have it your way, Jackson. But I'm not falling asleep." To illustrate my point, I ghost my hands over his package before stepping away.

Jackson's deep chuckle as he throws a glance over his shoulder at me sets my heart racing, and I know I made the right move. If he doesn't leave those dishes half washed, I need to work on my seduction techniques more than he does.

With an extra swish in my hips, I make sure he's still watching as I remove my shirt before disappearing down the hall to the bedroom. His whispered curse confirms he was still watching and for the first time since the news of Aunt Agnes's fall, I feel like myself again. That I can manage anything thrown my way and it will be okay.

Right down to falling for a cowboy.

Stripping completely and foregoing my initial thoughts of more lacy underwear, I slide under the covers. I'll have to ask him if he'd like more lace or something else. But right now, I just don't want to be bothered. I want him against my nakedness the moment he steps into this room.

Which means I need to think this out better. I know he's going to want to give and I want him to receive, dammit. I flip the covers back, exposing myself completely. An almost restless energy has settled over me despite the exhaustion I lied about not having. I want to show Jackson just how much I appreciate what he's done for me.

Exactly seven minutes later, Jackson steps into my bedroom.

"I'm still awake, cowboy."

Running my hands down my body, I stop at my cock and give myself a slow stroke as Jackson's gaze burns down my body.

"I see that." He tears his shirt off, dropping it on the floor as he walks towards me. "You sure you don't want to go to sleep?"

"Jackson. Do I look like I want to sleep right now?"

He bites at his lip with a small smile. "You most certainly don't."

"Get your pants off and come here. Stop being so thoughtful for...like, twenty minutes or so."

He raises his eyebrows. "Only twenty minutes?"

Sliding to the edge of the bed and sitting up, I reach for his hand and pull him to me. "Look, I'll admit I'm tired. But I won't fall asleep until I make you come, and it won't take much for me to follow." Jackson passes his palm over my cheek and lifts my face. His lips part, but I press a finger over them.

"You've been taking care of me for two days, Jackson. Let me take care of you."

"Okay," he whispers, and the simple words spur me forward to draw his pants down, but the rest of his words stop me. "But I just want you to know that I never want to feel like I'm controlling you or whatever. I…" Jackson breathes deeply. "I don't like it when we don't feel equal."

Peering up at him as I sit on the edge of the bed, I wonder what exactly he means. But I remember his words while we listened to the bullfrogs and again at the hotel. He implied he never wanted me on my knees, but I didn't think it stemmed from something like this. I thought he was just being sweet and not wanting me to feel cheap.

"Wait a minute." Leaning in, I kiss his stomach before standing up. "Do you feel like if I kneel for you, something I want to do because I love it and it makes us both feel good, that in some way you're…" I don't even know the right word because I'm confused.

Jackson cups my face and kisses me. "It makes me feel like I'm taking advantage of you. I know that sounds silly, but…" He shrugs his shoulders and glances away.

"Do you trust me, Jack?"

"Of course."

"Let me show you how good it is. Just because I'm on my knees doesn't mean we're any less or that you disrespect me." Kissing his neck, I slide my hands up his chest. "You're a safe place for me. It means I cherish you and in no way do I feel like you're taking advantage of me. I promise you, this makes me just as happy as it will you." My hand drifts and wraps around his growing erection. Jackson moans and drops his head to my shoulder. "And I'm the one in control, Jack. Not you. So please let me do this for both of us."

"Okay, Rye."

His hands trail down my arms before dropping to his sides as his gaze tracks me lowering to my knees. I've been thinking about tasting Jackson like this since he ran the tub for me, but I don't want to rush it. His swallow clicks in the silence as I lower myself in front of his now very hard cock.

Leaning in, I lick up the underside of his dick and relish the stuttering sigh from Jackson's lips. After a flick of my tongue across the tip and his sigh turning to a loud moan, I'm done for.

"Holy shit, Rye." Jackson grips my shoulders as I take him down, swallowing around him as his mouth drops open with a gasp. One shaky hand reaches out to cup my cheek, and I lean into it. Jackson rubs his thumb across my cheek, and I glance up at him. His eyes are wide, chest flushed as his breaths come in short pants.

"Are you okay, Jack? Feeling good? I know I am. Look." I lean back slightly, stroking my hard-as-fuck length. "This is what tasting you on my knees does to me, Jack."

"Shit...then don't stop," he rasps.

But it's his shy smile that gets me. Somehow, he's turned this back to being for me and I can't even be mad about it.

I take him down with more gusto, burying my nose against his skin until my eyes water. I can't get enough of him in my throat, his flavour flooding my mouth and the weight on my tongue. Blowing someone is an immense turn on for me. I love the way I can turn a man to *Jell-O* with only my mouth.

Jackson's thighs tense and his fingers curl into my hair, pulling at the strands.

"Rye..." His raspy voice makes me moan around him. He's so fucking gone. My hand moves faster along my dick as I feel Jackson swell in my mouth. Glancing up, I watch his face transform as he unloads down my throat. The absolute bliss, followed by a tenderness that lights me up from the inside, washes over his handsome features. Some people might think having your lover's dick in your mouth as he comes is the height of intimacy, but that's not entirely true. Add on the complete adoration on Jackson's face while I swallow and jerk myself off. You can't get closer than that.

My orgasm hits me hard, almost stealing my breath. When I finally open my mouth to heave in a lungful of air and let his cock slide out, Jackson falls to his knees in front of me and surveys the mess. My hand overflowing with cum, my lips swollen and his cum on my chin and maybe even on my cheek.

"Are you okay?" he whispers and I can't keep the laughter contained.

"Jackson, that was the hottest blow job I've ever given." Leaning forward, I press my lips to his with a small sigh. "I'm *so* fucking okay. Are you?"

"I think I blacked out for a split second when I—" His eyes grow impossibly wide. "Oh my god. Did I hurt you? I didn't pull away or anything and I've never..." Jackson trails off as the tips of his ears turn red.

"You've never come down someone's throat before?"

"Um...no. I'm just...I mean, I'm not..." Jackson screws his eyes shut tight. "I'm not a prude or anything. I've just never let my partners do anything like this before."

Cold dread grips me.

"Jackson, shit. I'm an asshole. An irresponsible asshole. I haven't been with anyone in over six months. I still get tested, so don't worry. I've always been safe, even when I was with Chase. We should have talked about my status first, but I...I was so focused on making you feel good. I'm so sorry for not even bringing that up."

Jackson remains quiet for a beat. "You're not the only one at fault for that, Rye. I'm an adult and could've spoken up, too. But that's not why I've never done this before."

"Because you feel like it's some sort of power imbalance?"

Jackson touches his forehead to mine.

"I guess I've always thought if someone could do what we just did, it would be cheap and dirty and not be meaningful. I never want the person I'm with to feel like I'm only with them for sex." He rushes on. "And that's not a comment about your previous job."

Before I respond to Jackson, I need a moment to wrap my head around his words. It makes so much sense now. His caretaking and romantic tendencies, while they absolutely come from his heart, they've also skewed the way he views intimacy. Maybe all the Disney movies were a bad thing because Jackson could make me gag with his cock, and I'd still feel loved and cherished.

"Can we continue talking about this after I rinse the cum off myself? I want to talk about this more." He nods and stands, holding out his hand to pull me up to him. "But for the record, Jackson, I've never once felt like you were with me just for sex."

"Good. Because I never was. I'm here because I love you."

Twenty-Two
Jackson

*S*hit.

I was not supposed to say that right away. Not like this. But Riley stands and stares at me, still holding a handful of cum and some of it smeared on his face. Since I can't take the words back, I just change the subject.

Expertly.

"Did you know ostriches are one of the few breeds of birds to have a penis?"

Fuck. I shouldn't talk about sex. That's not really deflecting from what I just confessed.

"My mom used to worry I didn't eat enough protein. That's why I love hummus so much. It has just as much protein as steak, really." Grabbing a tissue box from Riley's dresser, I pull a few out and wipe the gob out of his hand before pulling him into the bathroom. This is the most disappointing romantic confession ever. And yet I can't stop talking.

"Hunter loves steak, though. Sometimes I worry about his red meat intake, you know? Like, he's a typical rancher. Beef all day long, that guy."

"Jackson."

Pausing outside the shower, I finally turn to face Riley. Tears threaten to spill from his eyes, and I drop my head.

"I'm sorry, Riley. I didn't mean to blurt that out."

This is the most epic failure of professing love ever. He must be so disappointed.

"Did you mean it, though?"

My head snaps up with the urgency in his voice and my heart flutters. "Of course I did. There's nothing I say that I don't mean, but I didn't mean to just say it like that. I wanted to give you the romance that'd you remember. Maybe plan some special date where I can tell you under the stars before I kiss every inch of your body. I wanted it to be a romantic moment like you plan for everyone else, but never yourself."

Riley steps closer until our chests almost touch and a wave of emotion crashes over me that's so thick I feel like I'm buried under a wet blanket.

"Tell me what else we'd do on this date," Riley whispers, his lips hovering over mine.

"I'd make sure you didn't have to work the next day. We'd drive up to this meadow in the mountains. Even farther up than Hunter's pastures."

"That sounds pretty."

"It is. I'd light a fire if it was too cold, and I'd put the better cushions in my truck bed so we could fall asleep if we needed. If we didn't see the Northern Lights, I'd show you the stars."

Riley's fingers dust over my abs, and he kisses my shoulder.

"What would you show me in the stars?"

Riley's hands drift to my hips, his thumbs rubbing along the bone there, and I pull back to watch as a single tear slides down his face.

"I'd bring my telescope and show you Saturn's rings. I'd give you a tour of the Milky Way and then I'd kiss you."

"Yeah? How?"

"Like this." My hands shake as I cup his face and take his lips in a slow and deep kiss. Riley melts into me as our tongues slide together and I hope I haven't ruined the evening. My heart ran before my brain, and it's been such a whirlwind of emotions since he showed up at the rodeo last week.

But I kiss him like how I wanted to the first time I said those words. A kiss to tell him he's the one. He's tied my heart in a knot only he can untie, but I want that knot to get tighter and never be undone.

When I finally pull away, I'm almost afraid to look at him, because what if he doesn't feel like I do? What if that kiss wasn't enough?

"Jackson, that was the most beautiful date I've never been on. Just because it didn't play out how you wanted doesn't make it any less special. Yes, I love romance, but you do it quietly every day. It's in the way you make my favourite foods and know how I'll need to unwind after visiting my aunt. I see it when you tell me random food and animal facts and how you always put my feelings and experiences before your own."

Riley swallows and takes my face in his hands like I had his before. "Not all romance is a big show that needs planning, Jack. You do it in every single action without even thinking about it." He presses a kiss to my lips before breathing a shaky sigh. "You made me fall in love with you with barely any effort."

"What?"

Did he just say what I think he did?

Riley smiles and slides his arms around my neck. "I love you too, Jackson. I didn't want to, because I was afraid. But I can't ignore how seeing you is the highlight of my day or how I think of you so much when you're on the road. We just did something big. Both of us. You trusted me with your feelings, just like I trust that you'll not do me wrong."

I feel like I could ride a bull better than Jamieson right now. My happiness bubbles out of me and I smash my mouth to Riley's.

"You love me. Holy shit," I mumble against his lips as he laughs against mine.

"I really do."

"So, we should probably get in the shower soon and get you to bed. Tomorrow is a big day for both of us."

Riley's smile fades. "Yeah. Reality sucks. I'd rather just lie around in bed with you."

Groaning, I press a kiss to his temple and turn us towards the shower.

"I'll take a rain check on that in about two weeks if the offer stands."

"It's a date."

Riley grins at me as he steps into the shower, and I follow behind him.

This wasn't how I planned the day to end, but I'm certainly not complaining.

"I *knew* you had a secret hottie!"

Jamieson slaps me on the back, almost knocking me over.

"When do we get to meet him?" Griff leans against the fence in Hunter's yard and his smile is one I've not seen in a while.

"I think at the banquet after this rodeo."

"You think?"

"He's a romance planner, and he has a few events of his own on the go. His aunt also had a hip replacement, and he's spending a lot of time with her. Actually, I need a favour from you all."

"You know we'll be here for whatever you need, Jack." Jamieson looks to his best friend Griff, for confirmation.

"Of course we can help you. What do you need?"

Hunter walks up to our group and passes out drinks. Beers for them and an iced tea for me. "Who is helping who with what?"

"Jackson needs help," Griff says before he takes a swallow of beer. "So do you, but you never let us."

Hunter purses his lips and ignores Griff's comment. Instead, he focuses on me. "What do you need, Jack?"

"Well, I need some capable men to renovate a darling older woman's house so she can move around and remain independent. Nothing too technical. A plumber is already lined up for that part, but we'd do the interior stuff and heavy lifting."

"Is this for your hottie's aunt?"

Griff elbows Jamieson. "Dude, he has a name. Don't call him that."

Jamieson frowns. "Did you actually tell us his name?"

"It's Riley," Griff informs him and I raise an eyebrow Griff's way.

He shrugs. "I pay attention and listen. You talk about him a lot." Huh.

"I guess I do. You're not wrong. It's Riley."

"We've got the Kissing Ridge rodeo this week and then we have one more road trip before the season ends. When do you want us to help?" Hunter is already scrolling the calendar on his phone and waits for my reply.

"I know it's short notice, but if we could do some demolition before we leave on the road trip, it would get the plumber in faster. We can do the rebuild when we return. She'll be in a rehab facility for a minimum of two weeks, but Riley wants her there until the house is completely finished. If the four of us work at it, we can have it done in a day or two."

"We could demo for a few hours Thursday. None of us have events on and we all compete Friday evening and Saturday. We could maybe sneak in a few hours on Sunday, but we might need the time to prepare for the following week."

Griff nods as he looks at his calendar while Jamieson peers over his shoulder. "I have less to do than you three. I could always drop in on my own while you guys pack on Sunday."

"Honestly, I'm grateful for whatever you can all spare. I know the timing is shit, but I want to help keep her costs down."

Hunter jams his phone in his pocket, and I catch his eye. Hopefully, he picks up on my unspoken words that I'd do the same for him. He shakes his head briefly before gesturing back to the house.

"I have lunch started and we can hit the practice ring after."

He leaves and Jamieson tags along after him rambling about grilled cheese sandwiches. Griff gestures to join him and I step over to the fence and lean next to him.

"Thanks for offering to help. I really appreciate it, and Riley will, too."

"Of course. You're welcome."

He stares off into the mostly empty pasture now. Hunter has sold most of the rodeo stock and cattle. Only a handful of broncs and bulls remain. The older stock that breeders aren't as interested in.

"Are you okay?"

Griff kicks at the dirt and stares at the ground.

"I don't know if I can keep doing this. The bull fighting. It's too much."

"What? Why? I thought you loved it."

His jaw works and I touch his arm. "For my ears only, Griff. If you want to talk, I'm here. If not, I'm still here later."

"It's not the bull fighting I love." His eyes meet mine, and while Griff is normally less than sunny, he's never troubled. "It's Jamieson."

"Of course you love him. He's your best friend."

Griff sighs and raises an eyebrow, giving me his best *are you that stupid* look.

Oh.

Oh!

"You're *in* love with him?"

"Yeah, Jack. I am, and it's too hard on my heart. I got into bull fighting to protect him, you know? He thought he couldn't be good without me and it kept us together. But seeing him with other men or women sometimes when we're away? It's too much. I can't keep doing it."

I don't know how to process what Griff just told me. I know he and Jamieson are best friends, practically attached at the hip since the day I've met them, but I'd never have guessed Griff was in this deep. Or this affected.

"Have you ever..."

He shakes his head. "No. I've never brought it up, because... shit, I'm a coward, maybe?" He kicks at the dusty ground with the toe of his worn sneaker. "We had an almost threesome once, and that was too much for me. I excused myself as best as I could while naked with a hard on and left them. I didn't talk to him for two days after that. Made up some kind of story about not enough condoms and split."

I've known Griff and Jamieson for five years. We've all spent so much time together on the circuit, but not once did I ever think feelings were involved.

"Can I do anything?"

"Unless you have any tricks for me to separate Jamieson from work, I don't think so. I just wanted you to know, so you're not surprised when I quit."

"You're really serious about quitting? You're so good at what you do, Griff, and you enjoy it. Maybe if you talked to him, he might understand. Jamieson would never want to hurt you."

Griff stares into the field for a while and Jamieson yells from the house to get our asses down there or he's eating our share, too. Griff chuckles with a sad shake of his head.

"Yeah. I think I'm serious. Unless I figure something else out, I need to create some separation so I can move on with my life. I can't keep pining after him forever. It's...I feel like I'm drowning, and I just can't do it anymore." His last words trail to a whisper, and he blinks fast. "I don't want to hurt him either, but I think this time I need to put myself first."

I squeeze his shoulder before we push away from the fence.

"I'll miss you around, but I understand whatever you decide." We walk back towards the farmhouse, and I can't imagine Jamieson taking the news well. He depends so much on Griff, and they mesh together even better than Hunter and me.

My phone chimes and when I glance down to see Riley's name, the smile on my face is automatic.

"That right there." Griff smiles and gestures to my face. "That's what I want. I'll see you inside." Griff hustles up the porch steps and I hope he finds what he needs without hurting too much to get there.

"Your parents are incredible, Jackson."

Riley bumps me with his shoulder as we clean up the kitchen. My mom made a full roast beef dinner with all the fixings and

Riley was in heaven. Mom asked him a million questions about weddings but managed to not ask about what we would do for ours. Not that we're anywhere close to that yet, but I know my mother. She's dying for it to happen.

My dad just smiled a lot. He's a smiley guy, but tonight he was extra happy, and it wasn't the pre-dinner drinks that did it.

"They love you, Rye. I told you they would."

Riley stares off with a smile on his face as he dries a pot. "I bet you had great family holiday dinners."

"We did. Lots of food and lots of laughs."

"Do you think your mom wanted to ask about our wedding? She was getting a little specific with her questions."

I snort a laugh as I pull the plug on the sink and turn towards Riley. "She was definitely fighting to keep from asking. She's always wanted me to get married. I think you being into romance and weddings has her extra excited."

Riley sets the pot down and turns to me.

"Do you ever want to be married?"

Nodding slowly, I step over to him and pull him into my arms. "Yes, I do. I want to be married and get a dog. I want to dance with you in the kitchen at midnight to music that only we can hear in our hearts." Riley loops his arms around my neck, and we sway like drunk teenagers at a high school dance.

"What about kids?"

"They don't need to be my own, but I'd be open to foster kids if needed. I'm not sure if I can handle babies, but older kids maybe. What about you?"

"I've always wanted a family that I didn't have. Marriage definitely, but I never thought about being a father. I like your idea, though. I work too much, and I'd like to give back somehow. You inspire me."

"I do?"

We sway in a circle, and he pecks my lips with a kiss.

"Yes, you do. You stuck with me when I told you I don't date cowboys. You came when I needed you without even hesitating and you don't give up. Not to mention all your help with Aunt Agnes and renovating. You're so...generous and kind. It inspires me to be better."

I swallow the lump in my throat.

"That's just me being me."

"I know, and it's what I love about you."

It's still so new to hear those words from Riley that I can't stop the smile forming.

"I love hearing you say that."

Riley kisses me again and I back him up against the kitchen counter as his fingers slide into my hair and a leg wraps around my waist.

"God, Riley...you drive me wild. How do you always make me forget what I'm doing?" I murmur between kisses and Riley smiles against my lips.

"Talent?"

We both laugh and make out like we have all the time in the world. Until a throat clears behind us and I remember my parents are here.

"Sorry, son. I just came to see if you needed help with the tea, but I see everything is under control here." He chuckles when I groan and hide my face in Riley's shoulder. "If you two want to get home, we don't mind. We'll catch up again after the rodeo tomorrow. Riley, you're going to sit with us, right?"

My dad walks over to the kettle, not at all bothered to catch us making out like school kids and talks like it's not awkward at all.

"Yes, of course, Mr. Sutherland. I can't wait."

Dad pulls two mugs from the cupboard and tilts his head towards the door. "Call me Dean and Jackson will show you to our seats before his event. Get out of here, you two."

"But Mom—"

"She'll be fine, Jack. Unless you want her to start telling stories about you as a toddler, you might want to split."

Riley perks up. "Oh? I bet he was a darling. Maybe we should stay."

"No. We're leaving." I tug Riley towards the door. "Thanks Dad. Say goodnight to Mom and I'll see you tomorrow."

Riley looks disappointed, but I press a kiss to his mouth.

"I'll make it up to you."

Before he can say anything else, I push him out the door.

Twenty-Three
Riley

It's so wonderful to see my aunt looking less frail.

She's only a few days post surgery, but she's more herself. With her improvement, a large slice of my stress slides away.

"Is Jackson picking you up today?"

She's moved out of bed with my help to sit at the table for her supper that should be here soon. She's stronger than I thought she'd be and seeing her already adjusting to her new walker, even with a casted arm, further eases the worry I've carried since her fall.

"No, Gabe will. Jackson is already at the rodeo grounds. They do this big meet and greet thing and because he's a hometown competitor, he takes part in anything they ask."

"That sounds like the boy I know. He really is a wonderful man, Riley."

"He is." My sigh is almost embarrassing, but my aunt only smiles bigger, and I don't remember ever feeling this light and happy over another man before.

"Knock, knock." Gabe enters my aunt's room with a giant houseplant and a happy face balloon. "I'm not interrupting, am I?"

"Not at all, Gabriel." My aunt hugs Gabe when he leans in, and I take the plant to set it where she can see it from her bed.

"I just stopped by your place. It appears a few local cowboys have already started some renovations for you." He peers over her head at me. "You didn't tell me you had so many attractive friends, Riley."

My aunt chuckles and I shake my head.

"Gabe, we aren't talking about this right now and you don't live here, anyway. I don't need you breaking hearts and making my friends sad."

He mock gasps, but I know Gabe. He'll never commit and while he's always up front about it, I always feel bad for the men he leaves behind.

"Are you staying in town much longer?" my aunt asks as he squeezes her hand.

"Just a few more days. Riley is all set, and I approve of Jackson, so I feel better leaving you two now that I see it's under control."

He winks at me, always teasing me about having to give his stamp of approval. I don't even hate it, because his approval means the world to me.

But I don't tell him that.

"I think there's a compliment in there somewhere."

He grins. "There is." My aunt laughs as Gabe sticks out his tongue as I reach for my jacket.

"Anyway, we'll let you get your supper in, Auntie, and I'll be back tomorrow." After kissing her cheek and Gabe making her laugh with bawdy cowboy jokes, I shake my head at their antics and we leave the hospital.

"Do you have to get back to the office soon? Not that I don't appreciate you being here for me, but I feel bad. You're probably behind at work."

Gabe's smile fades as he glances my way.

"No...not behind. I can work from anywhere usually. I have to appear in court next week, but most of my work I can do anywhere."

Gabe doesn't look at me. Instead, he peers off in the distance and if I didn't know him as well as I do, I wouldn't recognize his body language.

"I feel like you're leaving a few things out."

"Not really. It's all unknown, so I'm not leaving anything out. But don't worry about my work. It's fine."

I also know that he'll share when he's ready. We have enough going on with my aunt, my business, and now being involved with Jackson. If he doesn't want to add to the pile right now, I'll respect that.

We reach Gabe's rental vehicle, which is a huge SUV, and I need to use the handle to pull myself up and inside.

"Are you missing the *Lexus* yet?"

Gabe groans as he buckles in.

"You have no idea. The rental place only had trucks and SUVs. When the hell does that ever happen?"

"When you live in a country town, Gabe. It's just how it is here."

"I suppose if you live here, you get used to it, but I miss my luxury car." He steers us out of the parking lot and bumps the curb with a curse. "Are you excited to see your man in action tonight?"

My belly swoops and what must be the loopiest smile ever forms on my lips. "Yeah. I can't wait. I'm sitting with his parents, and I think his mom wants us married already."

Gabe laughs softly. "I told you if you let go of hating what Chase represented, you'd find the prince you've dreamed of. You're so happy, Rye. For the first time in...god, years, you're truly happy. I love that for you."

"It's all happening so fast. Some days it feels like it's not real."

Which is the understatement of the year. I thought once I finally opened up and let Jackson in, we'd have this slow, warm romance. Like sipping hot apple cider on a chilly fall day. That he'd do exactly what he said he would and romance me off my feet as we slowly and sweetly fell in love.

Instead, he blurted out his feelings in the most simple yet poignant way and had me spewing my emotions right back. None of it scripted like the events I plan or written on cue cards by nervous lovers. All of it in real time, straight from the heart.

It wasn't perfect, but it's perfectly Jackson and I wouldn't change a thing.

Even if Aunt Agnes hadn't fallen and Jackson didn't charge into my condo in the wee morning hours, it would have happened in the easiest way. Because that's who Jackson is. Easy like lazy mornings in bed or the snuggle of a puppy.

Gabe parks in the overflowing rodeo lot, somehow squeezing the giant SUV into a space with a satisfied grunt, and together we amble across the lot to the fairground entrance. Much like the rodeo I went to in Big Rock, this one is huge. The riot of noise carries from the midway, complete with the aroma of deep-fried foods. To the left is the entrance to the rodeo grounds, and gradually the scent of fried foods dissipates as we walk, only to be replaced by the smell of animal shit, leather, and something unique to rodeo that I can't quite name. But I love it.

Earlier today, Jackson showed me where to find his parents and, as odd as it seems, this rodeo has a boxed seat section.

The Sutherland family sponsors it every year just so they have guaranteed unobstructed seats to watch Jackson and his friends all weekend. Dean and Linda hold court like royalty in the special grandstand seats that have comfortable chairs with backs and not the bench seating of normal stands.

Every year, the Sutherlands donate rodeo tickets to the Boys and Girls Club so kids who can't afford to come could experience a real rodeo in as much luxury as a small-town rodeo can give. It shouldn't surprise me that Jackson's parents are still involved in the community. Like Jackson, they're kind people and love to help. When Linda notices me climbing the stairs with Gabe, she waves off the person checking for our entrance wristbands.

"This is my future son-in-law! He's fine to allow in." She rushes over to pull me into a hug. "I'm so happy you're here! How's your aunt today?"

Her son-in-law comment pulls a chuckle from Gabe, and I have to stomp on the butterflies rioting in my gut. "She's so much better. Still on some pain meds, but she's more herself today."

"Wonderful to hear. She's a lovely woman." Dean chimes in and motions to a chair next to them. Gabe shakes their hands and takes a chair behind me, chatting to some teenagers sitting in the back hosted by the Sutherlands.

"Jackson is awfully excited you're here," Linda says as she squeezes my hand.

"I am too. He's a natural."

"He wasn't always," Dean chimes in from the other side of Linda.

"What do you mean?"

"When Jack was little, he was so fearful. We didn't know why, and we just accepted that was his personality, but it was so hard to watch him miss out on things because of it." Linda's gaze is wistful as her eyes roam the rodeo ring for Jackson, who isn't around yet. "He just had this odd fear of new things. Almost like he refused to believe he could succeed, so he never tried."

"And he was just like that from the beginning?"

Dean nods, but with a smile. "He was a very sensitive boy. We just accepted it and tried to make him comfortable while gently introducing him to new things. It wasn't until one of the neighbours' horses got loose when Jack was maybe thirteen. He saw the horse and just went to it. Somehow, he got over whatever the fear was and threw a rope around its neck to walk it home safely. I remember him telling us what happened and how he almost grew right in front of us. He was so full of pride from helping that horse." Dean glances at Linda, who nods in agreement. "He came out of his shell more after that and finally tried rodeo the following summer."

My mind plays a movie of a cute young Jackson just growing into himself and helping a creature who couldn't help itself. My heart nearly bursts thinking about how brave he had to be just to do that. Perhaps that's what started him on the version of Jackson I know.

Now he throws himself onto running cattle and bakes cakes when I need him. He still blurts random facts when he's nervous, but he has the confidence now that he clearly lacked early on. Is this where his reluctance to have someone on their knees for him comes from too? I wouldn't doubt that it's related. A fear of maybe upsetting someone he cares about.

And while I'm not about to ask his parents, the insight is powerful.

The rodeo announcer's voice blasts over the speakers and our conversation comes to a halt as we all focus on the ring. A local musician sings the anthem and an older gentleman leads us through the cowboy's prayer.

I'm barely paying attention to the events happening before Jackson's turn arrives. My mind keeps wandering to life with Jackson in the future. Dogs, dates and cheering him on ringside until he decides it's time to become a spectator. When the clown finishes his show, there's movement in the chutes at the end of the ring, and I search for Jackson.

There's no sneaking into the ring this time. A hometown boy, just like many others tonight, gets the spotlight and is introduced. Of course, Dean and Linda are mad proud, and hoot and holler as the announcer makes Jackson and Hunter wave.

Jackson waves and when his gaze finds mine, it's like the rest of the world doesn't exist. The cheers of the crowd vanish and the only thing in this world right now is me and the most amazing man on the back of his chestnut horse. A cowboy, a steer wrestler, and the man who deserves a thousand stars served to him because I've never known a better person.

Jackson's lips tilt in a small smile as he glances away.

"You just made the cowboy blush, Rye," Gabe whispers in my ear and I swat behind me to shut him up. "But who's the guy next to him?"

Turning quickly, I gape at Gabe. "His best friend and hazer. That's Hunter."

"I'm just looking, Rye. Calm down."

I know Gabe and he's not just looking, but I'll think about that more after.

This rodeo is much larger than the last one for the number of competitors and they've been divided into groups to wait behind the chutes. The competition is steep. Many of the cowboys have travelled farther than usual to get a shot at the very rich pot of prize money.

I know this because, during my online searches for information on Jackson, I fell into a rabbit hole of steer wrestling stars. Maybe that makes me an official groupie, but I'm not at all ashamed about it.

"These guys are super good, Linda."

The times posting early are all below four seconds and only one team missed out with a penalty and eliminated themselves.

"They sure are, but Jackson always does great here. He's in the zone. He'll have a great time." She squeezes my bouncing knee. "You'll see."

Four more teams go out and post four more incredible times. Two sit tied for first place and my anxiety blooms bigger for every extra minute I have to wait for Jackson. Finally, his and Hunter's names are called, and I see them both moving their horses in the chutes.

The noise settles around us as most of the spectators ready themselves for the hometown duo. Clear as a bell, Jackson's voice stands out over the murmur of the crowd.

"Yep!"

My heart lurches into my throat along with the steer that bursts from the chute with Hunter and Jackson alongside it. Jackson slides off his horse, smooth as butter melting on a pancake and the steer is on its side with feet in the air before I have time to take a breath.

Dean and Linda jump to their feet with cheers, and I do the same, because how could I not? I don't even know the time, but it has to be in contention to win. With my cheeks aching from smiling and my throat raw from cheering, Jackson does something that makes my knees weak.

He smiles that boyish grin and points at me before tapping his chest and forming a heart with his hands.

"Jesus, Rye. I'm not even romantic and that made my heart pitter patter," Gabe whispers in my ear, and I can't even argue with him. Because the announcer booms out the time as it flashes on the board.

"Ladies and gentleman, give our hometown boy a standing O because he just broke the Kissing Ridge rodeo record with a time of 3.1 seconds and is your new leader!"

Jackson's mouth parts in surprise as the crowd grows impossibly louder, and this time when he points my way, I know what he's saying.

That's for you, Rye.

When Jackson is finally out of the ring on his horse, I plunk back in my chair and savour what just happened.

My cowboy boyfriend just broke a record and in front of all these people, told me he loved me, and that he did it for me. Then he rode off on his horse in his perfectly worn denim jeans with a tip of his hat.

Holy fucking swoon. Top that, Disney.

"That's the most technical I've seen those two in years. Such a perfect execution." Dean is smiling and slapping me on the shoulder and shaking Gabe's hand like he just found out he's a grandfather.

"That was amazing." Gabe's voice sounds far away, and I shake my head to come back to reality. "I've never paid much attention to rodeo before. It wasn't my thing, but I can see why it's popular."

Gabe and Dean talk about rodeo and Linda bumps my shoulder.

"You're good for him. Thank you for being there for my son."

"He's good for me," I murmur, and Linda pulls me into a hug.

This rodeo can't end fast enough because it's not his mother's arms I want around me.

I want my cowboy.

Twenty-Four
Jackson

Hometown rodeos are great.

Until all you want is for it to be over so you can get the man of your dreams naked and celebrate a victory in private. But local celebrity status requires shmoozing with sponsors and greeting fans. Both of which I love, just not right now.

After I accepted the prize money for us, I did three separate interviews. My favourite was the local 4H club who asked if I could come talk to them sometime about caring for steers. The least favourite was the man from the championship rodeo panel who asked me far too many questions about who I was acknowledging in the stands and not enough about my actual sport.

Then there was an autograph and meet the cowboy session that I never turn down. It's usually kids just wanting to be like you when they grow up and I can't say no to that. I love answering their questions and encouraging them to get involved with the sport.

As the session winds down, the one person I want to see the most steps in front of me at the signing table.

"Do you sign body parts? They ran out of glossy photos for me to buy just to get in here."

Riley grins at me, and I slide my chair away from the table to meet him in front.

"Will a kiss be enough to make it worth your while? I'm all out of photos."

"Perfectly acceptable substitution, yes."

Thankfully, there aren't any kids left in the area because our kiss quickly turns into something very X-rated. The burning inside me to get this man home is fierce.

Riley comes up for air first and pats my chest with his hand.

"Wow, cowboy. You sure know how to make a man feel good." His cheeks glow and he radiates a pure happiness I've not seen from him since we met. Yes, he's laughed and been happy, but right now... he's next level and the most gorgeous thing I've ever seen.

"I can make you feel even better."

Riley's gaze drifts to my mouth, and he licks his lips. "Yeah? Does that mean you've fulfilled your cowboy duties for the night?"

"The banquet I must attend is tomorrow. Tonight, the party is optional, and I opt to spend it with you. Alone."

Riley swallows with a soft sigh.

"Lord, I was hoping you'd say that. Ever since you did your show and pointed at me from the ring, I've been..." Riley trails off with a soft laugh. The people securing the area for the night shuffle around us and he glances at the exit. "I've been anxious, maybe. It's weird. There's no word I know to describe what I'm feeling right now, Jack. It's all so new to me and you make me feel like I'm floating one minute and burning up the next."

Riley closes his eyes and exhales slowly, all while keeping his hands anchored to me. One on my hip and the other flat on my chest... over my heart. When he opens his eyes and meets my gaze again, I draw him closer.

"Baby, I get it. It's okay." Pressing a soft kiss to his mouth, I bring my lips to his ear. "It's hard to understand big feelings, but I promise you that you're not alone, Riley. It's like you're a part of me I need to breathe."

"Will you take me home now?"

"Of course."

Grabbing my hat and thanking the few lingering staff, I take Riley's hand and lead him out of the tent, where we almost run into Gabe.

"Oh, there you are. I'm going to the big party thing, if you don't mind?"

Riley shakes his head. "No. Why would I?"

"No reason. Just wanted to make sure you found Jackson and have a way home. Jamieson, I think, he found me and invited me along with the group, so I'm doing that."

"Jamieson likes to sing sea shanties when he's drunk, FYI," I add with a laugh. "But they're good people and it's a fun event."

Jamieson rounds the corner with Griff beside him and throws an arm around Gabe.

"You disappeared! Ready to party? There's even a mechanical bull! I can teach you!"

Riley raises an eyebrow when Gabe laughs and agrees, just as Hunter ambles up to the group.

"Come on. There's an *Uber* waiting. You know how hard it was to find a ride to fit all of us? Don't waste it goofing off here," Hunter barks as he motions to follow him, and Gabe looks positively pissed.

"Is he always an asshole?" Gabe quips.

Jamieson laughs. "Yeah, but he's our asshole, so we just let him do his thing."

"Have fun, Gabe. Seems like you might have your hands full," Riley chirps, but Gabe just shrugs and follows my friends. "I'm a lawyer. I'm used to assholes."

Riley grabs my hand again and pulls me towards the lot where my truck is parked.

"Let's get out of here, Jack."

We stop and kiss far too many times, if there is such a thing, in the short distance to my truck. Riley is an expert flirt. Touching just enough to light the fuse, but not enough to make it flame to life and burn the house down.

Finally at my truck, he tries to dash ahead and slip into the passenger side, but I catch him and easily pick him up by the hips and spin him around to pin him against the truck door.

"Jesus, Jack," he breathes as his hands grip my shoulders and his legs wrap around my waist. "Kiss me."

My lips meet his and his body squeezes around me tighter.

"Oh god, Jackson..."

"Riley..." My hands support him under his ass, and when I pull away, the moonlight shines just enough to illuminate him against the truck in just such a way that his once-guarded features are now naked.

I have all of him. Those ocean blues no longer have that tiny cloud of uncertainty.

Resting my forehead on his, I sigh a shaky breath.

"You unravel me, Riley. I'm never this out of control."

"If you're unravelled, then I'm already in a pile on the floor." His shaky hands cup my face. "Take us home, Jack. Quickly," he whispers, and I lower him to his feet. I want to kiss him again and not stop, but he shoves me away with a laugh and opens the truck door.

"We'll never get home if you keep doing that. Drive, please."

After what feels like an eternity with Riley smashed into the passenger door to not touch me, I pull into the parking space at his condo and kill the engine.

Then I burst out laughing.

"Are we just extra horny, or is this something else? I can't believe you spent the entire drive pushed up against the door to avoid touching me."

Riley snorts and laughs as we grin across the truck cab at each other.

"I don't know Jack. It's weird, but I love it."

Riley slides out and speed walks to his building, with me trailing two steps behind. If I can't risk touching him, I'm going to look. And imagine. Thank fuck for my vivid imagination.

After he punches in his security code, he glances over his shoulder to find me adjusting the front of my pants. The elevator slides open, and he immediately squishes into one corner and points to the other side without a word.

"When do I get to touch you again?" My voice is so jagged, he turns to look at me as he bites his lip.

"The minute the door of my condo closes behind us."

The second the elevator doors open, Riley is out like a shot and entering the code to open his door. I linger a half a step behind... I don't want to break the rule he set.

We both step inside and Riley spins, pushing me into the door and forcing it closed with my body.

"*Oof.* You know the door wasn't really closed."

Riley pauses for a breath. "Really? You want to split hairs on that now?" His hands are already under my shirt and forcing it over my head and I've never felt so damn comfortable with someone before. We have this connection that shouldn't be so solid this soon, but it's the most right thing I've ever felt.

My hat gets tossed on the coffee table and my shirt hits the floor all before I can even react to Riley mauling me like a bear in search of food after hibernation. His mouth is on mine before I can reply, and then I forget the question, anyway.

Like a match to gasoline, Riley's hands on my exposed chest send a shiver through me and I'm grabbing at his clothes with zero finesse, pushing him back from the door as we race to undress.

"I've wanted you naked since I saw you ride into the ring tonight," he pants as he wrenches my jeans down my legs.

Somehow, I get untangled from my pants and pull his face to mine. I can't stop kissing him. I need his kisses in a way that throws all rational thought out the window... so I bend and lift him over my shoulder in a fireman's carry and jog down the hall to the bedroom.

"Jackson! What are you doing!?" He laughs and makes a half-assed attempt at struggling, but in the end, just lets me carry him until I flop him on the bed.

"Sorry, Rye. I just—" Riley shimmies out of his jeans and my mouth drops. "You've had that on this whole time?" My voice breaks like a teenager in puberty.

Riley lifts his legs, and I pull his jeans off the rest of the way, pitching them somewhere behind me before kneeling between his legs on the bed. My hands run up his thighs and stop at the band of the intricate black lace jock he's wearing.

"You approve?"

"Damn right, I do." My palm brushes over his lace-covered cock, and he closes his eyes with a soft sigh.

"I didn't think you'd go all caveman on me. I thought you'd want to go s-slow." His voice hitches as I press a kiss to his navel and run my nose along the edge of the lace. Lace on a man has always been something I kept inside. I can't really say why. Maybe because I never felt comfortable enough to ask for it. Then Riley just shows up wearing it like a second skin and probably has a drawer full.

Karma came through.

"I did. Still do, but it feels like you've edged me for hours and I fucking need you, Riley. Like the air I breathe, I need to be make love to you or I might die."

"That's a little dramatic." He reaches for me and pulls me to his lips. "But I feel like that too," he whispers. "You make me feel like the biggest treasure on the planet, and I just want to give you everything I have."

I don't know how long we stay like that, but I'm stuck on his comment about feeling like a treasure because that's exactly what he is to me. A treasure with an unlimited value that I'm damn lucky to have.

I'm swinging between the desire to rip these lacy things off and claim him right this second to making slow passionate love to him the way I've fantasized about since I met him. Both options are good, and it's like trying to decide between the chocolate-coated donut and the chocolate-coated donut with sprinkles.

"Jackson?" Riley rolls us over and straddles my hips. "I can feel you overthinking. Will this help?"

Riley slides down and removes my boxers. He tosses them over his shoulder with a sexy smirk before bending over to remove his lace and display his gorgeous ass. Okay, new option, chocolate-coated donut with sprinkles and a cherry. Riley taking over is kind of hot. He crawls back over me and reaches into his nightstand.

"I'm putting a condom on you. Any objections?"

"No," I squeak as he rips the foil.

Oh god. He's not using his hands. Riley rolls the condom down my dick with his mouth, and I might spontaneously combust.

"Now you're ready. You can handle the lube. I like to use a lot. Do what you want to me, Jackson."

My breath shakes as I kiss him once before flipping him onto his back. After slicking myself and him, he practically purrs when I bend his legs back to expose his pretty hole. Not trusting myself to speak intelligible words, I notch myself at his entrance and press into him slowly.

His hands clutch at my shoulders and his eyes radiate a lust I understand, but underneath that, the softness for me he displayed earlier sits. The silent message of trust to take him like he just gave me permission for and to stop fucking around about it. Dropping his legs down, I collapse on top of him and gasp when he wraps his legs around me, pulling me fully into him.

"Jackson, I promise we can do this slow and romantic later. Just fuck me right now, like it's the last time you'll see me for a week."

"Um...it kind of is. I have that rodeo..."

Riley laughs softly. "I know, babe. So please...show me."

Loving someone like Riley is already easy, but when he reads me so well and makes me feel like I'm a whole person and not a hot guy in a cowboy hat, it allows me to let go and just be.

We move together, and I swallow his pleasured moans as I kiss him. His heels dig into me, urging me to give him more, and I do until the sweat dampens my hair, and I'm teetering on the edge of what I know will be a life-altering orgasm.

"Fuck, I'm gonna come, Rye."

"Touch me while you do."

He pushes me up and I grip his cock in my palm as I awkwardly continue moving my hips.

"Jackson!"

His cum spills over my fist moments before I explode. My orgasm is so intense my toes cramp and I almost crush Riley as I try to ease myself down, but my arms turn to jelly.

"Jesus, that was intense. Holy fuck, Rye. I can't feel most of my body."

Riley's body shakes with a laugh. "Neither can I. You're crushing me."

"I'm sorry!"

Pulling out gently, I try not to make a mess of the condom with my shaking hands. I can't catch my breath and Riley swoops in.

He removes the condom with a tender touch and ties it off before dropping it on the floor.

"Jack? What happened? Are you okay?"

He lies next to me, eyes brimming with concern, and I want to tell him I think I unlocked a new erogenous zone or something. Or maybe it's just him who makes my toes cramp and body turn to goo.

But instead, I say, "Did you know Hawaiian pizza isn't from Hawaii?"

Riley has the decency to not look shocked and before I can apologize, he nods. "Yeah. I do. A Greek Canadian, wasn't it? At his restaurant in Ontario. It's a Canadian creation."

"Yeah."

Riley smooths his palm over my cheek, and I swallow hard.

"Did you know I've never been in actual love before?" He brushes his thumb over my lip. "It's true. I thought I was once, but I was wrong. I didn't know true love until I met you." He kisses me and stares into my soul. "I don't mind that I make you nervous sometimes and you blurt your facts. You're you, Jackson. I'll never be mad about it if you can't find the right words because I can feel it and you show me. Every day since I've met you, you show me how you feel."

Ugh. That makes me all kinds of mushy, and I pull him in for a soft kiss.

"I wish I didn't have to go away so soon after this, Rye. I'll miss you."

"I'll miss you too. But you have video calling." He bites his lip. "And I have a whole drawer of lingerie to show you."

"I knew it!" I kiss him hard and wonder again if the universe knew what it was doing when Riley crossed my path. "I'll never say no to that."

"Wanna clean up and have a snack?"

Riley rolls off the bed, and I do too, gingerly testing my toes against the carpet. I don't think I've had my toes hurt like that before.

"That sounds perfect."

Riley leaves to turn on the shower, and I pinch my arm.

"Ouch." Rubbing the spot, I grin and follow the sound of running water.

Twenty-Five
Riley

"Are you sure you're okay with taking care of the new client on your own?"

The new assistant I hired has been a quick study. In the past week, she's proved herself invaluable and I'm grateful for Gabe kicking me in the ass to hire the help.

"Of course I am, Riley. I won't sign anything without you. It's purely information gathering. We can do the proposal together and you can meet them at the second appointment." Hailey pats me on the shoulder. "I've got this. Go see your aunt before your hot date."

My cheeks heat when she winks, and I don't know why. It's not like she can read my mind and know Jackson and I have been flirting over video the whole week he's been gone because he didn't want to do phone sex. I swear he couldn't get any sweeter when he finally stammered out facts about Korean beef when I angled the phone so he could see the dark grey lace shorts I was wearing.

At first, I thought maybe Jackson was old-fashioned and phone sex wasn't something he liked because he felt awkward. But when he told me he prefers a physical connection and sometimes needs it to be satisfied, I wasn't even disappointed. It just means I have many more steamy nights ahead of modelling lingerie in person for him.

The best thing I ever found online was the website for bespoke lingerie for men by a designer in northern Quebec. He does stunning work and has photos on his website with his husband in a plaid and lace piece that makes me drool.

"Okay, well, you have my number if you need anything. Lock up and I'll see you tomorrow."

"Will do, Riley. Don't rush in. I can handle it."

After leaving the office with a smile, I drive to the hospital, where my aunt is still recovering. She's been doing so damn well in the rehab wing there. Jackson's friends will finish the work at her house next week and she'll be back home before we know it.

There's a silver lining to her fall, which she's latched onto. Just like Aunt Agnes always does. She gets her main floor updated and painted, which I swear to god is more exciting to her than going home to sleep in her own bed.

Armed with paint swatches, I navigate the halls to my aunt's room, where she's just returned from her physio.

"Oh, perfect timing, Riley! Have you met Gary? He's my physiotherapist and absolutely charming."

In another world, I may have flirted with the buff young man. He's attractive, and I don't miss his lingering perusal.

"Hi. Nice to meet you. I hope she's not too much of a pain in the ass for you."

"Riley Maxwell Benton! If I were stronger, I'd paddle your ass for that!" She says it with a laugh, but I know for a fact she means it.

"I'd do it for her," Gary murmurs low for only me to hear.

"My boyfriend probably wouldn't go for that."

Gary nods with a grimace. "Can't blame a guy for trying."

"What are you two whispering about?"

"I was just telling Gary you're excited about the renovations and if there were any colours to set your rehab back."

Gary tips his head in appreciation of the subject change.

"She really likes the mustard yellow walls in our treatment wing."

"Oh, barf." My aunt gags as Gary laughs.

"I'll leave you two for your visit and I'll see you again tomorrow, Agnes. Tap dancing is the next activity."

Aunt Agnes snorts with a smile as Gary leaves.

"If you hadn't met Jackson, I'd have told you to go out with Gary. He's a nice boy."

"He is." Pulling a chair next to her at the tiny table in her room, I drop the pile of paint swatches on the surface. "As long as he's good to you right now, that's all that matters."

"Jackson comes home today, right?"

"Yep. In about three hours. He has to unload his horse and help Hunter with something, then I'm making him dinner."

My aunt forms a pile of hard nos for colours and pushes them aside.

"Is that what you're calling it? Dinner?"

"It *is* dinner! And I'm not discussing sex with you," I snap.

She makes another pile of maybes and reaches for a pen to number and label the colours she likes for each room.

"That's fine. I think you're beyond the safe sex talk and all that stuff, anyway. You know I just tease you. If it's making you uncomfortable, say something." Aunt Agnes sniffs and avoids eye contact.

Shit. I didn't mean to be so rude and now I've hurt her feelings.

"I'm sorry, Auntie. I didn't mean to be rude. I just..." Glancing towards the door, I lower my voice. "Jackson is very private about that stuff, and I think he'd be uncomfortable if he knew we talked about it."

"That's okay, Riley. I'd never want to cross a line. We've always joked, so I just did what was natural, but I can dial it back."

"It's just...he's so sweet, Auntie." I take the hideous baby-shit-coloured swatch from her hand and shake my head as I drop it into the trash can. "Jackson is everything I didn't know I was looking for. He caught me off guard. I thought we could just be friends, but he's so..."

I don't even know how to describe Jackson properly to my aunt because there really are no words.

"You really love him, don't you?"

"Yeah. He's definitely the one."

Aunt Agnes slides her now smaller piles of colours in front of her and taps her fingers on a bright sunshine yellow.

"I've always wanted a yellow kitchen. I know it's not on the renovation list, but do you think the fellows could paint the kitchen for me, too?"

"I don't think they'd mind at all. If they did, I'd do it for you. It's a good choice."

For the next hour, we talk about paint colours and what room will get each colour, and as much as I hate the reason for all this happening, I'm almost happy it did. There's so much goodness on the flip side of her falling.

She's getting her old home upgraded, refreshed and remodelled for her to live in safely by herself. Our community has rallied for it to happen. The man at the hardware store remembers when Aunt Agnes used to bring in cookies on holidays to the Boys and Girls Club. Along with the cookies, she sometimes snuck small gifts to the children who had little. I haven't told her yet, but he gave us the paint for free and offered to help.

Jackson and his friends saved us so much in contractor fees, too. They'll finish the drywall and flooring once the plumber is finished in the new main-floor bathroom and laundry. Her accident has shown me how many people in this town truly care about her well-being.

It also made Jackson shine like the light he is when he jumped in, not just for my aunt, but for me. His constant support is not something I'll ever take for granted.

"Okay, I think I picked one for every room, but if you think they go better in other rooms, switch them around. But I definitely want a yellow kitchen."

After getting us both a tea in the cafeteria and chatting for a bit, Aunt Agnes's eyelids grow heavy.

"Take a nap, Auntie. I need to do a few things before Jackson gets here. I'll see you tomorrow."

"Don't rush back to see an old woman resting. He just got back. Go enjoy that, Riley. Live your life. I'll be fine."

She squeezes my hand, and I pull her favourite blanket up to tuck her in.

"I know you are."

She bats away my hands with a smile and adjusts the blanket.

"I love you. Now get out of here and go see that handsome cowboy of yours."

I lean in to kiss her cheek. "I love you, too."

After leaving the hospital, I drop by the hardware store with my paint choices and load the mixed gallons into my car before dropping them off at my aunt's. I'm not expecting anyone here yet, but the smashing of a hammer into drywall is unmistakable.

"Hello?"

Walking towards the sound, I find one of Jackson's friends, the bullfighter Griff, swinging a giant hammer into the wall around my aunt's bedroom.

"Griff?"

"Fuck. Shit. Riley...hey. I didn't hear you."

Griff drops the hammer and runs a hand through his hair. He reaches for the shirt he stripped off and pulls it back on. "I just needed to get some energy off and thought I'd finish up the last bit of demo here. I hope that's okay. Jackson said it would be fine."

"Yeah, that's totally fine. We appreciate the help whenever we can get it."

Griff chews his lip and nods. "You're welcome." He stares at his feet for a moment before opening and closing his mouth without a word.

"Um, I know we don't know each other well, but is there something you need to talk about? Are you okay?" I ask because the vibe here is...odd.

"No...it's...I'm fine. But thank you! Jackson's crazy about you. You're good for him."

Griff genuinely smiles, but it doesn't reach his eyes.

"Oh. Thank you. I'm gone for the guy, too." I smile back at Griff. "And thank you for your help here. My aunt and I sincerely appreciate it."

"Anytime." He cocks a thumb over his shoulder. "I'm going to head out, but don't worry. We'll get it all done."

Griff shoves a battered ball cap on his head and brushes past me with a muttered goodbye and I'm left wondering if I should have pressed harder to talk to him.

After carrying in all the paint and locking up behind me, I rush to the grocery store for what I need to cook Jackson dinner. I quickly find what I need and as I head to the checkout, a bouquet that reminds me of Jackson catches my eye. There's nothing more romantic than a well-chosen flower, so I add it to my purchase and head home.

I'm not much of a cook and I order in a lot because it's easier. But Jackson mentioned he loves to stay in more than go out, and one thing he's very open about is his homebody ways and a desire to have quiet evenings with the one he loves. I know he enjoys healthier food too, so after a lot of thought, I went with a simple stir fry and sticky rice. All the vegetables are organic—I know he'll approve of that—and the beef is from a local butcher downtown.

After starting the rice in the cooker, I play an instrumental music list on my phone. It's one I enjoy when I just want to relax and unwind. Which is how it feels as I chop vegetables while the sounds of pianos and harps fill the room.

Jackson told me he'd be right over as soon as he and Hunter did whatever it is they do when returning from a rodeo. I suppose if I'm making him part of my life, I'll learn what he does eventually, but right now I just want to feel his arms around me and his lips on mine. To have him next to me while we share about our days and cook dinner together. I never thought such mundane things would bloom such an ache in my chest.

I guess that's love for you. Always surprising.

The beeps sound on my door's keypad and I look up from my chopping to watch Jackson walk through the front door. His black hair, still wet from a shower, sticks up as his smile lights up his entire face.

"Hey, Rye."

"Hey, handsome."

Brushing my hands off on the tea towel, I meet him as he kicks off his shoes at the door and reaches for me.

"Smells good in here." His hands grip my waist as he pulls me closer. "Looks good, too."

"Kiss me first, compliment me later."

His deep laugh rolls as his lips meet mine and I melt into him. "Fuck, I've missed you," I murmur as our lips dance and taste. Jackson's hands slide up my sides to cup my face.

"Missed you more," he murmurs across my lips.

Laughing, I push at his chest.

"I refuse to be that kind of couple. It's not a competition."

"You're right. We both win." Jackson follows me into the kitchen and surveys my mass of vegetables and tray of beef. He picks up a slice of pepper and I smack at his hand.

"Want to help me finish? It's beef stir fry. The rice should be done soon."

Jackson leans his hip on the counter as he crunches on his pepper slice. His gaze is a caress on my skin and my breath quickens under his attention.

"Barefoot, cooking dinner, soft music, and your beautiful face are the best things to come home to, Rye. Tell me what you want me to do."

Cue my heart melting.

"Um, ah, you could start the beef. There's a recipe here with the sauce," I point to my iPad on a stand. "I'll finish chopping the vegetables."

Jackson nods and moves to the stove while I fan my face. Jesus Almighty, is his kink having me cook for him? Because I will gladly stay home every night and learn to cook if he looks at me like that every time.

"How's your aunt?"

Jackson adds oil to the wok and works on the garlic cloves.

"Wonderful. She's really looking forward to the makeover of her place. We picked paint colours today."

Jackson dumps the minced garlic in a bowl and begins adding the liquid ingredients I laid out to the same bowl. Pausing, I notice he's not measuring. He's free pouring and mixing.

"You've made this before, haven't you?"

He grins and bumps my shoulder.

"It's one of my favourite meals. It's a lot of preparation to chop it all, but it's so easy to make. And healthy. You picked well."

The rice steamer pings that the rice is ready, and Jackson moves back to check the wok. The meat sizzles when it hits the oil, and I watch mesmerized as he moves so easily around my kitchen.

"Give me your vegetables, Rye. You can fluff the rice and plate it."

"Fluff the rice." I snort a laugh, and he raises an eyebrow, but the tiny smile is there.

"You're impossible."

Jackson takes my offered vegetables and continues to cook as he hums the damn song from Lady and the Tramp again and it almost brings me to my knees. He's so full of joy and comfortable in this element. It's hard to imagine this man ever feeling like he can't conquer whatever he puts his mind to.

I fluff the rice as instructed and giggle the whole time. Jackson tosses the cooking food in the wok like a professional before plating it on the bed of rice. He kisses me softly after placing a fork next to my plate.

"Tell me about your week. I know we talked on the phone while I was away, but talk to me. What else happened?"

"This is fantastic, Jack. You didn't even measure stuff."

"I told you. It's one of my go-to meals. Don't always expect me to cook that easy."

We talk back and forth. Jackson tells me about how big the squirrels were at the campground they stayed at, and I tell him how I got caught in the rain because my umbrella fell apart.

We talk about the rodeo more and he tells me how well his friends are doing, but not once does he tell me he's the circuit champion and has an invitation to the National Finals. I already know this because I looked it up online after he won the last rodeo.

The music still plays while we clean up our dinner mess, and even though it's early September, part of me longs for a roaring fire to settle in front of with Jackson wrapped around me. Nothing in my life prepared me for the crushing wave of feelings that have just dragged me under while we cleaned up the kitchen together.

"Rye? You okay?"

"How come you don't want to tell me you're going to the National Finals? Aren't you happy about it?"

Jackson hangs the towel on the handle of the stove and bites his lip.

"I'm thrilled about it." He holds his hand out to me, and I step between his legs. "But I'd be happier if you'd come and watch me. I was going to bring it up later, but since you asked...would you want to spend four days with me in Elk Meadows?"

"You want me to come?"

"Of course I do. I want you to be the first one I kiss when I win that giant buckle."

"First one? Better be the only one!"

I playfully try to shove him away, but he holds me tight.

His roughened thumb smooths across my cheek. "The first, the last, and the only one I ever want to kiss for the rest of my life."

Swallowing hard, I lean in to kiss him softly.

"I like the sound of that."

Twenty-Six
Jackson
Six Weeks Later

I can't believe I'm at the National Finals. After wrestling steers for almost twenty years, I've never made it before. I've been close many times and made a respectable living doing it, but I've never been to the pinnacle event of my sport.

Hunter sits on his horse, cool as a cucumber, while I'm almost vibrating out of my saddle.

"We're going to win, Jack. Relax."

"You sound pretty confident about that."

"Of course I am. If we aren't confident in our skills, we won't go anywhere. You're the best at what you do, Jack, and so am I. We wouldn't be here otherwise." His hardened gaze meets mine. "We're gonna win."

"You're right. We are."

Hunter returns to his hyper-watch state, and I suck in some deep breaths to settle my mind. It's something I've practiced since I started this sport and found to be helpful in many areas of life outside the ring.

My parents came up from Arizona to watch me and sit somewhere in the stands with Riley. Riley, who in the last month has accepted help with an assistant and was here for me while he let her handle his business.

After his aunt was released from the hospital, he helped settle her in. When he came home that night, he held me so tight I thought he wanted to become part of me. He later confessed that he wanted to be more flexible so he could watch me in the rodeo more and spend more time with his aunt. She may have only broken her hip, but Riley realized he'd missed so much. First by staying away when he moved out of town, and second by throwing himself into his new business.

I'm lucky he supports me so much, but I haven't missed how much fun he's having either. Two days ago, we had to qualify to make it to today's final round of twelve and he won't admit it, but I'm positive he tried to start the wave when the steer wrestlers were announced.

His assistant made him a T-shirt to wear that says, '*A steer wrestler stole my heart and his name is Jackson Sutherland*'. My mom found that entirely too precious, and frankly, so did I.

The man running the event behind-the-scenes motions for us to line up behind the chutes. Hunter and I are only two more riders out. Since the event is seeded 12th to first in order of riding, we're the last to compete after qualifying a mere one one-hundredth faster than second place. It seems like a long time for us to wait, but when it's the fastest event in rodeo it passes pretty quickly, even when they have issues setting the rope barriers.

In a blink, it's already our turn, and together, we fall into our mental zones. Hunter nods that he's ready, and I take a moment longer to visualize my run. Lady stops fidgeting and her muscles coil underneath me. The crowd noise melts away.

"Yep!"

The steer bursts out of the gate with Hunter on him keeping close, and me right alongside him sliding off my horse, barely two strides out of the gate. With everything I have, I plant my feet and twist the steer onto its side. It happens so fast that I don't even know if I took a breath. My entire body quakes with adrenaline as Hunter circles back with Lady and we wait for our time.

Time passes far too slowly and then the bright numbers flash on the board.

2.8 seconds. We've never broken three seconds. *Ever.*

Hunter's arms are around me, and he's crushing the air from my lungs.

"We did it, Jack! Fuck, I knew you would! Holy shit!"

I've won a lot of rodeos in my days, and they've all been amazing. But this one sits differently. After taking the reins for Lady, I remount and listen to the woman as she points us over to grab the rodeo flag for our victory lap. Hunter normally passes it to me, but this time I give it to him.

"I wouldn't be as good as I am without you. Take the flag, Hunter, and you go first. Don't argue."

If I'm not mistaken, his eyes get a little wet as he nods and takes the champion flag.

"Thanks." His face splits into a giant grin. "We fucking won!"

"I love this sport!" I howl, and together, we ride like demons out into the ring for our victory lap, and then I see him. Riley with my parents in his newly purchased cowboy hat we had specially fit for him here and a smile so wide I could see it from space.

Instead of following Hunter around the ring to meet him at the platform to receive our oversized paper cheque, I stop in front of the area with Riley and my parents. Hopping off Lady, I run to the barrier and climb to the top.

"Get down here!" I shout and point at Riley.

My mom shoves Riley towards the stairs and the crowd parts to let him down. When he finally reaches the fence I'm perched on top of, his laugh is the most beautiful thing I've ever heard. Someone helps him climb the few steps on the fence to reach me and he grabs a hold of the top. Joy and a tinge of fear spark in his eyes and I cup his face in my hands.

"No cowboy will ever love you like I do, Riley." I press my lips to his and kiss him with a fierceness that takes me by surprise. The crowd roars its approval, and I pull away to let Riley breathe. Resting my forehead against his, I whisper, "When we get home, move in with me. I want to see you first thing in the morning and last thing at night, Rye."

"Jackson…" One hand releases the fence and slides against my cheek. "You climbed a fence for me in front of thousands of people to ask me to move in with you? You need to collect your prize."

"It couldn't wait. I had to ask you right now and there's no bigger prize in this arena than you, Riley Benton."

He exhales a shaky breath, but his smile never fades.

"Everyone is staring at my ass up here."

"Let 'em look and see what they're missing. So, what do you say, baby?"

Riley's fingers slide down and clutch the edge of my shirt.

"On one condition."

"I'll give you anything."

"I get to name our dog."

I laugh against his lips, happier than I've ever been.

"It's a deal."

"Now, how do I get down in one piece so I can help pack boxes?"

Looking to the side, I see one of the security guys and motion for him to spot Riley as he climbs down. Once his feet are firmly on the ground, I make my way back to Lady and swing myself up to gallop over to where Hunter waits with the event coordinators.

"That couldn't wait?" Hunter says, but his smile is genuine.

"Nope. He said yes, though."

His jaw drops. "You asked him to marry you!?"

"Oh, no. To move in with me, but I'll ask him that too one day."

"Gentlemen, let's take photos, please. Mr. Sutherland has us running behind schedule."

We smile and hold the giant cheque for one million dollars and accept our fancy belt buckles before getting swept away for interviews. Both of us answer questions for various reporters for what feels like hours and finally we leave the media area to find my parents and Riley.

After we celebrate with some drinks and a late supper, my parents head to their hotel room with a promise of breakfast in the morning and for us to celebrate like we don't have to work tomorrow.

Hunter even fucks off to leave us alone, saying he's tired, which is not like him at all. But I have a full day of driving back home with him while we haul the horses. I'll get him to talk.

"So, how do you want to celebrate, Jack? Fancy champagne? It's pretty late. I don't know what's open other than bars."

"Honestly?"

"Of course. I only ever want you to be honest."

"Okay." I pull him into my arms and kiss his nose. "I want us to soak in the giant tub in our hotel room and use the bubble bath. Then I want to fuck you in front of the mirrors because I've always wanted to do that." Riley's breath hitches and I kiss him slowly. "Then I want to research puppies while we eat dill pickle chips and overpriced snacks from our mini bar."

"That's really what you want to do?"

"It really is."

Riley pretends to think about it before shaking his head with a smile.

"I love your randomness. Don't ever change."

"So, you're down with my plan?"

"Can the plan include me going down on you?" He wiggles his eyebrows, and I groan when he licks his lips with a seductive smile.

"I told you, Rye, whatever you want. I'll always give it to you."

His face softens, and he presses a soft kiss on my cheek.

"I know, cowboy. But having you is all I need."

We leave the restaurant hand in hand and walk the block back to our hotel. The city life still bustles around us, but we're about to cocoon away in a hotel on the biggest night of my career. People wearing brand-new boots and colourful hats still roam the street, the party atmosphere in full swing in this rodeo city.

But that life still doesn't appeal to me. I've always been an introvert of sorts and fully expected to remain alone because of my awkward tendencies. Until one day, who knew my life would change over a plate of hummus and stories of baby carrots?

Riley peers over at me.

"Whatcha thinking so hard about?"

You, me, a dog, and a million sunrises together.

"Nothing. Just thinking about carrots."

"Okay." We walk along in silence for a beat until Riley breaks it. "Jack?"

"Yeah?"

"I really love carrots."

Epilogue
One Year Later

Riley

"Are you sure that's what you want to name the puppy?"

Jackson grips my hand in his on the console of the truck. We're on our way to pick up our new puppy, who is an adorable beagle mix, at the animal shelter in the next town over.

"The deal was I could name the puppy and yes, that's the name I want."

Jackson flicks a glance at me.

"What if she doesn't suit her name?"

"Oh, she will. I know it."

I also know that Jackson really wanted to adopt an older dog he fell in love with on the website after we already agreed to take the puppy. He insisted one dog would be enough, and this was the dog we were meant to have.

But I disagree.

After pulling into the lot, Jackson opens the back door of his truck and checks on the puppy's kennel. He's like a new dad obsessively checking a car seat, and I take a moment to watch him more closely.

He's wearing a small smile as he adjusts the blanket inside and pets the comfort animal we placed in the kennel. It's supposed to help young puppies adapt to being away from their moms and make them less homesick. When the woman at the pet store explained what it was for, Jackson didn't even look at the price tag.

This man's tenderness makes me fall more in love with him every day. Whether it be something he did for me, his parents, or even Aunt Agnes, his heart only knows how to give and it's no wonder he didn't take to the bar scene like his friends. Jackson loves with all his being and he struggles with it sometimes.

He knows it's not a terrible quality, but it brings out the quirks he hates. Like random facts when he's nervous and stuck on what to say. I love it when he gets overwhelmed with me and still tells me things like how grapes need to freeze at a certain temperature to make ice wine.

It's both educational and his signal that he needs a moment to gather his thoughts and recalibrate.

"Ready, babe?"

Jackson nods, satisfied with the puppy setup, and joins me to enter the shelter.

"Hi! You made it!"

The shelter co-ordinator, a friend of Hannah's from Avocadabra, has been such a help with organizing my surprise.

"We wouldn't miss our puppy pickup date, Carla." Jackson shakes her hand and I go for the full hug because we've gotten to know each other a lot over the past three weeks. Jackson furrows his eyebrows, but I quickly move the conversation along.

"We're super excited to take Carrot home."

Jackson smiles as we follow her to the adoption meeting room. "I still can't believe that's the name you want to go with."

"It's special to me. I love it."

Jackson squeezes my hand. "I do too. Might be weird calling her that while we make salads, though."

"So Riley tells me you're a famous steer wrestler. That must be exciting."

"I wouldn't say I'm famous, but it is exciting."

They chatter a bit about rodeo and after we settle in the adoption room, Carla leaves to bring us Carrot.

"I'm kind of excited." Jackson rubs his hands on his pants.

"I know. You've always wanted a dog. I can't wait until she's underfoot while we make dinner together."

Jackson closes his eyes and inhales a deep breath. "I want that so much."

God, I hope I don't break him when he sees the surprise.

"Okay, guys, here she is. Miss Carrot."

Carla enters the room with a bundle of brown and white fur that's all ears and feet, and both Jackson and I sigh. He reaches out and Carla places Carrot in his arms.

"I'll let you both visit and be right back with all the paperwork." She winks behind Jackson's back and I turn my attention to him.

"Look at her ears, Rye! Oh my god, she's so cute." Carrot snuffles all over Jackson and his smile melts my heart. "I think she fits her name."

"Me too." I reach out to scratch her ears and she licks at my hand.

"Here you hold her. We should stop for an extra dog bed on the way home. When I'm away next year, you could bring her to work with you if needed."

"I don't think that will be necessary, but we can get her another bed. It's good to have choices."

There's a knock on the door and Carla pokes her head in.

"Do you have room for one more?"

She doesn't wait for an answer and instead opens the door to reveal the older grey dog Jackson fell in love with.

"What?" He turns to me and back to the dog, who instantly wags his tail and goes to Jackson. "I thought he was already adopted?"

"He was. By me."

"What?"

Carla left as soon as she brought the other dog in and if she's following the plan, she has all the dog accessories for an older dog gathered out front for us to take home.

Carrot squirms to get down, and I place her on the floor. She runs to the other dog, who immediately woofs and plays with her.

"Jack, look at me." Yep, I might have broken my boyfriend. Jackson's looking at me and back at the dogs, but he's still dazed. Cupping his cheeks, I force him to keep his eyes on me while the puppy races around the room with the other one chasing in play.

"I saw the way you wished for this dog when it came up for adoption and I couldn't not try to make your wish come true. He's yours."

"But now you have two dogs to look after when I'm away. That's a lot of work."

"Jack…I will do anything to make you happy. Taking care of two dogs while my cowboy boyfriend does his farewell rodeo circuit won't be difficult. Then you'll be home and we'll have the hydroponics and my business to focus on. It might be difficult at first, but it's worth it." I press a kiss to his lips. "You deserve the future you dreamed of, too, Jack. This is what you wanted."

The older dog barks and we both turn to find him standing and watching us. Jackson drops to his knees and calls him. "Here, boy. Come here."

The dog bounces over and almost knocks Jackson over. His laughter as he reaches to hug the dog closer melts my heart.

"Can I call you Tramp? You sort of look like him." The dog licks Jackson's face and bounces away with a bark. "Here, Tramp!" He immediately sits in front of Jackson.

"Rye…I think he likes that name."

"I think it's perfect for him." Carrot pounces at one of Tramp's feet with a puppy bark and we laugh. "I had Carla put them together before I made a decision. Tramp already acts like a big brother. They're perfect together."

Jackson pulls me into his arms and buries his face in my neck.

"I love you, Riley. I can't believe you did this."

"It was hard to keep it a surprise. I almost spoiled it a few times."

Jackson steps back and watches the dogs again. Tramp lies on the floor and Carrot keeps jumping over him while puppy barking.

"You know you have to be the stern parent, right? I can't say no to those faces."

Laughing, I scoop up Carrot and knock on the door to signal Carla.

"I know, Jack. Again…worth it."

I already picture him sneaking them treats and letting them sleep with us and all kinds of other things we talked about and agreed that we wouldn't do. But any time he breaks the rules with the dogs, something tells me I'll probably just love him even more and let it slide.

After wrangling both dogs into the truck, stopping at the pet store for yet more dog toys and discovering Carrot gets car sick, Jackson's smile never fades.

Carrot crashed out hard once we got them settled at home. Curled next to her kennel, of course, not in it. Tramp leans against Jackson's leg with a giant dog smile as he gets his ears scratched.

It's all so domestic and happy that I have to pinch myself.

"Ouch." I rub my arm and Jackson's gaze catches mine. He wraps his arm around my shoulders and pulls me close to kiss the top of my head.

"Me too, Rye. Me too."

Jamieson and Griff are up next as they try to adjust to the possibility of becoming more than just friends.
Bull Riders Don't Swoon is coming soon!

Want more of Jackson and Riley?
Get the bonus scene – Puffer fish and Porcupines!

Need more cowboys while you wait? The men of the Broken Horn Ranch Series have cameos coming. You can read about them while you wait!

Acknowledgements

Thank you so much for reading Jackson and Riley's story. I hope Jackson made you swoon. He wasn't meant to be a gentleman cowboy. I had more...filthy plans for him, let's say. As characters often do, he took over almost immediately and told me he wasn't like that.

So I rolled with it, and Jackson came to life. In a world where we often get lost in the photo shopped moments of Instagram and Tiktok, Jackson was unapologetically real. I think that's what I love most about him. While he hates all his awkward rambles and wishes to be different, Riley notices he's perfect as he is. I think that's how we should view ourselves: perfect the way we are.

I like to poll my reader group for suggestions, and this time I owe a thank you to Lia McKnight, who offered the name of Avocadabra as Riley and Jackson's favourite bistro. It's such a perfect name for what I envisioned. Thank you, Lia!

If you're wondering who has a story next, it's Jamieson and Griff! Don't worry, Hunter has a story too, but be warned that one might break your heart. I'll always put it back together, though.

Dear reader, I'm extremely thankful you give my books your precious time. Without you, I wouldn't be able to keep doing this.

If you missed the dedication, go back and look, because this book is for you.

Make sure you don't miss out on my book news and sign up to my newsletter. With all the uncertainty in the world, I'd hate to lose track of you.

Newsletter: https://www.rmneillauthor.com/newsletter

Of course, you can always follow me on Amazon and Bookbub, but if you like sneak peaks and want to connect, consider my newsletter to stay on top of things.

Much love,

RM

About the author

RM is an introverted Canadian author who likes to write about love while freezing in the winter. Her mission is to always make you swoon and snort laugh, sometimes even in public.

She talks to her cat, Moon, and sometimes people. She married her prince charming, who often inspires her characters, but still can't place dirty clothes in the hamper.

When she's not writing swoony men to fall in love with, she's in her garden providing mosquitoes with an alternative food source. She can also be found inventing new swear words on the golf course.

Also By

Want to read more by me? Scan the code to find my back list.

Visit my website for signed paperbacks and merch!
rmneillauthor.com